Emily Lowe,
PUBLIC HEALTHICAN

MASCOT BOOKS
an imprint of Amplify Publishing Group

www.amplifypublishinggroup.com

Emily Lowe, Public Healthican

For more information, please contact:
Mascot Books, an imprint of Amplify Publishing Group
620 Herndon Parkway, Suite 220
Herndon, VA 20170
info@mascotbooks.com

Library of Congress Control Number: 2023923978
CPSIA Code: PRV0224A
ISBN-13: 978-1-63755-919-2

Printed in the United States

For Alice

Emily Lowe, PUBLIC HEALTHICAN

REBECCA FANANY

MASCOT® BOOKS
an imprint of Amplify Publishing Group

1

The grayish white sky and discolored snow piled up along the streets made Emily Lowe think that this must be what it would be like if the whole world were somehow encased inside an egg. The dull white sunlight of winter, trying to penetrate a heavy layer of equally dull white clouds, ought to be exactly what one would see from inside a not-very-clean shell. In a month or so that shell would crack, and the golden sunlight of spring would pour down on the streets of New York, giving birth to a new existence full of color and movement.

Before that, however, the city would have to get through the winter. December had been one of the snowiest in recent memory. People in the stores and on the streetcars had complained constantly about the noise from the snowplows and the frozen trenches and icy furrows they left behind. The first two weeks of January had been mercifully without more snow, but then the temperature fell to record cold levels and had remained there.

A massive snowstorm on February 4 crippled the city for three whole days, bringing snow, sleet, and freezing rain the likes of which had not been seen in living memory. Seventeen inches of snow fell from the fourth to the seventh of the month, accompanied by below freezing temperatures and bitter arctic winds. Now, at the end of February, the public was still complaining about the inadequacy of the city's steam heat in their apartments and tenement rooms to cope with the cold.

Emily knew this kind of talk circulated every year, and people's perceptions didn't necessarily mean anything. Nonetheless, she listened and took note of what folks were saying because now it was part of her job, a job that she was determined to do well. For six months now she had been working as assistant to Nathan Kent, the Director of the Bureau of Child Hygiene for the whole city of New York. The position, according to Emily's mother and some of her friends from college who had immediately married upon graduating and began adding to the city's ever-growing population of infants, was merely clerical. In their eyes, Emily was just a secretary, albeit in an important office reporting to an influential man. It was hardly commensurate with the four years she had spent studying at Barnard College. That time had been truly liberating and had shown her there was a world of possibilities beyond her childhood home in New Rochelle. The twenty miles or so that separated her parents' house—where nothing ever changed—from her room at Hewitt Hall was like a vast ocean, where neither shore was visible, or even imaginable, from the other. Emily had taken to college living and as she became increasingly able to manage her life and affairs, she knew she would not be returning to New Rochelle in spirit. As attached as she was to her parents, home, and the town she knew so well, she was a woman of the world and planned to use her knowledge and abilities in a way that mattered to more than just her family. That would be through her job at the New York City Department of Health.

Emily reached the office slightly out of breath. It was heavy work pushing through the snow in a thick coat, hat, and scarf. The warmth of the foyer enveloped her and she began without thinking to unwind her scarf and open the top buttons of her coat. The past few years had been rough on the city and its people. The war had hit them hard. Emily had read about plans to commission a number of memorials to all those who had fallen during the years of fighting in Europe. If the prolonged conflict had not been enough of a trial for a population whose life was shaped by the competition to get ahead, the influenza that appeared almost magically in 1918 and lasted until spring of 1919 had killed some thirty thousand New Yorkers. Other cities had fared less well, but this, Emily knew, was due to the diligence and aggressive control measures adopted by her own department through the Bureau of Infectious Disease. Its job, like her own and that of everyone who worked for any of a myriad of branches of the department, involved a constant battle against infection, contagion, and death.

Emily's boss, Dr. Nathan Kent, frequently reminded her of this. Kent was a reasonable, even-tempered pediatrician with long experience of the many illnesses and problems that beset babies and children and interfered—as he put it—with a good start to a long and prosperous life. Emily found her boss easy to work with and shared his single-minded attitude toward disease in the young that left no room for laxity, carelessness, or lack of knowledge on the part of anyone involved. He had explained to Emily on her first day in his bureau that it was their responsibility—as if the entire bureau consisted of himself and his new assistant—to reduce the appalling mortality rate among infants and children and control various kinds of disease, especially among the teeming offspring of the city's large immigrant population. Kent believed completely that mothers needed constant supervision, and inspection of those who were expecting must begin from the earliest possible point in their pregnancy to make up for what he called "a disturbing lack of knowledge and education." This level of management should continue as the children matured and could be accomplished through cooperation between the schools, the Department of Health, and, if absolutely necessary, the parents of these young people themselves. Kent did not think highly of parents, especially mothers, who embodied all the accumulated superstitions and old wives' tales of generations past. He believed this blinded them to the benefits science and modern living had to offer. Despite this rather pessimistic view of human nature, Emily felt Kent was a kindly man who forgave the beleaguered mothers of the city for their shortcomings as he hoped the Mayor's Office would forgive his failings in bringing down the statistics on death and disability.

Encouraged by Kent to learn all she could about the operations of their section, Emily had been systematically reading the annual reports of the bureau going back to the early 1900s when she herself was just a toddler. She gradually came to understand the meaning of the terms the profession used and, increasingly, began to see why her boss was so motivated to stamp out all forms of ill health. Thousands of cases of infectious disease were identified by city schools every year. The nurses who visited the poorest neighborhoods preaching cleanliness and offering advice on hygiene and other matters recorded numerous cases of malnutrition among infants and young children. The number of children suffering from mental or physical defects reported by schools, hospitals, and clinics was truly shocking. Emily had never seen a hint of any of these things in her own school years, although she was aware they must have been present, affecting at least some of her schoolmates or neighbors. New Rochelle was a wealthy suburb, but her reading had shown her that the hardships of disease appear everywhere among people of all classes and backgrounds.

Emily reached her office and, as always, could not help but be impressed by the name and title carefully stencilled on the frosted glass, the black letters outlined in gold. Dr. Nathan Kent, Director. Emily could not, of course, hope to see her own name on an office of this kind but, in a way, this was more thrilling. She was one of the few individuals who had unrestricted access to the director and the suite of rooms where he did his work. Once inside, she went directly to her own desk and began taking off her heavy winter clothing. As she hung up her coat on the coat tree behind her desk, she became aware that Kent was already in his office. This was unusual for although he started work early, the first items on the director's daily agenda were almost always meetings with the directors of other bureaus within the department or with the Commissioner of Health, a man so widely feared by the employees of Emily's level that it was almost impossible to obtain any information about him, other than what appeared in the newspapers when he was quoted on some question of health in the great city. Emily imagined the Commissioner of Health to be a figurehead, like Richard the Lionheart or George Washington, leading the whole department into a future age of boundless health and vitality for all. That was how her boss portrayed him anyway.

This morning, however, Kent was in his office, the inner room that lay behind an imposing internal door made of pale oak. The door was almost always closed, but Emily knew this was more for the sake of impression. If any visitors came to the office, including employees from other sections who had some business with Kent, they were treated to the scene they expected. Emily would be working at her desk, reading files or transcribing notes from the many meetings she attended alongside Kent. The man himself would be in his personal office, no doubt occupied by some very important matter relating to the city's infants and children. Emily would silently open the door a crack and announce in a hushed voice that Mr. Kent had a visitor. Inevitably, Kent would look up, wink and smile, and the visitor would be let in. It was a code that had developed between the two of them to ensure the proper gravity of the situation was maintained. Emily often thought about this game she and her boss played and wondered what he actually did in his office all day when there were no meetings and no callers. Whatever it was, he was never too busy to stop and speak to anyone who came to see him. Emily was generally not asked to participate in these informal meetings, but Kent would tell her what he felt she needed to know once the visitor had left.

"Is that you, Miss Lowe?"

"Yes, Mr Kent. I'm coming." Emily glanced at her watch. As she suspected, she was not late. It was still two minutes before nine a.m., the time she officially began work. She knew something unusual must have occurred.

"I'm glad you're here," said Kent as Emily entered his office. She stood in front of his desk like a child called to the principal's office. "Sit down. Don't stand on ceremony," he added kindly.

Emily seated herself in one of the visitor's chairs and turned to a new page in the notebook she always carried. This was another behavior she had adopted because her boss recommended it. He was a strong proponent of "writing things down," as he called it. Emily had found it useful to make notes about everything she did as part of her job. She was still new enough to be overwhelmed by the wealth of detail and complicated health codes and also wary of forgetting something important that her boss wanted her to do or to remember.

"I'm ready, sir," Emily said, now very curious about what was going on. It was clear that Kent was not angry or about to scold her for some mistake she had made. She had not seriously expected this, but it was hard not to think about the possibility.

"We have a problem, Miss Lowe. A very serious problem." Kent looked directly at Emily to make sure she was paying attention. "I spoke to the commissioner this morning. He has received some very concerning reports about some children in one of the immigrant neighborhoods."

New York was a city of neighborhoods, where crossing a street could take a person from the new world to the old, across a class boundary, or into an enclave where no one spoke English. Needless to say, New York's wealthy had their own neighborhoods as well, but they seemed to cause the bureau much less concern. Emily had even heard it mentioned at one of the meetings she had attended with her boss that very little was known, in a public health sense, about the cream of the city's society. They tended not to register births with the department, or rather, the physicians who attended them did not. Their children did not go to public schools and, as a result, were almost entirely outside of the city's public health establishment. This was a slightly worrisome state of affairs but apparently not seen as serious enough for anything to be done about it.

The immigrants were another story however and represented a population of constant concern to Kent and the directors of other bureaus. There were so many of them. They seemed to come from every corner of the earth and have a million different customs most people knew little about. Many seemed to speak and understand no English at all, despite having lived in the city for decades in some cases. Others were indistinguishable from so-called native New Yorkers and tended to change their names to hide the fact they had been born overseas. Most lived in neighborhoods with others from similar backgrounds in tenements and apartment buildings packed as full as possible. Kent saw these living conditions as breeding grounds for disease and a kind of perpetuated ill health that struck children from birth and prevented them from surpassing the condition of their parents in which they, too, were brought up.

"Are the children ill, Mr. Kent?" Emily asked. Outbreaks of infectious disease were common among the youngsters of the working classes.

"They're dead," said Kent. "Seven young children all dead in the last two weeks. And the problem is, we don't know what they died of so we have no idea whether it might be contagious or how to handle it."

"How can that be? Weren't the deaths investigated?"

Emily knew the law stated that any unexplained or suspicious death required an investigation. The health department sometimes worked with the police and the courts to accomplish this. Once it was established that no infectious disease was present, the department would withdraw, but the risk of contagion and even a possible epidemic was never far from anyone's mind. This was Kent's concern this morning.

"They should have been, but it's the Jews. They won't allow it," Kent explained. He frowned, turning his normally cheerful countenance to one of deep anxiety. "They've closed ranks. When one of them dies, much less a child, they want to bury them immediately and will not tolerate any type of investigation." Investigation, in this case, meant an autopsy as well as laboratory analysis of tissues from the deceased.

"How is that allowed?" Emily asked. "Isn't it the law?"

"Well, yes," Kent replied. "But if they go ahead with the funeral before anyone knows what's happened, what can be done? We only know about the seven cases because the children in question happened to be taken to the hospital. There could be any number of others that haven't come to light. The commissioner is reluctant to pressure them, even though the law says we can."

Emily thought about this. While the community Kent was talking about was undoubtedly the recently arrived Eastern European Jews who lived in densely packed, Lower Manhattan neighborhoods where they had inadvertently created a semblance of the towns and villages they left behind in the old country, New York was also home to another kind of Jew. This community was highly educated, eminently respectable and a bastion of city politics and society. During the war, they had rallied to support victims of the conflict in Europe. According to the newspapers, they had raised more than sixty million dollars in relief funds and had even had a representative at the Paris Peace Conference that decided the terms for the defeated Central Powers and ended the Great War.

While there were very few similarities between the Jews Kent was talking about and those who were part of old established New York and had been there, in some cases, since the city was the Dutch colony of New Amsterdam, everyone knew the Jews always stuck together against any outsider. Ever sensitive to discrimination and increasingly restrictive quotas, the older community with its largely German background was growing more protective of the newcomers who mostly came from Eastern Europe. Emily knew her boss and his bosses were worried that any attempt to investigate the unusual deaths among the immigrants would likely spark vicious criticism from the longstanding community. They would speak to the press, accusing the department of persecution and harassment in preventing their compatriots from following their customs. What exactly these customs were seemed to be largely a secret. But, Emily considered, perhaps protecting their traditions in this way was necessary as so many New Yorkers seemed to dislike and mistrust Jews of any background.

Kent was speaking again, drawing Emily back to the conversation at hand.

"I want you to find out what you can about this. Here is a list of the names and addresses of the families we know about," Kent was saying.

"Me? How can I investigate, sir?" Emily asked, shocked. Her job involved acting as an assistant to Kent and doing paperwork. The department employed trained investigators to identify cases of disease so that appropriate control measures could be taken.

"Yes, Miss Lowe, you. We need someone these people will speak to. Someone who will not put them off," Kent explained.

"What about the Public Health Nurses?" Emily asked. She was confused as to why this task would be given to her when there were other more qualified people available.

"Deeply resented," Kent explained. "The public health nurses are seen as forces of disruption and interference. Always telling people what to eat, where to go, how to wash, and so forth. From the point of view of the mothers, of course."

Emily nodded. She had often heard other employees talking about the resistance faced by staff who worked in the field. Despite the obvious benefits to those the nurses visited, many of the recipients of their care did not want any intrusion into their lives. Consumptives too sick to work would nonetheless sometimes chase away the well-meaning nurse who came to check on them. New mothers, who often had several other children to take care of in addition to the infant whose welfare was a concern to the department, would refuse to open the door, fearing perhaps that the nurse was there to take the child away. Even a program to teach mothers in the poorer neighborhoods how to care for their children's teeth had been met with hostility when it started ten years before. Under these circumstances, how could she, Emily, succeed where professionals had been unable to gain a foothold?

"But Mr. Kent, I wouldn't know what to do. I wouldn't have any idea what to say to these families," Emily protested.

"You don't need to know anything. You aren't giving anyone health advice. You are there to find out what happened. From the families' side of things. All you have to do is report back to the department so the proper action can be taken. You know how serious it could be if this is an unrecognized infectious disease," Kent stressed.

Like everyone in New York, Emily knew that only four years previous the city had experienced a very serious epidemic of infantile paralysis. More than six thousand deaths resulted from an obscure virus that had never caused much illness before that very unusual summer of 1916. As if from nowhere, as the weather warmed and the public began to swelter, the disease rolled through neighborhood after neighborhood, beginning in the borough of Brooklyn and spreading across the city and beyond with blinding speed. The health department reacted as it had to other diseases in the past. Those who were sick were isolated and given what was felt to be the most effective treatment, their friends and family members were found and quarantined, new regulations on public hygiene were rushed into the books and aggressively enforced. Nonetheless, the hospitals were full to overflowing within a matter of weeks.

Emily, who at that time had finished her first year of college and should have been enjoying summer vacation, was thrown into a state of constant anxiety, largely because everyone around her was so fearful. While New Rochelle, with its small population and cooler, open spaces and greenery was much less severely affected than the city, in July alone there had been ten cases in town. All of the sick were very young children, which was the reason for the extremely high level of panic. No one knew how the disease spread, and this led to suspicion of everyone and everything on the part of parents with small children. However, all the early cases had occurred in one downtown neighborhood, which was rapidly quarantined by the Board of Health, which also began a program of fly and mosquito control. This seemed to have no impact and by August, eighty-six young people of various ages were in the hospital. This, it turned out, had been the peak of the epidemic. The patients were quarantined, their families isolated, and all events involving young people were temporarily banned. The start of the school year was postponed till October, and by then, the epidemic had passed, leaving the town much as it had been before, except for the lingering fear brought on by the knowledge that an unknown and unanticipated disease could attack its children at any time.

The city had fared much worse. By the time the epidemic passed, there had been more than nine thousand cases, and the health department's reputation had taken a serious beating. Quarantine measures had closed whole streets. When that proved ineffective, entire neighborhoods were cordoned off. Parents scrambled to send their children away to healthier areas. More than one thousand left the city every day, after being issued a certificate proclaiming them free of any symptoms of disease. Emily recalled that several of the early cases in her town had been brought in by such a group of children, all from a single Brooklyn family, that resulted in four hospitalizations and one death. Needless to say, children who had been well at the time of their medical examination could easily come down with the disease a few days later when they had already left the city and were staying in another location. The police guarded the railway stations, roads, and even the rivers to turn back anyone who tried to leave the city unlawfully.

At the same time, the health department began a campaign of handwashing and general cleanliness. The streets were sluiced with millions of gallons of water every day. Possible vectors, specifically cats and flies, were targeted for removal or eradication. People said the cause of the epidemic was the large population of Italian immigrants whose way of life was widely viewed as unhealthy and certain to breed disease. Official statistics showing a fairly low number of infections among children of Italian background did nothing to change people's certainty of this.

By the time autumn came and the epidemic was dying down, the fear it left behind had become permanent. People began to see summer as a time of extreme peril that science, medicine, and the Department of Health were powerless to control. Events of the few years that had passed since the epidemic had done little to restore the reputation of the experts and scientists at the department. Especially because just two years later an epidemic of influenza came to the city, carried by the crew and passengers of a Norwegian steamer that arrived from Europe in mid-August.

The next few weeks saw more ships arriving from major ports across the Atlantic bringing people who were already ill or, in some cases, the bodies of those who had died en route. By mid-September, the department had quarantined the whole Port of New York and made influenza a reportable disease. This required that all cases be isolated. At the same time, the department's laboratory scrambled to isolate the cause of the disease in the hope of being able to develop a vaccine. Despite strict orders to the public that anyone who was sick should be separated from the rest of the household, by the first week in October, there had been some four thousand cases reported. With the city government's recent failures in mind, the Commissioner of Health called for stores and businesses to institute staggered schedules so that fewer people would be in any one place at a given time and to reduce congestion on public transportation. Despite the best efforts of the department and the recruiting of a host of charity and social welfare organizations to help, the epidemic continued to grow. At the same time, criticism of the department and the commissioner personally arose in all sections of the city. The commissioner held steady, however, and after additional restrictions to cope with the growing number of bodies of the influenza victims, the epidemic finally abated in November. Even so, when it became possible to compare statistics, New York had done better than many other cities on the East Coast, even though more than twenty thousand people had died from influenza and pneumonia during the epidemic.

Emily nodded as she listened to Director Kent. His comment had reminded her of this recent history. It was impossible to deny that the city had a long and not very happy history of infectious disease, and Emily understood the pressure those in charge of the public's health were under to prevent another epidemic.

"Take this," Kent told her, handing Emily a typewritten list of addresses. "These are the families in question. Your job is to visit them and find out what happened and what they think about the whole thing. You'd be surprised what people know, even if they don't know they know it."

"I don't know where any of these addresses are, sir," Emily commented.

"They're all on the Lower East Side. Get yourself a map from downstairs and go and have a look."

2

Emily followed the instructions given to her by Kent and went downstairs to where the visiting nurses had a common room. Midmorning the large open room, with its rows of desks, was practically deserted as the nurses were almost all out on calls. An older woman in a white uniform who was transferring information from a small notebook to a large ledger offered to help Emily find a street map of the city. Emily nodded and the nurse spent a quick moment looking for one. After pulling a map from the desk, she asked why Emily needed it, so Emily briefly explained the assignment she had been given.

"I'm not sure I can give you any advice," the nurse said, smiling. "I just call at the houses in our records. I don't have to do any detective work."

"I hope this won't involve detective work!" said Emily, slightly worried at the woman's suggestion.

The nurse laughed.

"Why don't you ask someone in Investigations for help. Their job is to find cases of reportable disease, make sure they are isolated, and run down everyone who might have come in contact with them and become infectious. They will know what to do in a situation like yours."

Emily thanked the nurse for this suggestion and made her way deeper into the lower recesses of the building to find the Investigations section. It was located in a large room at the back of the building very much like the one used by the visiting nurses. Emily opened the door cautiously and found herself looking at a sea of empty desks, most of which were buried under piles of files and sheafs of paper. An enormous map of the city showing all five boroughs covered one wall. Only one of the desks was occupied by a blond man in his mid-thirties who was sitting next to the window typing furiously with a frown on his face.

"Excuse me," said Emily with some trepidation. Her first inclination had been to carefully back out of the office the way she had come, but her desire not to disappoint her boss emboldened her. Still, she was expecting a reaction of annoyance as she was obviously interrupting the man's work.

"Hello!" he said in a friendly tone, much to Emily's surprise. The man squinted slightly. "Can I help you?"

Emily quickly explained who she was and which part of the department she worked in. She was becoming adept at summarizing her assignment.

"So, you need some help with how to go about finding these people," the man concluded. "It's hard in the beginning. You've got to assume people don't want to be found and then, when you do find them, that they don't want to talk to you."

"Is it always like that?" Emily asked, alarmed.

"Well, no," the man admitted. "But more often than not, it is. Still, it's better to expect the worst. Then it's a nice surprise if things turn out different." He smiled broadly. "I'm Edward Morelli," he added. "One of the investigators. It's lucky you caught me. Most of the time, no one much is here."

"Thank you for taking the time to talk to me," Emily said, smiling to match Morelli's expression. "I'm sure you're very busy."

"It never ends. The department runs on records. The better the records, the more effective the response."

Emily nodded. She had come to much the same conclusion in the time she had been working for Director Kent. Knowledge was power in their field, or at least gave the possibility of control. Everyone's aim was the same—to try to avoid another terrible disease outbreak of the kind that was all too familiar to the public of the great city.

"I'm not even sure how to begin," she said. "I have a list of names and addresses but I don't even know where these streets are. I have a map, but there's so much territory. I don't know how to start."

"Let's have a look. I've been doing this quite a while. Maybe I know some of the addresses," Morelli said, reaching out a hand for Emily's list. She passed it to him and watched as he read each line carefully, appearing to think hard about each name and location.

"I can tell from these entries we need to be looking in lower Manhattan," he said after a moment. "These are Jewish names, as you know, but Jews live all over. Your boss told you these people live on the Lower East Side, but that's a large area with several different neighborhoods." He pointed to a section of the map that Emily had spread out on the desk. "You'll be down here along the East River, roughly from Canal Street up to 14th Street and as far west as Broadway. You're right, it is a lot of territory!" He looked up, as if expecting a reaction from Emily.

"I've never been there," she said nervously. "This is a slum area, isn't it?" Almost instantly, Emily regretted what she had said. She should have phrased it differently, as what she was really referring to was a widespread perception that certain parts of the city were unsafe, rife with crime and disorder, and not the kinds of places people she knew ever went. At the same time, she had been told many times by her boss that, no matter how they lived, the members of the public were the responsibility of the department to look after and protect from disease and ill health to the greatest extent possible. In this case, several children had died under mysterious circumstances, and the whole situation had to be taken with the utmost seriousness, regardless of Emily's own sensibilities.

Morelli laughed. "I understand what you mean," he said. "But it's perfectly safe during the day. There are always people on the streets. It's a long way from where you come from," he went on. "The important thing is not to judge them too harshly. They're poor. They're newcomers. Their lives are not easy."

Emily nodded. She was slightly familiar with the commentary written by the journalist and social reformer, Jacob Riis, that had been discussed in one of her college classes. Riis, himself an immigrant, had written a number of books illustrated with his own photographs documenting the lives of New York's ethnic communities in the 1890s. His later campaign, alongside prominent philanthropists and social observers, focused on creating "model tenements" in New York's teeming immigrant neighborhoods. Emily recalled the professor explaining that a number of modern apartment houses had been constructed in the early years of the century to provide healthier living spaces for the city's ever-growing population. These new-style tenements boasted light, airy rooms with good ventilation. They were fireproof, had steam heat, private bathrooms in each apartment, and built-in gas stoves. Rent was modest at the start, which was seen as a measure of generosity by the corporations that built them. There had even been a complex developed especially for residents suffering from tuberculosis where the healthier conditions, it was hoped, would lead to recovery and the disease would not spread. After a while, though, Emily recalled, the interest in providing better quality housing to the poor died down as other issues in the urban environment became more pressing, and the model tenements began to rent for market rates. None of this had affected the Lower East Side addresses she had to visit, however. That part of the city remained as densely packed and run down as ever.

"Now, the heart of this part of the city," Morelli was saying, "is Orchard Street." He poked a finger at the map on the desk to indicate the place in question. "It's one big marketplace from end to end."

Emily nodded. This section of the city, judging from the map anyway, was laid out very differently from the neighborhoods further uptown.

Morelli seemed to read her mind. "The streets don't form a perfect grid here," he said, referring to the rigid city planning that characterized much of Manhattan. "It's the oldest part of town and can be quite confusing."

Emily studied the map, noting there were several larger roads that cut across this part of the island at its narrowest but also others that formed diagonals, creating sharp angles and three-way intersections. Some streets ran for only a block or two before ending at a cross street slightly out of alignment with another street on the opposite side.

"I can see your addresses all cluster in this area," Morelli went on. "Here is Henry Street, Green Street, Essex, Forsyth, and so forth. What we don't know is where the individual houses are."

"What do you mean?" Emily asked. "I've got street addresses for all of them."

"So you do, but we can't be sure which way the numbers run."

"What do you mean?" Emily repeated. This was another complication that was adding to her confusion.

"Well," Morelli explained, "further uptown, odd numbered streets go west, and even numbered streets go east. The odd numbered buildings are on the north side of the street and the even numbers are on the south side. If you know an address, you can figure out the cross street with a calculation and go directly there. But not below Houston Street. There, the streets all have names, and there is no system to the house numbers."

"Is that important?" Emily asked.

"Very, if you're dealing with an infectious disease," Morelli told her. "You want to know how the contagion spread so you need to know how close these addresses are to each other and where people may have come in contact with each other."

Emily nodded. She had never thought about that. Suddenly, she realized that this information was something she should be writing down. After a moment's hesitation over whether it was better to risk looking like a country bumpkin who had no knowledge of the way the city's streets worked or to potentially forget important information that could help her succeed in her task, she decided the former was a better choice. Morelli paused, seeing her reach into her handbag for her notebook. Emily was grateful he didn't say anything. After a moment, he continued his explanation.

"You have an address on Green Street and one on Henry. These streets have an intersection, but they each run several blocks in both directions away from this point." Morelli looked up to check that Emily was following. "Your address on Green is number forty-two, and the one on Henry is 161. For all you know, these buildings might be blocks apart or they might be adjacent to each other at the intersection. They might even be the same building, with one address on the side facing Henry and another on the side facing Green."

"Can that happen?" She was used to a more orderly system of streets like those in New Rochelle or in midtown Manhattan where she and Morelli worked.

"Absolutely. There even used to be a few streets where the house numbers went up one side, crossed over and continued back down the other. Number one was next door to number two and opposite the highest number," Morelli said. "But I think those were all renumbered some time ago."

Emily just nodded. She had been worried about having to talk to the families at the addresses she'd been given. She hadn't realized that just finding them could be a problem.

"Which of these was the first case?" Morelli asked.

"I don't know," Emily admitted. "I didn't ask, and I wasn't told."

"You need to find out," Morelli told her firmly. "If you are dealing with an infectious disease, you want to track it from the first known case to the last. That way, you will be able to figure out where it came from." Then, more gently, he added, "Don't worry. It isn't hard to find out."

"How would I do that?" If possible, Emily did not want to have to ask Kent for any extra information. She wanted to prove herself up to this assignment and show her boss that she was capable of handling this unusual situation.

"You said that in each of these cases a child died. Is that right?"

Emily nodded.

"And we know about these cases because the deaths took place in the hospital or are possibly associated with a visit to the hospital?"

"That's right," Emily confirmed.

"In that case, you can go and look up the death certificates. They should already be on file, or you can ask the clerk to check the unfiled notices if they are too recent." Morelli smiled. "Vital Records is on the second floor of this building."

Emily blushed. Apparently, there was a great deal she did not know about the department, even though she had been trying to understand its workings from her first day in Kent's office.

"Thank you so much for your help," she said. "I don't know what I would have done if you hadn't been here to explain all this."

"I'm sure someone else would have helped you."

Emily wasn't sure about that, and she did want Morelli to understand how grateful she really was for his help.

"I can't thank you enough," she said. "You know so much about the city and how to go about investigating these cases."

Morelli laughed. "It says Investigations on the door. This is my job. I do it every day and have been for more than ten years."

"It's all new to me," Emily said. "Thank you again. I'd better go up to Vital Records and check on the dates."

"Good idea. It's best to move as quickly as you can in case you are dealing with something contagious," Morelli advised. "And I will get back to my reports."

Emily folded the map they had been looking at and closed her notebook before putting it back in her bag. Morelli had already turned back to the typewriter and was peering ferociously at the page as if what he had written previously had mysteriously changed in some way. Emily almost thanked him again but stopped herself. Gathering up her belongings, she left the office as quietly as possible, making sure not to let the door fall back with a bang. She was grateful for the time and advice and didn't want to cause her new colleague any further inconvenience.

3

Following the instructions she had been given, Emily made her way to Vital Records. This was one of the sections of the health department that was open to the public, and there were several growing lines of people waiting to be helped by one of the clerks behind the counter. Presumably these were citizens who needed a copy of a birth or death certificate or perhaps a marriage license. Emily was not sure what the procedures for obtaining any of these important documents were, but many of the men and women waiting in line looked like they had been there for some time. A kind of weariness was apparent in some of their faces, while others seemed bemused by the bureaucratic process. All of them were laden with thick coats, hats, scarves, and other garments to protect them from the extreme cold weather outside the overheated office. Since there was nowhere such items could be laid down or hung up, each person had to carry or wear a heavy burden of winter wool.

Emily looked around, unsure who she could ask about the death certificates she needed. She assumed she would not have to attach herself to one of the lines and wait. As she pondered this dilemma, an older women dressed in an impeccable dark blue dress with a crisp white collar and cuffs came up to her.

"I'm Mrs. Vogel, the supervisor of Vital Records," the woman said by way of introduction to Emily, whom she clearly had recognized as an employee of the health department, which Emily assumed was because she was the only one in the room without a coat.

"My name is Emily Lowe. I work with Director Kent in the Bureau of Child Hygiene," Emily began.

"What do you need from us?" the older woman asked somewhat impatiently. Emily got the impression other parts of the department often needed things from Mrs. Vogel and her staff.

Emily quickly explained that she needed information on the deaths of the seven children that had come to the attention of her Bureau and briefly told Mrs. Vogel that her boss was worried there might be a new infection of some kind spreading among the immigrant community.

Mrs. Vogel nodded knowingly, as if this sort of request came to her on a daily basis. But perhaps it did, Emily realized.

"If you only need to check seven records and they are all recent it should only take a few minutes. Normally, I would have you do it yourself." She gestured toward the room that was partially visible through an open door located behind the clerks' work area. Emily could see row upon row of filing cabinets, very much like the gigantic card catalog at the public library.

"These are all from the last three weeks," Emily told her. She was happy to be able to confirm Mrs. Vogel's prediction that the more recent records would be easier to locate.

"Fine. Those have probably not been filed yet. Come with me." The older woman led Emily around the long counter where the clerks stood, each speaking to a member of the public who had reached the head of his or her line. Emily noted that they seemed to have to spend a great deal of time checking the completed forms that were handed to them. Various blank documents were stacked in labeled trays on a table placed against the back wall next to the door Emily had entered. Every so often a clerk would send someone back to the table to correct a piece of information or perhaps start over on a clean form.

They reached the records room and Mrs. Vogel led Emily to a desk at the back. A number of clerks, all young women of about the same age as Emily, were filing documents or making typewritten entries on cards that would presumably be filed in one of the many drawers around them. Each nodded politely to Mrs. Vogel but continued on about their duties without a word.

"To issue a certificate, we require a certification from a physician that a death has occurred and what the likely cause was. There is a form for this," Mrs. Vogel said. This time, Emily was prepared and had begun making notes as soon as the older woman began to speak. "If no physician is in attendance, there are other ways a death can be certified, but you said all these cases you are interested in occurred in the hospital. Is that correct?"

"Yes," Emily told her. "That was how we learned of them."

"That's easy then. There will be a report from the hospital for each of them. We don't need to know which hospital it was, although that information will be on the report. Recent deaths are kept in date order. Later, one of the girls will type up the record in triplicate for filing by date, name of the deceased, and borough of residence."

Emily scribbled all this down in her notebook.

"All the cases we are looking into are from the borough of Manhattan," she said, realizing that Mrs. Vogel had just told her that information was not necessary.

"Have you a list?"

Emily handed her the list of seven names and addresses she had been given.

"From what you told me, these are the names of the children you are concerned about. You can get the date of death from the report, and the parents' names, the hospital, the attending physician, and cause of death will be listed as well."

As she spoke, Mrs. Vogel began leafing through the bundles of reports stacked on one of the desks. "Each of these files contains fifty reported deaths arranged by date. In a city this big, there can be several hundred deaths per day. During the Spanish flu pandemic, we had one thousand per day for a while." Mrs. Vogel looked at Emily, as if to ensure the younger woman understood the seriousness of this and the amount of work it had created for Vital Records. Emily nodded. "Needless to say, we do not, and did not then, get all the reports for all those deaths. Many came into the borough offices and were collated there. We received the compiled information and entered it into the master files," Mrs. Vogel explained. "Now, here is one of yours," she went on. "This will be the most recent as I started from two weeks ago today and am working backward. Annie Bornstejn."

Mrs. Vogel rapidly located the records for the Varsaver, Ojzerman, Dawidowicz, Rosenbaum, Gutstein, and Jablonski children. "Why don't you sit here and copy down the information you need?"

Emily obeyed. It had obviously been more a command than a suggestion. She decided to take advantage of being allowed to see the hospital death reports and write down all the available information for each case.

Turning to a new page in her notebook Emily began to read through the information on the first of the typewritten hospital death notifications. These forms, she was aware, were used by the department to issue a death certificate to the grieving family. However, she had not realized how much information was included and quickly decided to make a note of everything on the form, even if it didn't seem relevant at that moment, in case it was of use later in her investigation.

The process was time consuming; there were names, dates, places, the personal information of the deceased, the name of the certifying physician, and, because these were children, similar information for both parents. As she worked, a realization came over Emily—these were real people, not just the subjects of a mass of data. The names and places that were so strange to her reflected different lives and experiences she knew nothing about. The parents: Dovid and Tauba, Abram and Ester, Samuel and Blima, and others difficult to read much less pronounce; the towns where they were born—Chruslin, Krakow, Tykocin, Bialystok, and some that seemed even more distant and unknown; and even their nationalities, which for most was simply

'Russian'—all hinted to Emily the existence of another world as remote and unfathomable as Mars or Venus, where the things she knew about had no meaning and her own life provided no anchor points to enter into theirs. The children, however, had all been born in New York. The oldest of them had been eleven at the time of his final illness. The youngest was only four, practically a baby.

Emily was not so naïve as to imagine that children never fell ill or died. Everyone knew these things only too well as a fact of life. There were so many diseases that could carry off a young child at what seemed like a moment's notice. Some of these were old problems, like tuberculosis that was the subject of an ongoing fight to suppress and treat. Others were new, like the raging influenza that was only now dying down. Emily recalled reading in the newspapers that the recent flu epidemic had been unusual in that large numbers of young adults—people her own age—had fallen victim to a disease that should have struck the elderly and the very young the hardest. Now, looking at the pages of information she had transcribed, Emily wished she had some kind of background in medicine or public health or at least had paid more attention to the public discourse of recent years. The strangeness of the people she was assigned to investigate intensified her feeling of being at sea without direction or guidance to reach the shore.

Once again, she found herself worrying about whether she would be able to complete her task and what exactly Director Kent expected her to find out and do with the information. She desperately wanted to meet his expectations, having convinced herself that her job depended on this outcome, despite Kent never having mentioned anything of the kind. More than any of that, however, Emily felt fear of a kind that was unfamiliar to her and also unwelcome. She realized she had never been in a situation where she had so little knowledge, so little preparation, so little that might help her. It occurred to her that her successes in life so far had been due to the fact that she had always been safe within the world that she knew, that was populated by people like herself, whose views and way of thinking were just like her own. Any differences were minor and could be put down to natural variation within the same frame, like the changing patterns of a kaleidoscope that seemed infinite but were actually created by a small set of colored crystals reflected over and over again by two adjacent mirrors.

For the first time, Emily knew, she would be dealing with people from outside her frame of reference. How would they feel? What would they say? Would she understand them? What would they think of her? All of these questions loomed unanswered, almost masking a tiny but perceptible thrill Emily felt at the prospect of exploring the unknown lives of people so distant from her that she couldn't even picture them in her mind. She had undertaken this and reiterated her promise to herself that she would try her best and not permit the fear—which was presently greater than the excitement—to dampen her resolve.

Now, however, it was Friday afternoon, and even the most experienced investigators, barring an emergency of some kind, took the weekend off. She would be visiting her parents as she did most weekends, and Emily planned to put her work out of her mind till Monday. Her father had always told her there was no point in worrying. "The things you worry about never happen," he had said many times. "And you can't predict the things that do happen." Emily had found this to be good advice, and it was especially relevant in her current situation.

4

"Drink this," said Emily's mother, placing a steaming cup in front her daughter as she sat at the dining table with her parents. "It will put color in your cheeks."

Without thinking Emily placed a hand on her cheek. Her skin still felt like ice from the frigid wind outside. It had been so cold on the train from the city that she had kept her coat on the whole way, as had most of the other passengers. The twenty-five minute ride from Manhattan's Pennsylvania Station had seemed much longer than usual due to the chill, making the trip to one of the most populous suburban areas of New York feel like a journey into the deep country. Emily's short walk from North Station to her parents' house had felt like a sojourn through the Arctic and she was very glad to get inside, even if that meant facing the herbal brew her mother was expecting her to drink. Still, her cheeks must have been bright red, and it was hard to imagine she lacked "color" as her mother implied.

"What is this, Mother?" Emily asked as she studied the fluid in her cup. It had a distinct green tinge and a strong smell, very unlike any tea Emily was familiar with.

"It's an herb tea," Margaret Lowe replied. "It's guaranteed to give you vitality and pep you up."

Emily took a tentative sip. "It's awful," she said.

Emily's father laughed. "Of course it is," Henry Lowe agreed. "Just treat it like medicine."

Emily noticed her father was not drinking the same stuff she was. Henry Lowe had his own steaming cup of what was very clearly hot chocolate. "Mother knows what's best for you."

Emily, irritated by the fact that her father had spoken to her as if she was a little girl, not an adult woman with an important job, said nothing. She decided, however, that she would not drink the tea. She tipped the cup slightly to look at the contents.

"Where did you get this, Mother?" she asked.

"I bought it in town. One of the ladies recommended it," Emily's mother told her.

The "lady" she was referring to, Emily knew, was one of the members of the temperance club her mother belonged to. The group had started years before as an offshoot of the ladies' auxiliary associated with their local church. Emily's mother, who had long been a follower of the clean-living movement that espoused health food, avoidance of alcohol and other stimulants, as well as cold baths and treating disease with diet, had found a natural home among the club women, and Emily could not remember a time when they had not played a major role in her mother's social life.

Henry Lowe humored his wife in this, although he very clearly did not share her ideas about good health and clean living. But Emily had long realized it was easy for her father to take all this as a long-running joke because he was never made to participate. Overwhelmingly, Emily's mother permitted her husband to eat and drink whatever he liked. Her approach to health had been mostly applied to herself and Emily, especially as one of the aims of clean living seemed to be to address the many health problems that seemed to plague women but not men. If asked, Margaret Lowe would explain that this had something to do with what she referred to as "constitution," with that of men being made of sterner stuff and hence much less susceptible to the chronic and painful afflictions familiar to all women. When they were alone, Emily's mother would inquire about cramps, feelings of faintness, dizzy spells, heart palpitations, and other vague symptoms and remind Emily, seemingly endlessly, about the importance of a healthy diet for the future benefit of the children she would one day produce. Emily, who felt herself to be a rather robust person, would agree and try to change the subject to avoid the embarrassment of discussing the functions of her internal organs.

Sensing a change of topic was now needed, Emily asked, "What are the ladies doing now that the Volstead Act passed and is in effect?"

The Volstead Act was of great interest at the health department, as it prohibited the sale and manufacture of alcoholic beverages anywhere within the United States. Emily had not paid a great deal of attention to the discussion and analysis in the newspapers until she began working for Director Kent. The consensus among the professional staff at the health department was that the removal of alcohol from the daily lives of the city's residents would be beneficial for the public health, no matter how they felt personally. Kent, for example, had explained to Emily that liquor often fueled violence and disharmony in families, which was damaging to any children involved in the situation. Mothers who drank could so easily lead to negligence in the care of their offspring as well as further abuse. The act itself had passed surprisingly quickly in 1919, having achieved the necessary two-thirds agreement from the states to ratify this 18th Amendment to the Constitution. The changes it brought to the law, however, as well as the economic and social life of the country, had only come into effect a few weeks before on January 17, 1920.

"Temperance is an ongoing battle," Margaret Lowe told her daughter primly. "There is always more work to be done."

Emily's father smiled but restrained any laughter. Like most men of his background and social class, Henry Lowe liked a drink. He owned a successful moving company that operated mostly in and around the Westchester and Putnam Country region. He had started out as a carter with two mules and a wagon long before Emily was born. As motor vehicles gradually shifted from expensive curiosities for the wealthy to affordable necessities for the self-made businessman, he had quickly moved to upgrade his business and capitalize on the growing trend of suburban living. More and more city residents wanted greater space within easy commuting distance of their Manhattan offices. As they moved out into the surrounding country towns like New Rochelle, Henry Lowe had been there to transport their crates and barrels, household furniture, and even the occasional piano. The town was, after all, "only forty-five minutes from Broadway," as George M. Cohan had reminded theater-goers back in 1906 when his musical by the same name debuted on the Great White Way.

"At least it's keeping the men sober," Emily's father commented philosophically. Drunkenness among his employees had been a common complaint that Emily and her mother had become used to hearing about. The main task the workers had to carry out—loading and unloading other people's possessions and driving large, heavily laden trucks—required care and precision that were not enhanced by the consumption of alcohol on the job. Still, there was no way to limit what employees did on their lunch break, and he had had to rely on the men's own good consciences to prevent them from drinking on the job.

Now Emily laughed. "I'm glad you can see the bright side," she said. This was a reference to a private conversation she had had with her father almost a year ago when the details of the Volstead Act were starting to reach the awareness of people not directly involved in the legal profession or the liquor industry. Henry had been angry and amazed that much of the country was willing to ban alcohol so readily and had never really believed that the activities of suburban women, through their churches and social leagues, could so strongly influence lawmakers and the public's outlook. It soon became clear that the local campaigning for temperance paralleled much larger social forces that had been at work in America for decades and accounted for the popularity of the Anti-Saloon League and Women's Christian Temperance Union. Like so many others, Henry's anger receded when he learned that the act, while banning manufacture and sales of liquor, imposed no penalties for possessing and consuming alcoholic beverages. And, also like so many others, Henry

Lowe had stocked up early. Emily knew the cellar of the house was filled with crates of beer, spirits, and fortified wine that her father had purchased in bulk and moved using the facilities of his own company. "It can't last," he had confided in her. "I give this whole business a few months. They'll soon realize the error of their ways and repeal this silly act."

Emily was less sure about all this than her father. Her observations, many of which came from the health department files she had been encouraged to read as part of her job with Director Kent suggested that 'they,' referring to those in government, were rarely willing to admit they had been wrong. For the moment most people seemed to be lauding Prohibition, which had quickly become the common name for this new era of no liquor, and were intently waiting to garner the many social benefits that its proponents had promised. Very little had been mentioned in the press about any potentially negative effects, even though violation of the new law had begun at 12:01 a.m. on January 17, only seconds after it came into force.

"So, how is your Director Kent?" Emily's mother asked, filling a break in the conversation. Margaret Lowe had immense respect for medical practitioners of all kinds and seemed to make little distinction between those with the training and experience of Nathan Kent and the self-proclaimed miracle workers extolling the benefits of raw foods and electromagnetic coils (claimed to supercharge the iron in the blood to produce wonderous results against ageing and natural deterioration). She in fact owned one of these amazing magnetons, to which she attributed the youthful appearance her friends often commented on enviously. She had also gone through a phase of using a tonic made of radioactive water. That miracle cure-all had not panned out, and Emily's mother soon decided it was not worth the expense.

"He's given me a very important task," Emily said with excitement. She explained briefly about the children and their mystery illness as well as what she had been assigned to do.

"I don't know that I like the idea of you going into those tenement neighborhoods, Emily," her mother said. "We don't know anything about those people."

"Your mother is right," Henry Lowe put in. "I've seen these places, and they're no place for a young girl by herself."

Emily doubted that her father knew anything about the people and places she would have to visit. While his business did occasionally take him into the city, and by its nature into people's homes, the company mostly handled moves for the more well-to-do residents of the city's Upper East and West sides nearer to Westchester County.

"I'm sure they're just people like us," Emily said. "Besides, I need to talk to some women who have lost a child. They are not going to murder me."

"These people are nothing like us," Emily's mother said sternly. "They are immigrants from God knows where, with customs no one knows anything about. I didn't suggest anyone was going to murder you, but anything could happen."

"It's no place for a young girl," Emily's father repeated. "I can't imagine what that director of yours was thinking."

"I am not a young girl, Father. I am a grown woman. I work for the Department of Health, and this is the work we do," Emily said defensively. She had many of the same doubts as her parents but was not going to admit it to them. Hearing them express these same thoughts seemed like a lack of confidence in her judgment and abilities, and Emily felt like a schoolgirl being chastised for choosing the wrong friends. "Director Kent would not have asked me to do this job if it was not very important."

Like their neighbors and many others in New Rochelle, the Lowes read the newspapers every day and kept abreast of the social and political climate. This was a matter of great concern to many residents of the town, which was growing rapidly. Many of the old houses had been bought by wealthy city people, torn down and replaced with luxurious homes designed by the architects of the day. New shops were opening on Main Street on almost a daily basis, and fancy hotels were springing up along the shore of Long Island Sound. It was understood that the newcomers to the town were leaving the city, in part because of increased crowding, crime, and inconvenience, all greatly contributed to by the legions of immigrants who had arrived over the past two decades, packing into the old neighborhoods and trying to get ahead in this New World. There could be no question, though, that the city's recent experiences with epidemic disease had a great deal to do with more and more of its residents seeking healthier, more spacious living conditions in the suburbs.

"But, Emily, these children may have had a disease you can catch," her mother protested in a change of tack.

"It's possible they had an infectious disease, but no one else seems to be ill. Not even other children in the same families," Emily said. She considered this objection on her mother's part to be more acceptable and also more refutable by logic.

"You've got no medical training," her father said. "Why are you the one investigating some strange disease?"

"I'm not interested in the disease itself. We need to know about these children's lives, where they went, what they did. That will help us understand why they fell ill and died. So we can prevent it happening again."

"That's a noble cause," Emily's father said. "But I still don't see why it has to be you who goes into the tenements to find out."

Emily sighed. "Many of these families are confused and angry about how the hospital treated them. They are not comfortable with doctors and nurses and they are very suspicious of the department's motives. Director Kent wanted to send someone who would not be threatening to them, and that is me."

"He should have sent a professional," Margaret Lowe concluded.

"I am a consummate professional," Emily said flatly with lightly suppressed anger. She realized there was no point arguing about any of this with her parents. But she was angry, and the knowledge that, in a few hours, she would be on the train and on her way back into the city was not cheering her up. She also knew that some of the things her parents had raised were valid considerations. The conversation had triggered all her fears and lack of self-confidence. This, in turn, was making her angry, upset, and pressured. But Emily also knew she should not allow herself to be made to feel like a child. She had a job to do, and Director Kent would not have assigned it to her if he didn't believe she could do it. That was what she had to keep focused on. In the moment it took for all this to run through her mind, Emily also decided it would be worth listening to her mother talk about the latest health craze rather than have this discussion turn into an argument. Regardless of what her parents thought, she was going to do this job and make the director proud of her.

"So, Mother," she began. "Can I get your advice . . . I have this back pain that will not go away. At first I thought I strained my back, but now I am not sure." Emily felt, rather than saw, her mother perk up at this. At the same time the excitement in her father's eyes seemed to dim, and he sunk back into the placid state of benign tolerance he always adopted toward his wife's interests.

Emily and her mother began a long conversation about the nature of Emily's pain. What she had to do on Monday morning slipped into the background. A quarrel had been averted, and Emily at least knew that she had done her part by telling her parents what she would be doing. She had anticipated their disapproval, but it had been milder than she expected, and having everything out in the open would make her job slightly easier, if not less frightening.

5

The electric streetcar in which Emily was riding buzzed down the avenue, passing through intersection after intersection on its relentless way to the southern tip of Manhattan. Many of the crossings were blocked by cars and buses, and Emily's progress was slowed as the streetcar crawled ahead when any space opened. This was a part of the great city she was unfamiliar with. Her few visits to the areas south of Midtown where she lived and worked had been with friends and were limited to a visit to New York University, located near City Hall at Washington Square, and a walk through Chinatown. On both these occasions, Emily had paid little attention to the trip itself, which had involved the subway and a great deal of walking. Her friends seemed to have very clear ideas about how to get around the city, and Emily had simply followed their lead. There had been no serious purpose to these outings, and it had not been important to Emily to note her surroundings.

She recalled having felt like an alien intruder as she and her friends strolled along Mott Street. Signs and shopfronts had Chinese characters on them, presumably advertising goods that Emily could only imagine. All around them, people of Asian descent were speaking unknown languages, the strange, sharp sounds of which were startling to her ears. It was like being a voyeur into a reality that had no meaning or relevance to her, Emily had reflected as she and her friends wandered through the neighborhood, pointing out various sights to each other as if no one else could see or hear them.

The two women she had been with, fellow lodgers at the hotel for women where she lived during the week and when she was not staying at her parents' home, were professionals like herself. One worked at City Hall. The other was a clerk at the New York County Court House on Chambers Street. They traveled to Lower Manhattan every day, and the almost surreal atmosphere of the city's more exotic neighborhoods didn't seem to make any impression on them.

This feeling of displacement returned as Emily stepped off the streetcar and made her way to Orchard Street where she planned to begin her investigation. In the few moments that took, Emily realized several things. First, she was only a few blocks from the Chinatown neighborhood she had visited before. Second, there was nothing essentially different about the city blocks and their stores and tenements here as compared to other parts of the city. And third, what made people refer to this part of town as "the ghetto"— a term Emily had seen on an illustrated map intended for tourists—was the amazing determination of the residents to recreate the places they had come from in "the Old Country."

Emily stopped to catch her breath. The Williamsburg Bridge that connected Manhattan to the westernmost edge of Brooklyn only a couple of blocks away dominated the skyline in one direction. In the other, a claustrophobic maze of densely packed streets stretched out before her. Every usable space it seemed was occupied by people selling, buying, some in stores, some from pushcarts, and others off tables set up on the sidewalk. Overhead, signs written in Hebrew letters presumably indicated to passersby what could be found below. Someone had told Emily that the alphabet was that of the Old Testament, but the language was Yiddish, a kind of German-Slavic vernacular used by Jews across eastern Europe. Regardless, none of this conveyed any information to her, but it must have been significant to the people who thronged the street. She heard English—heavily accented and natively used—heavy, guttural tongues she could not place, and even traces of German that she recognized from her school days. As she got her bearings and began to look around more calmly, Emily realized there was, in fact, a great deal that she could understand. Signs proclaiming "Rooms to Let," "Butter and Eggs," and "Ladies' Tailor" could have been located anywhere, even back in New Rochelle.

But it was the people who held Emily's attention. The street was packed to capacity with men, women, and a few children. All were busy, in constant motion, buying, selling, and making deals. Emily could see that without understanding much of the activity around her. No one noticed the interloper in their midst. Women with bulging shopping bags pushed past her, annoyed to find their way blocked by a gawking stranger. Men in overcoats and dark hats walked purposefully down the street, deep in conversation and seemingly unable to see anything around them except the almost identical individual they were speaking with. For their part, the sellers eyed each passerby, assessed whether they would be a potential customer, and focused their attention on those most likely to make a purchase. On the surface the majority of shoppers seemed like people anywhere, but there was nonetheless something exotic about most of them—a gesture that did not fit, a mannerism that was both European and outdated, and of course the heavy accents with which so many spoke. The shopkeepers—more than the customers—seemed to Emily to have emerged from a bygone era. The women in their long dark dresses, hair hidden under a colorful scarf or woolen hat, took payment and made change from the pockets of the large aprons they all seemed to wear. The men in dark clothing all wore hats as well, and many had the same sort of apron the women did, theirs reaching almost to the ground. They reminded Emily of old photos she had seen from before the turn of the century, but there could be no mistaking these people for the residents of New Rochelle, even those of twenty or thirty years before.

She had learned that this part of the city had come over the course of years to be referred to as "the ghetto" because of its supposed similarity to the old parts of many European cities and towns. The term was often used in the newspapers, and she had studied a map intended for tourists in the small reading room of her residence with fascination. It listed various points of interest, one of which was this neighborhood, where visitors to Manhattan were advised a wide range of goods could be purchased at very reasonable prices and where it was possible to dine on a variety of delicacies from eastern and central Europe. The nickname referred to the sections of Medieval cities in which European Jews had chosen or been compelled to live. Within the bounds of this modern ghetto they were free to recreate the densely packed, communal life their ancestors had experienced. The new ghetto, however, was adjacent to Chinatown and the Italian quarter, resulting in an odd rearrangement of world geography.

Somewhere in the warren of streets just beyond the hive of activity that was Orchard Street, Emily would find the families she had been assigned to investigate. She could delay no longer. Realizing she had been standing in the same spot for some time now just watching the scene around her, Emily knew she had to start her assignment, as terrifying a prospect as that was. Suddenly, she was aware that she had now lost her bearings and had no idea which way to go to reach the first of her addresses. Under other circumstances, she would simply have asked a fellow pedestrian or one of the many sellers on the street around her, but this was not her usual situation, and Emily was put off by the fact that most of the people around her did not seem to be speaking English and she could not judge who was likely to be the friendliest.

A small man pushing a heavy box on wheels whose side was gaily painted with the words "Hot Knishes" walked slowly past her. Their eyes met for a moment before the man turned away with an enigmatic smile. Emily could not tell whether he was amused at her confusion—which must have been visible in her expression—or had simply decided she was not a likely buyer of whatever it was he was selling. Emily looked around again, hoping to find a sympathetic face in the crowd. Everyone around her seemed busy and intent on what they were doing. A policeman would have been the ideal person to ask for directions, but there was none in sight. A woman would be easier to approach than a man, Emily thought, but the women working in the stalls and shops were busier than the men and appeared to speak less English. Finally, she decided to simply walk up to someone and ask for directions. No one could possibly mind that, Emily reminded herself.

Having generated this artificial courage, Emily boldly took a few strides to the corner where a man was sitting by an easel set up on the pavement. A handwritten sign proclaimed "Portraits and Silhouettes While You Wait." Several examples were tacked to a board that was propped up alongside his stool and supplies. The samples of the man's artwork were good and, to Emily's eye, showed talent, which perhaps there was no outlet for other than the street corner in the kind of life the people of the ghetto obviously led. The man smiled as Emily approached but did not rise.

"Paint your portrait, Lady?" he asked in heavily accented but colloquial English. "Or maybe a silhouette. It's a true work of art made with ordinary paper and scissors."

Emily smiled. The offer was intriguing, and she was tempted to see what the man could do in his impromptu street corner studio. But it was cold, and she had wasted enough time. "Can you tell me where I might find Henry Street?" Emily asked, referring to the first address on her list.

"It's behind here," the man told her, gesturing vaguely at the row of tightly packed buildings across the street. "But it don't come through. You go down to the corner, turn left and left again. It's right there. "

"Is it far?" Emily asked, wondering what she would do if it were.

"Three minutes' walk," said the man with confidence, as if he had personally timed it.

Emily thanked the artist and began to walk away.

"Hey, Lady," he called. "I'm here every day. Come back and get a portrait."

Emily smiled. Perhaps she would.

6

Number 161 Henry Street was a narrow tenement house, much like all the others on the street. It was built from reddish bricks, now dull and stained with age. The narrow frontage contained rows of windows, all curtained, that must have been the only entrance for light into the apartments, as the building abutted its neighbors on both sides. A stoop that had been carefully swept clean of snow and sprinkled with sand marked the entrance. Emily climbed the steps and entered a dark hallway dominated by a narrow staircase leading to the next floor. No one was around, and the building was very quiet. It had not been clear in Emily's mind what she was expecting, but it was not this comparatively clean, silent refuge from the commotion in the market just a few blocks away.

Judging by the numbers on the doors she could see, Emily determined the people she was looking for must live on the third floor, so she began the long, slow climb to the upper stories. As she trudged up the stairs she thought about how the residents must feel going up and down these narrow stairs several times a day, carrying groceries up, garbage down, and young children both ways. She could feel the depression in the center of each tread that told of where all the people who had lived here had stepped. She was out of breath when she reached the third floor and had to lean against the banister for a minute to rest. She could see apartment number six, the one she was looking for, and a wave of uncertainty washed over her.

Nonetheless, Emily steeled herself. Her mission was about to start. She had met no one up to this point, but now a serious encounter with the residents of the ghetto was inevitable, and she would do her duty. She knocked on the door and held her breath.

There was no sound from the interior of the apartment. In fact, the whole building was so quiet as to seem uninhabited. Emily knew that most of the city's lower classes worked—men as well as women. An abundance of low-paying jobs in factories and workshops, as well as the possibility of going into business for oneself, was what had brought them into the country in the first place. Still, someone must be watching the children who were the subject of her investigation. She knocked again and was again met with silence.

"They're not at home," said a voice to Emily's left.

"What?"

"They're not at home. They go out to work."

Emily turned to look at the speaker who had stuck her head out of the other apartment on the landing. A woman with reddish blonde hair that had been put up hastily was looking at her aggressively.

"What about the children?" Emily asked. This first family on her list, the Jablonski family, had two other children in addition to the one that had died.

"She leaves them with her sister," the woman said, referring to Mrs. Jablonski. She seemed to be examining Emily's clothing with a critical eye. "They won't be home till six, seven o'clock."

"I see," said Emily thoughtfully. She realized she should have been prepared for this situation but saw an opportunity in the person of this neighbor, who seemed to know quite a bit about the Jablonskis. "May I speak to you?" she asked politely.

The blonde woman shrugged.

"You'll have to come inside then. I can't talk out in the hall."

Emily nodded as the woman stepped back to allow her to enter the apartment. Emily found herself in a small room with the back corner set up as a kitchen. A closed door led to the next room. The space they were in was dominated by a table on which stacks of cut cloth were neatly arranged. A large pair of tailor's shears lay on top of one of the piles. A box of sewing thread and a large, bristling pin cushion suggested this was a professional set up, not just a home sewing project.

The woman was not alone. Four children were standing together in the kitchen area. A girl of twelve or thirteen, two younger boys who seemed to be almost the same age, and a much younger girl of perhaps four were all watching Emily with great interest. They were eating thick slices of bread, carefully spread with butter all the way to the edges. The uneven slices, along with the way the younger children pressed against their older sister, suggested that she had made their meal and was responsible for them while their mother worked. All four of them had the same hair color as the woman. They were carefully dressed in clothing that was worn but spotlessly clean. The girls' hair had been neatly braided.

"They go to school," the woman said defensively when she realized the children had attracted Emily's attention.

The idea that they should have been in school had not crossed Emily's mind up to this point, but now she realized that was why the building was so quiet. It was a school day, and attendance was rigidly enforced in the city's public schools. These children, however, seemed perfectly healthy so it was not illness that had kept the three oldest at home. The little girl smiled at Emily, seemingly unaware of the threat a stranger might bring. The older girl eyed Emily with the same mixture of fear and aggression as her mother.

"I'm not the truant officer," Emily told them all. One of the little boys laughed and poked his brother. The older girl quieted them with a gesture. They all looked at Emily with wide, watchful eyes.

"I'm Emily Lowe. I'm . . ." Emily paused. What was she doing here? She could not claim to be a public health investigator like her friend Edward Morelli. As Assistant to the Director, which was her job title at the Department of Health, she had no plausible reason to be here, except that her boss had directed her to be.

"Yes?" the woman inquired.

"I'm a Public Healthican," said Emily forcefully. The made-up term that had sprung into her mind in an instant conveyed exactly how she felt—she was champion of the public's welfare, a professional of a kind that crossed the traditional lines of discipline and training.

The woman nodded, accepting Emily's self-proclaimed identification without question.

"What do you want with the Jablonskis? she asked.

"Do you know them well?" Emily asked, ignoring the woman's question.

"Of course. We live in each other's pockets here."

Emily paused and thought about the unfamiliar expression. The woman spoke English well, but her pronunciation was slightly strange and her intonation somewhat off.

"It's about the little boy who died," Emily explained. Then, seeing the expression of curiosity and alarm on the woman's face, she added, "I've been asked to look into it. We are concerned he might have had an infectious condition."

This did not seem to put the woman any more at ease.

"No one else is sick. Not their children and not mine."

"I can see that," said Emily quickly. She did not want to give the woman the impression that she was interested in the four children now huddled even more tightly together in the corner. "The health department is always concerned about any sickness that we can't identify. It could spread, and many people could become ill."

The woman relaxed visibly. Emily smiled, but the woman remained stony.

"Do you know what happened?" Emily asked, hoping to draw her out.

"The boy was sick. He got worse and died."

"They took him . . ." Emily glanced at her notes on the Jablonski child. "Samuel, wasn't it? They took Samuel to the hospital," she prompted.

"That was at the end. Sam had been sick for days. Finally, there was nothing more that could be done for him here."

"What was wrong?"

The woman shrugged. "Children get sick."

"I meant, did he have a fever? What other symptoms were there?"

"Oh, it was the cough mostly. He had a deep cough. After a while he couldn't stand up and could barely stay awake. He had terrible stomach pains and began to vomit," the woman explained.

"I see," said Emily thoughtfully as she scribbled this into her notebook. "Did you see the boy?"

"No," the woman told her as if it should have been obvious that she had not. "She—Mrs. Jablonski—told me."

Emily nodded. "So, they took him to the hospital?"

"When he wouldn't wake up. He was perfectly alive, of course."

"Then he died in the hospital?" Emily knew this from the death record she had seen but wanted to hear what the woman might know about it.

"He must have."

"That was it then? What about the other children?" Emily pressed.

"What about them?" the woman asked.

"Were they sick as well?"

The woman seemed to ponder this. "I think they were all coughing. The parents, too. Sam was sicker than the others though."

Emily made a note of this as well. She wondered what else she could ask this woman.

"The rest of the family was sick, but they recovered," she repeated. "What happened then?"

"What do you mean? They buried the boy. The other children are fine," the woman told her forcefully. "I don't know any more."

"Isn't Mrs. Jablonski a friend of yours?" Emily asked, confused. It seemed to her like the woman knew a great deal about her neighbors.

"They're Russians," the woman said with a snort of derision. Behind her, the children began to whisper, and one of them giggled. The woman whipped around and shushed them. Obediently, the group of children fell silent and stared at Emily with a piercing intensity. She noted that they had not moved since she entered the apartment. They had even forgotten to finish their meal.

"*A kind in shtub, ful in alleh vinkelech*," said the woman more to herself than to Emily.

"What does that mean?" Emily asked.

"It's Yiddish. 'A child in the house, all the corners are full,'" The woman told her. "We don't get much peace around here."

"I understand," said Emily. She could see how cramped the tiny apartment would be, especially at night when the children's father was at home as well. "You were saying the Jablonskis are Russians," Emily went on.

"Yes. They have their ways. We have ours," she said matter-of-factly, as if this difference should be obvious to Emily.

As Emily tried to think about what the woman might have meant, other than that she perhaps did not get along very well with Mrs. Jablonski. She looked down at her notebook, hoping to formulate her thoughts into a coherent notation.

"I have to get back to work," said the woman suddenly. It was clear she was ending their conversation, so Emily allowed herself to be led to the door and ushered into the hallway.

While she had compiled several pages of notes about the illness suffered by Sam Jablonksi that led to his untimely death, Emily felt she had not learned much that could be put to use. She was afraid she had asked the wrong things, but she had not even been able to speak to the affected family. This was all secondhand information that may or may not have been accurate. She wished she had spoken in more detail to Edward Morelli about what to say and how to get information from people and that she had written out a list of questions.

It was as she turned back onto Orchard Street where the marketplace was still just as busy as it had been earlier that day that Emily realized she had not asked the woman her name or anything about herself. The woman had not introduced herself, nor had she spoken to any of the children or referred to them by name. Suddenly, it occurred to Emily that this was a form of defensive behavior that would make it Emily's word against the woman's that they had even met. Fear of the authorities in any form ran deep, Emily knew, even among law-abiding people. The simple act of being spoken to by a police officer caused many people to lie automatically, even when they had done nothing wrong. Emily hoped her oversights would not turn out be a serious problem and promised herself to do better with the other families.

7

Emily sat at her desk on Friday morning, puzzling over the notes she had made during her visits to six of the seven families who had lost one of their children. Director Kent was at a monthly meeting with the various bureaus that made up the health department. He had departed for his engagement with the instruction for Emily to "get on with it." For her part, she still had not been able to see the Jablonskis, but, at each of the other addresses on her list, she had found a distraught mother, often trying to add to the family's income by taking in piecework, while caring for other children, and, to a varying degree, managing her own emotions.

They all had felt the loss of a child acutely and only had been able to give Emily very little information. There did not seem to be anything distinctive about the dead children's illness—a fever, cough, general malaise. It had seemed like just a bad cold of the kind that plagued the city's residents every winter. There was nothing to suggest that this illness would be any different from the illnesses this child or the family's other children had suffered from in the past. In each of the cases Emily had been told the child seemed stable but then had suddenly taken a turn for the worse with a new set of symptoms serious enough for the family to seek medical care. Ordinary illness was nothing new to them, but when the children began to complain of weakness, dizziness, vision problems, and two experienced frightening seizures, there had seemed to be no alternative but to take the child to the hospital and hope for the best.

Emily felt a measure of sympathy for the women she had spoken to. They seemed to be reasonable and caring mothers beneath their foreignness. All had been born outside the United States and spoke heavily-accented English, some quite well, others notably lacking fluency. They lived in conditions of deprivation and squalor, and it was this that tempered Emily's response to them. They were poor, they were immigrants, but surely there was more they could do to improve their lot. Her own upbringing had taught her the importance of personal responsibility, especially for one's health and that of one's children. She wondered briefly about how the sick children had felt, coughing and fevered, trying to rest in a crowded apartment surrounded by noise inside and outside of the building and the contrast between that and her own childhood experience of illness, lying in a darkened room, the rest of the house in silence as her mother sat reassuringly by her bed until she felt better. That line of thinking was getting her nowhere, however, so she turned back to her notes.

Emily thought that writing everything out might help her make sense of what she had seen and heard from the bereaved parents. They had all been willing to speak with her, if wary and on the alert for any sign of trouble. None of them had noticed any warning signs that there might be something different about this illness as opposed to any other in the past or in an older or younger sibling. Interestingly, in each of the families the child who died had been the only one who became seriously ill. Anyone else in the family who seemed to have the same disease recovered without incident. Beyond this, Emily could make little sense of her own findings. As one of the mothers had told her:

"Children are always sick. This wasn't any different."

Nonetheless, Emily knew there must be something different. She simply couldn't see it. As she pondered this, there was knock at the outer door, followed immediately by the appearance of her friend Julia Brown who worked in reception.

"Miss Lowe," she began formally. She and Emily were on a first name basis under normal circumstances, often eating lunch together in the employees' rest room. The formality was an indication that Julia was not alone. "There's someone to see you."

"To see me? Not the director?" Emily asked with surprise.

"The lady asked for you by name," Julia explained, smiling. "Shall I bring her in?"

"Uh, yes, of course," Emily replied. This was the first time anyone had come to see her and the prospect of a visit from a member of the public was both frightening and intriguing. She just had time to wonder how someone would even know about her before the woman was standing in front of her desk.

Emily studied the visitor for a moment. She was about fifty and was wearing a well-cut and very thick black wool coat and a soft cloche hat that completely hid her hair and extended over her ears and well down her neck. She moved rapidly with self-assurance.

"Please sit down, Mrs. . . ." Emily realized Julia had not introduced her guest.

"My name," said the woman, "is Miriam Kandel." She sat down in the chair Emily indicated and placed her handbag on her lap. She did not move to open her coat even though the anteroom was heated. The woman showed no discernible sign of nervousness or hesitation, despite being in the heart of a major government organization of a type that made most people anxious. She folded her hands in her lap and eyed Emily critically.

"How can I help you, Mrs. Kandel?" Emily asked.

"I want to know why you are harassing and haranguing women all over town about their children." The woman's English was barely accented. Over the past few days, and for the first time in her life, Emily had become consciously aware that many New Yorkers did not speak much English or spoke in a way that was distinctively based on their native language.

Emily gasped. This attack on her investigation was not at all what she was expecting from this elegant and composed woman.

"I haven't harassed anyone," Emily cried in self-defense.

"Have you not been going around town, calling on women, and asking about their sick children?" Miriam Kandel pressed.

"Well, yes, I have," Emily protested. "But I am not harassing anyone. I am investigating what happened to the children who died."

"Why are you interested in this?"

"My superior, Director Nathan Kent of the Bureau of Child Hygiene, is concerned these children may have had an unknown infectious disease. I am investigating," Emily said formally. Then she added, "How do you know about this?"

"I know two of the families you went to see, the Varsavers and the Gutsteins. The mothers came to me and asked me to help them."

This explanation stunned Emily. It seemed too unlikely that in a city of five and half million this woman could know two of the affected families. She seemed to be of a completely different type than the women Emily had met. They had been much more like the typical immigrant often discussed in the newspapers—poor, timid, and hostile, separated from the rest of society by their experiences and living in conditions most of the public could never even imagine. Mrs. Kandel, by contrast, was stylish, self-confident, and appeared prosperous despite the obvious air of foreignness about her. This confusion must have showed in Emily's expression because her visitor went on:

"I know a great many people, Miss Lowe. My husband is a rabbi. He has a significant congregation. I know all the women, the children. They come to me with their problems. But these two families, it's more than that. We go back to the Old Country. They come from the same town my husband and I do. Our parents knew their parents. Over here, we have *landsleit*, people from the same place as us."

"Do you know all the families or only the Varsavers and the Gutsteins?"

"Just those two. But I know there are others involved. You told them, and they told me."

Emily thought this over. She realized she had mentioned to some of the women that she was investigating seven similar cases of illness and death.

"As I said, Mrs. Kandel, we are only concerned that the children did not have a contagious disease. We all know only too well how quickly something like that can spread and become out of hand," Emily explained, referring to the influenza epidemic that was still fresh in the minds of all New Yorkers.

The woman looked at Emily impassively. "If they were contagious, there would already be dozens of cases," she said calmly.

This, Emily realized, was probably true. There had been only the seven unexplained deaths she knew about. Her investigation thus far had not revealed any clue that might suggest an outbreak was brewing in the densely populated neighborhood where the victims had lived.

"We still want to know the cause of the children's illness," Emily said. "Seven children have died."

"Do you think I don't know that? Do you think the families are not aware? The women you spoke to have personal tragedies to deal with. You should leave them in peace."

"We need to know what happened," Emily told her with as much confidence as she could muster.

"Why?" The question was unexpected.

"Well . . ." Emily thought for a moment. "If we know what happened, maybe we can prevent it happening again."

"Do we get to know everything? Is that our place in the universe?"

"I don't know. We have to try to learn as much as we can."

"We can only learn as much as is within our capacity," Mrs. Kandel said as if speaking to a child. "Many years ago, there was a rabbi who longed for justice in the world. One night, the prophet Elijah came to him and said he wanted to go out among the people to see if they were still hospitable to strangers. So, the two of them set out disguised as beggars. By nightfall, they came to the hovel of a couple who were very poor but managed to live by selling milk from a single cow. This couple invited the two strangers to stay the night and shared with them the best of what they had. The rabbi noticed the prophet slip out in the night but said nothing as he had been instructed before they set out. In the morning, they awoke to a terrible scream when the farmer's wife went out to milk the cow but found she had died in the night, taking away the couple's only source of livelihood. The rabbi tried to console them, and the prophet blessed the man and his wife.

"Leaving the poor couple in despair as to how they would survive, the rabbi and the prophet went on their way. By evening, they arrived at the home of a very rich man. A servant told them an engagement party for the man's daughter was taking place, but they should continue on their way because his master did not like beggars. Nonetheless, the prophet told the servant that they would ask for a bed for the night. The householder was very hostile, but the prophet persisted and eventually the man said they could sleep in his barn, but to stay away from the party and keep out of sight.

"The rabbi and the prophet went to sleep in the cold, drafty barn. In the morning, the prophet pointed to a hole in the wall of the barn and said it was the reason it had been so cold. He took up some tools that were lying there and began to fix the hole. The rabbi was shocked, but he had been warned not to ask any questions, so he kept quiet.

"Then, without saying anything to the owner who was busy with his house guests, the rabbi and the prophet left and began the trip back to the rabbi's home. 'I know you are thinking about how unfair it was that the farmer's cow died in the night and that I fixed the miser's wall for him, but there is much more to this than what you can see,' the prophet explained to the rabbi.

"'The Angel of Death came for the farmer's wife in the night, but I was able to convince him to take the cow instead. I blessed the couple when we left and, even though they did not know it yet, another cow was wandering lost near their hovel. They will find it and take care of it. And, on top of that, God will bless them with a child.'

"'What about the miser?' the rabbi asked.

"'As for him,' the prophet replied, 'there was a jar of gold buried under the wall. If I had left the hole, he would have repaired it himself and found the gold. Now it will stay buried until some more deserving person comes across it. Also, his daughter's marriage won't bring him any happiness. She will die before the wedding.'"

"What does that mean?" Emily asked in frustration. She had listened to this long, strange story carefully but could not see a point.

"It means that the world is not what it seems to be to us. We do not have the ability to know everything, and things happen for reasons we may never learn."

"That story cannot have happened. It's a parable, a moral lesson," Emily protested.

"Must it have really happened for it to be true, Miss Lowe?"

Emily was becoming tired of her visitor's constant questions. She felt she had lost control of the conversation and was acting out an unknown script directed by the older woman.

"What are you asking me to do?" she said finally.

"Only to respect the privacy of these families and leave them in peace. They have enough hardship without visits from the authorities and a lot of questions that scare them. They have no answers," Mrs. Kandel told her.

"I have to do my job," said Emily weakly. It was not much of an argument against the other woman's eloquence.

"I have taken up enough of your time," said her visitor, rising. "I left my husband in charge of the store. I have to get back and see what's going on. He isn't good with the customers. He gets distracted and can't find what they want."

"The store?" Emily asked. "Isn't your husband a rabbi?"

"Yes, he is. The congregation does what it can, but his work doesn't put bread in our mouths. We have a store on Hester Street. I sell ribbons, buttons, sewing thread, embroidery silk, pins, whatever. If you need something like that, Miss Lowe, come to me."

With this abrupt change of topic, Mrs. Kandel stood up, smoothed her coat, and disappeared into the corridor without another word, leaving Emily to wonder at this strange meeting and what it meant. A feeling of unreality had come over her, which she attributed to the story of the prophet Elijah and the miraculous events her visitor had described. While she had inadvertently gained some potentially useful information about the Jews of the ghetto, such as the fact that there were unexpected social connections between unlikely individuals, Emily felt an even greater confusion about the sick children, what had caused their deaths, and what she should do next. It occurred to her that she once again needed expert advice, and Edward Morelli was the obvious source, assuming he was willing to help her, which Emily dearly hoped he was.

8

The investigators' work room was quiet as Emily carefully pushed open the door and stepped inside. To her delight, Edward Morelli was at his desk just as he had been at her last visit. He was putting a large pile of index cards into order and did not look up when Emily entered. She had not considered seriously until that moment that Morelli would likely be out of the office on a case. As she thought about this possibility, she felt embarrassed at her own assumption that the investigator would be sitting there waiting for her. But miraculously he was at his desk, and she hoped he would have time to speak to her.

Two other investigators, both older men who seemed worn down by the burdens of their profession, were sitting at desks at the back of the room. One was reading a thick file, while the other was copying notes from loose sheets of paper into a bound notebook. They seemed not to have noticed Emily and gave the impression that they had always been in those exact spots doing those same tasks and would be for as long as the department and this office existed. Emily knew this was not the case but she quickly looked away anyway, as if her gaze would interrupt their eternal toil.

Morelli looked up as she approached his desk and greeted her with a big smile.

"Miss Lowe. How goes the case? Have you made progress?" he asked.

"I'm not sure," Emily said truthfully. She sat down in the same chair she had used when she spoke to Morelli before. "I have interviewed six of the families and have spoken to a neighbor of the seventh but I can't make anything of what they told me."

"How do you mean?"

"Well," Emily began, "the sick children seemed to have had colds, bad colds, but no one was especially worried. All the mothers insisted this was just an ordinary illness like what children get all the time. There was no reason to think it was anything more serious, but then the child died."

Morelli nodded seriously.

"You told me these children were taken to the hospital," he said. "What made the parents feel that was necessary?"

"That is interesting," Emily told him. "In each case, the sick child developed a new set of symptoms." She glanced down at her notes, which she had taken out of her bag and had been holding on her lap. "Stomach pains, dizziness, confusion, and two of the children had fits."

"And before that happened?"

"Before that, they all seemed to have a bad cold, with a cough, sore throat, aches and pains. The type of winter illness all children get."

Morelli nodded thoughtfully.

"May I read over your notes?" he asked after a moment.

"Of course. I don't have much. I really wasn't sure what to ask, and the mothers were very upset," Emily replied.

"I can imagine," Morelli agreed. He reached for the notebook Emily had laid on the desk, sat back and began to read.

Emily looked around the room, avoiding Morelli's two colleagues who had not reacted in any way to their conversation. After a few minutes, Morelli put down the notebook and looked up at Emily.

"You did well for your first investigation," he said. "But I see you haven't been able to see the first family, the one with the first death."

"That's right," she said, encouraged by Morelli's praise. "I've been there twice, but apparently they are out all day. I did speak to a neighbor, but she didn't have much to say, except to confirm the sick boy had a bad cold. She didn't seem to know any more about it."

"That isn't really surprising. A neighbor wouldn't know much about a child's illness. You need to talk to the parents." Morelli smiled, indicating to Emily that this was not a criticism of her actions. "It can be very hard to find people. Even if they are not trying to avoid us, they go to work, they visit friends, they're out shopping, whatever. An evening visit would be best for these folks," he said, tapping the page Emily had allocated to the Jablonskis with his index finger.

Emily was startled. She was uneasy during the day in the strange part of town where the Jablonski family lived. She had not considered visiting them at night, and everything her parents had said about that neighborhood and its residents flooded back into her mind.

"I'm not sure . . ." she began, uncertain how to express her fear without seeming either unprofessional or unwilling to do what was required to solve this case, something she realized Morelli and his colleagues did on a daily basis.

Instead of the criticism of her work ethic that Emily expected, Morelli laughed.

"I know it's frightening. I go into places that scare me every day. What if we go together? Maybe I can give you some help."

Emily's heart leapt in excitement, and she realized this was what she had secretly been hoping for. She had come to a dead end and would not be able to proceed without advice and assistance, as well as knowledge and experience that she did not have. But Morelli did, and would be able to provide the information and support she needed.

Realizing he was waiting for an answer and that her facial expression must have been one of surprise and concern, Emily quickly replied, "Could we really do that? I would be so grateful for your help!"

"Of course," Morelli told her. "This looks like a difficult case. Sometimes another pair of eyes and ears makes all the difference."

Emily knew he was going out of his way not to mention her inexperience and wondered whether she had made serious mistakes in the interviews she had conducted. But she just nodded, resolved to follow Morelli's lead and count on his expertise to move the investigation forward.

"Today is Friday," Morelli was saying. "A lot of these Jews are religious and won't talk to us on Friday night. They won't even answer the door. Even if this Jablonski family is not observant, we can't go calling on them on Friday night. It is not respectful."

Emily nodded in agreement. This was the kind of consideration that could only come from long experience, and she was grateful for Morelli's insights.

"But tomorrow night might be the time," Morelli was saying. "Saturday after sundown, everyone will be more relaxed and maybe more willing to talk to us." He paused and looked at Emily. "I am sorry, Miss Lowe, I should have asked whether you are busy tomorrow night."

"I'm not," Emily told him. "And I would have canceled my plans anyway. This is very important."

"Of course." For a split second, Morelli looked embarrassed, but his expression returned to normal quickly. "Perhaps I can pick you up somewhere and we'll go downtown together."

Emily blushed. Even though she knew this would be the most desirable plan, especially as she herself had admitted she was hesitant to travel around the city at night, she was worried about imposing too much on Morelli's generosity.

"I'm staying at the women's hotel on East 29th Street. The Martha Washington. But surely that would be very inconvenient for you," she said.

"Yes, very."

Emily, who had been looking at the notebook in her lap to hide her uneasiness, snapped up to see Morelli grinning broadly.

"I'm sorry," he said, laughing. "I'm just teasing. You looked so serious."

Emily smiled tentatively, unsure whether this was a further joke.

"I mean it," Morelli said. "I know the place."

"Do you live in the same area, too?"

"No. I live in Brooklyn. But the subway goes right to your place."

"It seems awfully far out of your way," Emily said. She suspected it was not at all easy to travel from the borough of Brooklyn into Manhattan and that it was unlikely a single subway would suffice.

"Not really. I live in Williamsburg," Morelli told her. "With my parents," he added, as if he could read the unasked question in her mind. "I'll meet you outside your hotel at six p.m."

"If you really wouldn't mind," Emily said finally. "I would be very appreciative."

"My pleasure. I have to come into the city anyway, and we can go downtown together."

"Do you often have to call on people at night?" Emily asked. The awkwardness of making arrangements to meet in a way that had coincidentally—Emily reminded herself—seemed like a date had passed.

"It's common," Morelli conceded. "We have to catch them when we can."

"Can't you find them at work during the day?"

"No, we generally don't know where a person works anyway. We have a home address at most. Even if we did know their employer or place of business, we couldn't show up there to ask them questions about some disease. That would get people fired and would also violate their privacy. How would they manage if the people they worked with found out we suspected them of having tuberculosis or something worse?" Morelli explained.

"I didn't think of that," Emily said. As she turned the matter over in her mind, she realized that Morelli was right. Being suspected of harboring an illness people feared would be catastrophic. True or not, such a suspicion could only lead to dismissal by an employer and ostracism by friends and coworkers. This realization put a different light on the interviews she had conducted with the six families whose child had died.

"At least there is a better chance of people being home in the evenings,"

Emily said.

"That's true, but you wouldn't believe some of the lengths people go to to avoid us. I've had people I wanted to speak to insist they were someone else and that they had never heard of themselves. I've had people climb out of windows and hide on the fire escape. Plenty of people just refuse to speak to us."

"Why is that? Don't they realize you're just concerned about the public's health?" Emily asked.

"In short, no they don't," said Morelli cheerfully. "They don't see us any differently than the police. It's all the government, and the government exists to cause them trouble. That's how the average person understands things. They are just trying to get ahead, and we are trying to stop them by telling them what to do and how to live their life."

"But that isn't right. You are just trying to protect people from disease."

"Most people don't feel there is a risk of disease. I mean, they do, but that risk has always been present. It's like the influenza," Morelli said. "Sure, a lot of people were sick, and everybody talked about how terrible it was. But they didn't really want to change what they did because of a disease. Most people don't really believe they or their loved ones will become ill. Everyone does get sick eventually anyway. It just isn't that big a deal to many people."

"You're very cavalier," Emily commented, more disapproving than she meant to be.

"I'm telling you what people think. If I believed that myself, I wouldn't be in this line of work."

"I'm sorry," said Emily sincerely. "I didn't mean that as a criticism of you. It's just that I don't understand why people don't take serious illness more . . . seriously," she added finally.

Morelli nodded. "You and I come from stable backgrounds. We have a place to live, enough to eat, these jobs." He gestured around the room. "A lot of people in this city have none of those. They can't worry about getting sick tomorrow. They have to eat today. They figure if they do get sick, they'll deal with it then."

What Morelli had said was true, Emily realized. This assignment was giving her a glimpse into a part of society she had never really thought about before. Considering this, she knew she had often been uncharitable and intolerant in her thinking about people like the families she had spoken to in the past few days, wondering why they didn't just shape up and be more like the people she knew. She now wondered whether this was her boss's true intention in giving her this assignment. Perhaps he had recognized how sheltered she was and wanted her to understand the problems of the people they dealt with in the bureau. Thinking about Director Kent gave her an idea.

"My goodness," Emily burst out. "I am so sorry . . ."

"What?" Morelli asked with a start.

"I hope I haven't gotten you into trouble with your boss. You've spent so much time helping me already. It's too much to expect you to come with me to see the Jablonski family."

Morelli smiled, his face lighting up.

"It's fine," he told Emily. "Part of our job is to help the other sections. I've done a lot of work with the visiting nurses, for example. They see all kinds of things on their visits and often come to us for help in running down cases of polio and so forth. I spoke to my boss about you last week the same day you came here the first time. I had already decided your assignment would be an interesting one, so I told my boss I had been asked by Director Kent's assistant for help on the case. He said 'fine' of course."

Emily was stunned.

"But how did you know I'd come back?" she asked.

"Well, I don't want to boast," Morelli said, looking down at his hands. "But I assumed you would need help. It isn't easy to get information out of people, and I thought you might be out of your depth with the people you would be seeing. It takes a long time to really learn how to deal with the public and get information they may not want to give you or that they don't even know they have. Frankly, I didn't think you could do it alone." Morelli looked up hopefully, as if he feared Emily would be angry at this admission.

"I'm very grateful. I guess no one really likes being told they're a novice, but it is true. And I do need your help." Emily's desire to complete her assignment and impress Director Kent was far greater than her ego. She was very much aware that she lacked experience, and her knowledge of her profession was much less than it should be. She had often wondered why Director Kent had hired her when there must have been other applicants with formal training in public health or at least medicine or nursing. "It was very kind and generous of you to think of me."

Morelli beamed again, and Emily matched his smile.

"So there is nothing standing in the way of our arrangement to talk to the Jablonskis tomorrow night?" she confirmed.

"Nothing whatsoever. I will pick you up at six. We can get something to eat on the way downtown before we seek out where this family lives."

Emily laughed at this light way of describing what was actually a very important visit to investigate a very serious issue, but her mind was already racing ahead to her preparations for the meeting. She had to remind herself several times that she and Morelli would be at work, but she kept slipping into a mode of thought more associated with what felt a lot like an important date.

9

By five-thirty Saturday evening Emily was ready. She sat with one hand in her lap and with the other self-consciously fingered the edge of the newspaper she was trying to read. She had spent a considerable amount of time during the day setting her short dark hair and deciding what to wear. This was definitely an occasion for workwear. Most of the time she wore a skirt and blouse or sweater to the office, but her best outfit—a dark brown woollen suit—seemed more appropriate. For one thing, it was a much warmer choice for a winter night, and Emily had no idea how long it would take to speak to the Jablonskis. By about nine o'clock the city could be bitterly cold as arctic winds swept down the long avenues from the north. Another reason was that the suit was skilfully cut and fit her well. She knew it was flattering attire and also very professional looking. She would have preferred something brighter, but the austerity of the war years had not yet given way to more cheerful colors. There was no alternative to the winter boots and heavy coat that would have to go over the suit; spring remained a long way off.

Having decided on her wardrobe and personal appearance, Emily was now thinking about the job ahead and the information she and Morelli would have to obtain from the Jablonskis. She had no idea what the nature of that information might be, but this was her last chance, she felt, to solve the problem Director Kent had put before her. She had spoken to the other families and, while she could return to question them again, she had no idea what to ask to draw out the crucial point that would shed light on the confusing mystery of the children's deaths. Emily did not especially care for detective stories, but she had read enough of them to know there was always a moment when the detective stumbled upon the clue that would unlock the solution to the murder he or she was investigating. Sherlock Holmes, the greatest of all literary detectives, always seemed to know exactly what he was looking for even before he started investigating. Emily wished she could somehow step back and observe her assignment from a distance like one of those murder mysteries. This might give her the vantage point to see deeper into the situation and start to understand what had made the children so ill. She wondered whether Morelli had this kind of insight, which brought her back to the beginning of the thought cycle and whether her hair would still look nice when she took off the close-fitting felted hat she wore to cover her ears and neck above her coat collar. She had no answers to any of these questions, and there was nothing to do but read the paper as the hands of the clock on the wall crept around to six o'clock.

At one minute to the hour, Emily stood up with forced restraint. She glanced out the window of the reading room where she had been sitting. She caught a glimpse of Morelli standing under the streetlight outside the main entrance to the hotel. Despite his heavy coat, thick scarf, and black fedora hat pulled down over his blond hair, Emily easily recognized her friend's profile and watched him light a cigarette as she pulled on her own coat and hat. As she stepped out the door onto the street, Morelli turned around as if he had eyes in the back of his head.

"Good evening, Miss Lowe," he said, creating a cloud of condensation as he spoke.

"Good evening," Emily replied, smiling. The cold air was biting after the warmth of the building.

"I'm glad to see you're warmly dressed," Morelli continued. "It's impossible to know how long it will take to find these people and interview them, even though you know where they live."

Emily nodded. "I suspected that might be the case," she said.

"Let's get moving then," said Morelli. "Miss Lowe . . ." he began. Then, "May I call you Emily?"

"Of course, Edward," Emily replied with pleasure.

"Oh, just call me Ed. Everyone does."

"Thank you, Ed," Emily said. She was glad she had taken the trouble with her appearance. As she had hoped, Morelli saw her as a friend, not just a work colleague he was doing a favor for.

"Do you have a nickname or do they always call you Emily?" Morelli was asking.

"My parents always use Emily, but when I was in school my friends called me Em."

"Em and Ed," Morelli laughed as they turned the corner onto the cross street that in another block would take them to the downtown streetcar line. "We could be a vaudeville team."

"I'm afraid I don't have much talent in that direction," said Emily. Morelli was right, however. It was not just the ready-made stage names—Morelli was tall and blond while Emily was short and dark. "Perhaps I could be the straight man," she added.

"I was thinking more of the old soft shoe," said Morelli, giving a small hop to demonstrate. "It would help keep us warm," he went on, jamming his gloved hands into his pockets.

Emily had to agree to this. They continued on their way downtown with Morelli leading her on and off the streetcar, across streets, and around corners. Emily had long since lost track of where they were, despite Morelli's attempt to orient her by pointing out various stores and buildings in a kind of personalized travelogue. Finally, they arrived in front of a small but brightly lit restaurant that was already very busy despite the early hour.

"Let's get something to eat," Morelli suggested.

Emily nodded in agreement. "Where are we?" she asked.

"This is Delancey Street. The heart of the Italian Quarter. I hope you like this restaurant. It's a favorite of mine." Morelli led the way inside. Almost all the tables were occupied by family groups and couples of various ages. Everyone seemed happy, and the level of noise indicated a good time was being had by all.

"*Buona sera.*" A waiter came up to them. Morelli spoke rapidly in Italian. The waiter replied and immediately led them to a table in a back corner of the restaurant.

"I said we needed to eat right away because we have an appointment," Morelli told Emily. "Luckily, there is an empty table."

"You speak Italian very fluently," Emily said admiringly.

"Well, my parents are immigrants. They still don't speak English too well after forty years. That's what comes of living among your own countrymen. It was important to them that we kids spoke English, but of course we had to speak Italian, too," Morelli explained.

Emily was fascinated by this. Apparently, Morelli came from a very different kind of background than she did, although she would not have guessed this to be the case if he hadn't told her. He seemed as American as the people she had grown up around, most of whom came from families that had been in the United States since colonial times.

"I'm ordering us spaghetti," Morelli told her. After waiting a moment for Emily's agreement, he spoke again to the waiter who had reappeared to take their order and then vanished into the kitchen.

"Tell me more about your family," Emily said.

"I have an older brother and two younger sisters. We all live in Williamsburg, but I'm the only one still at home with Mom and Pop. The others are all married and have their own children, so I guess I'm the ugly duckling." Morelli paused, as if waiting to see how Emily would respond to this comment. Seeing she was still smiling, Morelli went on. "My brother works with my father in his fruit and vegetable business. 'Morelli and Son,' it's called. I think Pop would have preferred 'Morelli and Sons' plural, but it just didn't interest me. We all did plenty of that kind of work when we were in school, so I knew what I would have been getting into."

"Don't your parents approve of what you do?" Emily asked.

"I don't think they approve or disapprove. But they are confused and a little uneasy that I have become some sort of official agent, as they see it. It's like I've gone over to the other side."

Emily considered this. It now made sense to her that Morelli had a much better understanding of the way of thinking of the people involved in her case as well as his sympathetic view of their situation.

"I know all about parents and their perspective," Emily said. She quickly told Morelli about her own mother and father and how they didn't seem to take her work seriously. She had not consciously thought about it until she began to explain, but Emily suddenly realized her parents treated her job as if it were a game of pretend, with the inevitable outcome she would eventually do what they thought she should and enter into an appropriately staid, middle-class life with a husband, home, and children. This was what her friends from school and college had all done as well as her cousins, and her parents saw no reason Emily should be any different.

Explaining all this to Morelli brought Emily a great sense of relief. She had discussed these same issues at length with her friends, who nowadays were largely working women like herself. They tended not to understand the problem and believed the solution was for Emily to do exactly what she wanted without consideration of either her parents' feelings or how they treated her. Morelli, by contrast, seemed to understand the real problem.

"Sometimes you can't convince people," he was saying. "You have to accept that they see it their way and you see it yours. For me, I try to compromise. That's why I haven't moved out on my own after all these years. It's not the way things are done, and it would break my mother's heart. I feel I can make this concession to their feelings in exchange for being allowed to live my life."

"So, you have an agreement with your parents?" Emily asked.

"No, nothing like that. Everything just sort of settled in this way. We don't discuss it. I help out around the house and Mom gets the pleasure of having me at home. I come and go, for work or whatever. But I know they would prefer something else."

"Something more like them," Emily supplied, as much to herself as to Morelli. "My parents are the same way."

During this conversation they had eaten their dinner. The spaghetti and meat sauce Morelli had ordered was not the kind of food Emily was used to. She found it to be very rich and somewhat spicy but not unpleasant. In fact, she liked it, she decided. The dish reflected the many new experiences she was having and the new knowledge she had gained.

"Let's plan our attack," said Morelli, pushing his empty plate away.

"That sounds very serious," said Emily apprehensively.

"We need to be prepared. They may be expecting to be questioned by someone, not by us specifically and not tonight, but at some time by someone official."

"How could they be expecting that?"

"We don't know if they know any of the other families who might have told them someone came calling and was asking questions about the child's illness," Morelli explained. "Or they may have heard about it on the grapevine, so to speak."

"Can it really happen that all these people know each other?" Emily asked in surprise.

"Absolutely it can. People who come from the same place and speak the same language often know each other and stick together in this country because there aren't many of them," Morelli said.

Like the rabbi's wife, Emily thought. Miriam Kandel had said much the same thing.

"On top of that," Morelli went on. "You talked to these people's neighbor. We have to assume she told them all about it."

"I'm almost positive she did," Emily agreed. "I got the impression the neighbor didn't care for Mrs. Jablonski and might go out of her way to frighten her. Even though I'm not very frightening," she added.

Morelli laughed.

"I'm sure you were terrifying to the families you spoke to. They see you as the health department in human form. In their minds nothing good can come of that," he joked. "The important thing is we find out all we can and in as much detail as possible," he went on more seriously.

Now Emily knew this was where she had made a mistake with the families she interviewed. She had asked what had happened and had made notes of what she was told, but she had not thought to press for more information. In this case what had been misplaced sensibility had prevented her from pushing the grieving mothers further.

"One of the problems in a situation like this," Morelli said, "is that it is hard to separate fact from people's opinion and impression. We need both, but we have to be able to tell the difference. People often tell you something they believe as if it were a proven fact. For instance, someone might say the child had influenza, but are they saying so because they think that was the case or because the doctor told them so? It makes a difference, and it's an important one."

"I understand," Emily said. "If the person only thinks so, we might be dealing with something completely different. If they were given a firm diagnosis, we might expect to see other cases among their circle of friends and family."

"Exactly. We also need to know as much as possible about the progress of the illness, what they did about it, what did the child tell them about how he felt, and anything else that might be important. Sometimes a very small clue can break the case wide open."

Emily smiled to herself. Apparently, Morelli was also comparing their investigation to a murder mystery.

"Now, what would you like me to do?" Morelli asked.

"What do you mean?" Emily was confused.

"This is your investigation. Do you want to ask all the questions, and I'll just be there for moral support? Or, if you don't mind, I might ask something that happens to occur to me."

"I would be grateful for any help you are willing to give me," Emily said truthfully. "I am really at sea."

"Of course. When I began this job, the man who was training me just sat back and watched as I floundered. He let me make all kinds of mistakes and criticized me afterward."

"That's very hard," Emily said.

"Yes, but I learned quickly. It's like your boss. The department doesn't coddle its employees," Morelli said.

Emily certainly agreed with that. She felt Director Kent had thrown her in at the deep end with very little instruction or guidance about what to do. She carefully turned over in her mind the question of whether the director wanted her to succeed or was actually hoping that she failed. The second possibility did not seem to make sense, but the lack of direction he had provided did not support the first. Or, she finally concluded, Director Kent had given her no support because he had none to give and knew as little about all this as she did. For this reason, Morelli's experience seemed like the best guide to what she should do, especially in the event that the children's deaths did turn out to have been caused by some infectious disease the health department did not know about.

They talked for a few more minutes about specific questions they would need to ask and how to phrase them best. Emily hoped the Jablonskis would cooperate. They were her last chance to find the key that would unlock the whole case.

"We'd better start going," Morelli said, standing up and pulling on his overcoat.

"Are we far from the Jablonskis'?" Emily asked. She had lost her bearings on the trip to the restaurant.

"We're on Delancey Street," Morelli told her. "It runs right into the ghetto in a couple of blocks. Keep going east and you come to the Williamsburg

Bridge. I could practically walk home from here," he added cheerfully.

Emily nodded. She had a lot to learn about the city. The map she pictured in her mind still had many blank areas about which she knew nothing.

As they were leaving the restaurant, Morelli suddenly spoke.

"Did you enjoy your dinner?" he asked, as if he had just remembered.

"Very much so," said Emily truthfully. "I'm not used to this kind of food but it was delicious."

Morelli smiled a relaxed, genuine smile.

"I'm glad. A meal like this needs a nice bottle of wine, but I guess we won't be having that for a while."

10

The tenement on Henry Street seemed both familiar and alien to Emily as she and Morelli approached. At this time of the evening the building, like all of its neighbors, was brightly lit with a light burning in every window. Even from the street the sounds of people living their lives could be plainly heard. A baby cried, somewhere else a door slammed. People talking sounded like a dull rumble of unintelligible syllables punctuated by sporadic laughter. A man in a heavy coat and dark hat carrying a paper-wrapped parcel shuffled along the icy sidewalk ahead of them. To Emily's surprise, he labored slowly up the steps of Number 161 ahead of her and Morelli. Though they were only seconds behind him the man had already vanished into one of the ground floor apartments when they entered the building.

"What floor?" Morelli asked softly, starting up the stairs.

"Third," Emily told him. She noticed Morelli was stepping carefully on the outside edge of each tread to minimize any noise from creaking floorboards. "There's no point in alerting everyone in the building that we're here," he whispered, indicating that Emily should follow his lead.

In this way they crept up to the third floor, which seemed quiet despite the sounds coming from other apartments below and the fact that Emily knew children lived here. She was slightly out of breath when they reached the landing, so she pointed at the Jablonskis' door. Morelli nodded that she should knock. Steeling herself, Emily rapped sharply on the door.

From inside they heard a shuffling and the sound of a chair being pushed back. Suddenly the door flew open and they found themselves facing a short, slight man with round eyeglasses and a look of extreme anger. Behind him, a woman of surprisingly similar appearance stood limply in the middle of the room.

"So, you've come," the man said sharply. "It was always just a matter of time."

Like everyone connected with this case, the man spoke with a pronounced accent that indicated he came from some part of Central or Eastern Europe. His English was fluent, rapid and colloquial, and Emily had no trouble understanding.

"Were you expecting us?" she asked with surprise.

"You. Someone like you. You were bound to show up." The man glared first at her and then at Morelli. "Who are you anyway?"

Morelli glanced at Emily, who nodded to indicate he should speak for them.

"I am Edward Morelli. This is my associate, Miss Emily Lowe. We're from the Department of Health."

"What do you want?"

"We want to ask you and your wife some questions," Morelli said calmly. "About your son, Samuel."

Emily was impressed that Morelli had memorized the facts of the case and did not need to refer to any notes. She resolved to do so as well if a chance came up again.

At the mention of her son's name Mrs. Jablonski began to weep silently behind her husband. She sniffed loudly and said something to him in a foreign language Emily didn't recognize. Whipping around, Jablonski hissed at her to be quiet and said something in the same tongue. He turned back to Emily and Morelli.

"My wife says you are here to arrest us. She is afraid you'll take me away and no one will ever see me again. I told her that can't happen in this country. And besides, we haven't done anything. Am I right?"

"You are right, sir," Morelli said in the mildest tone. "We do not have the power or authority to arrest you. You are not required to talk to us. We were just hoping you would answer some questions about your boy."

Jablonski nodded with satisfaction. In the background, his wife was still crying silently. After a moment, she wiped her eyes with the back of her hand and looked at them with the watchfulness of a cornered animal.

"Why do we need to answer questions? The boy is gone. The hospital knows all about it." Jablonski's tone made Emily think the man blamed the hospital for all his problems, perhaps having caused his son's condition rather than trying to cure it.

"Sir," Morelli began, speaking slowly and deliberately, "when a child dies and the cause is not known, the health department is concerned that child may have had an infectious disease. We investigate in the hope of preventing others from becoming sick."

Emily was increasingly happy that Morelli had accompanied her to speak to the Jablonskis. She could not imagine having to confront this furious man and his tearful and obviously frightened wife by herself. She would have had no idea what to say or how to deal with any of this.

"What infectious disease?" Jablonski snapped. "No one here is sick."

"I understand that, sir. But we are just trying to find out what happened with your son."

"He got sick. He died. Nothing happened."

Mrs. Jablonski spoke for the first time. Her accent was much stronger than her husband's and Emily had to strain to follow what she was saying.

"Can't you just leave us with our troubles? There is nothing to tell," she said plaintively.

Emily had been looking around the room from her vantage point just inside the door. It was almost identical to the apartment next door she had seen when she visited the building before. The only real difference was that the sewing supplies were missing and instead, the table held several covered dishes and a number of empty plates, presumably the remains of the family's dinner. A small pile of newspapers lay against the wall. Emily could see one written in Hebrew letters that she had learned was Yiddish, the language spoken by most Eastern European Jews but without an alphabet of its own. A copy of the more familiar *New York Sun* was also visible, carefully folded back to preserve the reader's place. The door to the next room was tightly shut, and Emily could imagine the two remaining Jablonski children cowering in a corner like mice while their parents dealt with the strange intruders.

"We investigate situations like this to prevent other people from becoming sick. You could be helping the whole city by telling us about your son's illness," Morelli was saying. He spoke in the most reasonable voice imaginable, as if no one could possibly object to what he proposed. Jablonski, however, did object.

"Why should we help the whole city?" the man blustered. "No one has ever helped us. We mind our own business and don't expect anything. Nothing has ever been offered anyway."

Morelli nodded and appeared to think this over.

"Perhaps you would explain it to us as a personal favor," he suggested.

Emily saw Jablonski soften visibly. She knew this was an example of what Morelli had told her about using your voice to calm a hostile situation. Somehow Morelli had known the idea of them doing a favor might sit better with the Jablonskis.

"Fine," Jablonski said, not very graciously and with a glance at his wife. "We will do you a favor."

"Thank you," said Morelli, with his usual good humor. Emily murmured her own thanks as well and took out her notebook to record anything the Jablonskis might say.

"Maybe you can start by telling us about Sam's illness," Morelli said. "How did he get sick?" he added, directing this question to Mrs. Jablonski.

"The children go to my sister's after school when we're at work," Mrs.

Jablonski explained. Emily recalled this fit with what the neighbor had told her about the family. "One of her children caught a cold at school and gave it to the others. Of course, Sam and my older two caught it as well."

"So, it was just a cold?" Emily asked, trying to replicate Morelli's tone of voice that implied this was as ordinary a situation as eating a meal or waiting for a bus.

"Yes, we thought so anyway. They all had a sore throat, stuffed nose, and a cough," Mrs. Jablonski explained. "The cough was the worst part. None of them could sleep with the coughing. It kept us up at night as well," she said, looking to her husband for confirmation. Jablonski nodded in silent agreement.

"Was there any reason to think Sam might be sicker than your other children?" Morelli asked.

Mrs. Jablonski looked at him in confusion.

"What I mean is, you had no doubt he had the same illness as the older children?

"Oh yes," she said. "It was just the same."

"And the same as your sister's children?"

"Yes, of course."

"What are you getting at?" Jablonski put in.

Ignoring the question, Morelli went on, "What did you do for it?"

"Do? What's to do? Children get colds, coughs all the time."

"The school is a hotbed of germs," said Jablonski, echoing a sentiment Emily had heard many times from her own friends, her parents, and their acquaintances, and even a former classmate who had become a teacher at one of the city's public schools. She had even read this in the newspapers, often accompanied by criticism of her own department.

"Did you give the children any medicine? Cough syrup, for example? Did you take them to the doctor?" Morelli asked, again using his most mild tone. He made the questions sound as if the answers were unimportant details to the case, when, in fact, Emily knew from their discussion after dinner that these were crucial points in establishing the facts of the situation.

“Of course we didn’t take them to the doctor for a cold,” Jablonski said before his wife could respond. “And we didn’t give them medicine either. They weren’t that sick.”

Emily was about to protest that a child had indeed been taken to the hospital and had subsequently died, so he must have been very sick. But Morelli spoke first.

“Didn’t you try to stop the coughing somehow?” he asked.

“I gave them *gogl-mogl* . . .” Mrs. Jablonski trailed off and looked at her husband, apparently at a loss for words.

“It’s a home remedy. A sweet egg drink,” Jablonski said.

“Did that help?” Emily asked.

“Yes, but Sam was still coughing. It would have been better with brandy, Heering or Slivovitz,” Mrs. Jablonski explained.

“Did you try that?” Morelli pressed.

Mrs. Jablonski’s expression suddenly became worried. Again, she looked at her husband for reassurance.

“I had none in the house. I couldn’t buy any because of the Prohibition. All the liquor stores have closed,” she said in a quivering voice.

Jablonski looked at her sharply. Then turning to Morelli and Emily, “We agreed that this is a personal favor. You said we won’t get into trouble.” The aggression with which he had greeted them initially had returned.

“That is right, sir,” Morelli assured him. “We are not the police, and we will not be speaking to the police. We are interested only in the child’s illness.” He addressed his next statement to Mrs. Jablonski. “But you managed to get something anyway,” he suggested.

“I asked my sister, my friends, but no one had anything to spare. Their children were sick, coughing as well,” she explained.

Emily bit her tongue. Her first impulse had been to express shocked outrage that the Jablonskis, as well as everyone they knew, were dosing young children with strong liquor. She restrained herself, knowing that this was exactly the kind of behavior Director Kent was committed to wiping out.

"But you got some anyway," Morelli said, leading Mrs. Jablonski to tell them everything.

"Yes, I did manage to buy a bottle of *palinka*." She looked again at her husband.

"It's some kind of fruit spirit made with cherries," Jablonski supplied. He seemed resigned to the fact that Morelli and Emily had no knowledge of such items that made up the daily life of people like him and his wife.

"May I ask where you got it?" Morelli said. Emily wondered whether Morelli was going to break his promise to Mr. Jablonski and report the violation of the Volstead Act. She knew from reading the files of the Bureau of Child Hygiene that any violations of the law or city regulations that did not relate directly to health were supposed to be reported to the relevant authority.

"I bought it from a peddler," Mrs. Jablonski said.

This Emily did understand. Even in New Rochelle many housewives and also younger women bought various items from the occasional salesman passing through town with his wares. She and her friends would sometimes buy inexpensive hair ribbons and handkerchiefs from such people, even though their mothers discouraged the practice. Emily's mother thought that peddlers were dishonest and the goods they had to sell were likely to be flawed, but even she did not protest too much as the peddlers did play an important economic role in the country, especially in the days before the town had grown and so many stores opened up.

"So, you gave your children this cherry liquor for the cough," Morelli confirmed.

"No, only Sam," Mrs. Jablonksi corrected him. "The others were already much better by then."

"How did the child end up in the hospital?" Morelli wanted to know.

Both the Jablonskis seemed to shrink. He looked at the floor, while his wife's eyes filled with tears.

"Sam seemed better," she said. "But then he got much worse. He complained he was weak. He couldn't get up out of bed. His stomach hurt, he said.

Stabbing pains. He started vomiting and complained he couldn't see right. We had to take him to the hospital."

"What did they say at the hospital?" Morelli asked.

"Nothing," Jablonski told him. "They didn't know what was wrong. They put him in a bed and sent us home. The next day he was worse. Then he died. They didn't do anything at all."

"Were you told anything after he died?" Emily asked as gently as she could.

"Nothing. They didn't want us to bring him home. They wanted to do tests, to cut him up," Jablonski said with evident disgust. "But I know my rights. And we have traditions. We have laws we live by," he added indignantly.

Neither Morelli nor Emily spoke for a moment, contemplating this sad story.

"And no one gave you any further information about the child?" Morelli asked finally.

"Not a word. When we refused to let them do what they wanted, they were only too glad to see us go. Some of my friends helped and the rabbi came. He was buried that same day, as he should have been."

"You wouldn't happen to have any of the brandy left? Or even the bottle?" Morelli asked hopefully.

Jablonski scowled at the suggestion.

"Of course not," he said flatly. "It was used up, and the bottle went out with the trash. Enough is enough. My wife is deeply upset."

Mrs. Jablonski was now weeping openly. Emily felt like crying herself. The story they had been told was one of misfortune, frustration, and bitterness. In her mind, the childhad died needlessly. She was sure that would be what Director Kent would have said if he were here. At the same time, a chance to understand the child's illness and perhaps prevent an epidemic had been lost. For the moment she had forgotten about the six other families who were part of this investigation and the fact that she was supposed to be looking for a common thread that ran through all seven cases.

Emily did not recall the other people involved in the case until much later that evening when she was back in her room. When Jablonski had ushered them out with a reminder that he had done them a favor and they should now leave the family in peace, Morelli had insisted on escorting her back to her lodgings. It was late, he said, and she might have trouble as a woman alone. Despite her protests, he assured her he did not mind returning to Brooklyn on the subway so late on such a cold night. They had spoken very little about the Jablonskis or any other aspect of the investigation on the way back uptown. The conversation, which Emily had found to be very pleasant, was general and included Morelli telling her a number of stories about his student days more than a decade before at Brooklyn College, where he had studied biology in the hope of one day becoming a laboratory scientist. When he graduated, however, a paying job was more pressing than his desire to complete a doctorate, so he had taken a position offered to him at the Department of Health, the same position he still occupied. Public health investigations suited him, Morelli had explained to Emily, and he earned a good living. Emily wondered if she herself would feel the same way in another ten years or if she would have long since left Director Kent's office for another kind of life.

11

Having gone over all seven of her interviews, including the most recent with the Jablonskis, at least a thousand times in her mind on Sunday—which was otherwise a day to relax and do chores—Emily was no further along in understanding what had happened to those children. She wondered what Morelli thought. He had witnessed only one of the interviews, which Emily had to admit had produced more information than any of the others, but he had read her notes and may have formed an opinion based on his much greater experience. Her desire to solve this mystery had grown far beyond the need to please her boss or avert a public health emergency. The case had become an absorbing puzzle that she felt she must understand.

When she arrived at work on Monday morning, Director Kent had already left for a series of important meetings to evaluate the city's ongoing efforts to fight tuberculosis, which, despite their best efforts, was still a major cause of disability, especially among the poor. The discovery almost forty years ago that the dreaded "White Plague" had been caused by a microorganism, rather than a defect in the individual's physiology, had done little to reduce the stigma of poverty generally associated with sufferers. The disease most commonly emerged among people who lived crowded together in unsanitary conditions with few amenities and could be practically epidemic in such areas. Director

Kent had explained all this to Emily and stressed the impact of the disease on children. They often suffered from tuberculosis themselves but frequently became orphans when it resulted in the loss of one or both their parents. He had stressed that the number of people with the disease was declining in the city, but tuberculosis remained a serious concern for him personally as well as for the department. Emily knew that Kent was trying to give her a thorough grounding in modern public health, and she made a special effort to pay attention and think about everything he told her.

Emily quickly read over the list of tasks the director had assigned to her for the day. They were few in number and could be completed in less than two hours, she calculated. This would leave her free to work on her investigation and talk to Morelli.

By half past ten, she had finished the filing Kent wanted done and had also located a number of reports he would need the next day and laid them on his desk where he could not miss them. Taking her handbag but not her coat, Emily left her own office to look for Morelli in the investigators' workroom. Expecting to find him at his desk, Emily was startled for a moment when she did not see her mentor. She realized of course, that Morelli's work must mean he was out of the office more often than in. She had been lucky on the previous occasions that he was there. Several other investigators were at their desks, however, so Emily supressed her surprise and walked calmly over to Morelli's desk as if she had an absolute right to be there. She sat down in a chair set aside for visitors and began to write him a note.

Emily could sense the other investigators watching her and were probably wondering who she was and what she was doing. She thought one of them might ask, but none of them did. Knowing what people were like, Emily assumed someone would find a way to read her message to Morelli, and she didn't want to embarrass him. She also did not want to give even a hint about what they were working on. For now, it should remain between the two of them. Even her director did not know the full story. Emily had given Kent a summary of what she had learned and was hoping to present him with the solution to the mystery in the near future, especially since he had instructed her to "keep at it." However, she did want Morelli to know she appreciated his help and felt warmly toward him, so she started her message with "Dear Ed" and signed it "Em." She hoped the reference to their shared joke would convey her feelings. The note itself simply said: "If you have time, perhaps we can discuss the case this afternoon."

Placing the note in the middle of Morelli's desk where it would be the first thing he saw when he came in, and where it was in plain sight of anyone else who happened to look, Emily stood up and prepared to return to her own office, purposely moving slowly as if by delaying for a few seconds Morelli might return and she could speak to him directly. As she was opening the door to leave, one of the other investigators, an older man who looked like he had seen everything and life could no longer surprise him, called to her:

"He's gone down to the First District to check something," the man said referring to one of the branch offices of the health department. "He'll be back after lunch."

Emily nodded her thanks and the man turned back to what he was doing. She wondered how many cases each investigator worked on at one time. Most of the twenty or so desks in the large room were empty each time she had visited, so Emily knew the investigators must be very busy.

Back in her office, Emily sat down at her desk and took out her notes on the case. She had practically memorized her own words by this time, but she tried to read them again as if she had not pondered them a thousand times before. Seven children appeared to have had a fairly bad chest cold, took a turn for the worse, and died. This might not have attracted any attention had the children not been taken to the hospital by their parents as a last resort when it became clear they were not recovering at home. Oddly, all of the children had siblings who had gotten over what seemed conclusively to be the same illness. Emily could not see anything in her notes that indicated a difference between the dead children and those who had returned to health, nor did anything stand out that might shed light on what had caused their death.

The only consolation in all of it that Emily could see was that no more deaths had been reported, and every day that passed lessened the possibility that a new disease was lurking among the public that might suddenly grow to epidemic proportions.

The time passed slowly but Emily made no headway. She was back at her desk turning the pages of her notebook after having a sandwich in the employee's rest room when there was knock at the door, followed by the appearance of Morelli's smiling face from behind the doorframe.

"Is he in?" he asked, gesturing toward Director Kent's private office.

"No," Emily said, smiling in an attempt to match Morelli's relentless cheer. "He's gone all day."

"So, I can come in," Morelli said. He walked over to Emily's desk and moved the visitor's chair from its position at the end of the desk so he could lean on the far side opposite her seat. "I don't get to come upstairs too often," he added.

"You're not missing much," Emily told him. The furnishings of the various Health Department offices were largely the same, regardless of section or location. The private offices of directors and other higher ranking officials were more luxurious as well as more formally set up, but as far as Emily could see, her desk was exactly the same as Morelli's, and the filing cabinets and a small table opposite her desk were duplicates of similar pieces she had seen in the investigators' room.

"Still, this is the big time," Morelli joked. "How's the case going?" he asked more seriously.

"It isn't," said Emily in a tone of discouragement. "I've been over everything again and again but I just can't see anything."

Morelli considered this.

"Well, it seems like there are two possibilities," he said after a moment. "The first is that the seven deaths were a coincidence, and there is nothing more to report to your director. The second is that we are missing something important that would allow us to understand everything if we could find it."

"Which possibility is right, do you think?"

"Two children could be a coincidence, but not seven. I think we must have missed something, and we need to look for it," Morelli told her.

"I agree, although it would be nice to be able to say there was nothing unusual in all of this," said Emily. She realized what she had said sounded like she wanted her cooperation with Morelli to be over, which was not the case at all, so she quickly added, "I meant it would be good to be able to say there is no new disease the department has to worry about."

"I knew what you meant," said Morelli, smiling yet again. "I am enjoying your case, but it would be good if we could be sure there was no possibility of another epidemic," he went on. No one could forget those events, Emily knew, and the memories of widespread illness and death lay like a pall on the great city.

"What do we do now?" Emily asked. Surely Morelli would have ideas, considering his job centered on investigations of this kind.

"I think we need to look at everything from a different angle," Morelli told her. "Change our perspective, so to speak."

"How do we do that?"

"The best way to identify a disease is by its symptoms. We know quite a bit about these children's symptoms from their parents. I think we can take that as accurate in the sense that the parents have told us the truth as they understand it," Morelli began.

"Yes, I think they have. There would be no reason not to," Emily agreed.

"Maybe that can help us, then," Morelli went on. "We need to try to see where things don't fit."

"What do you mean?" Emily asked. The idea that there was a way forward amidst all these seemingly meaningless facts was intriguing.

"For example, everyone knows any kind of respiratory infection will have certain symptoms: a cough, sore throat, maybe a fever, possibly congestion of the head or chest," Morelli explained.

"Right," Emily agreed tentatively.

"So, if someone has those symptoms but then also has, say, nausea and vomiting, is that part of the same illness?" Morelli asked.

"I see," said Emily, brightening up. "Because the nausea and vomiting are not part of the respiratory infection, maybe the person has a wholly different illness or even has two separate ones."

"Exactly! So, since all the parents thought their child had a bad chest cold, let's look at the symptoms they told us about. If there are any that don't fit, maybe we can see something else that might have been wrong."

Emily nodded in agreement. "It's hard to believe the doctors at the hospitals didn't do this," she said.

"I'm sure they didn't have time. The children were only taken there when they had become very sick. There was probably no time to look into the history of the illness. The doctors would have accepted the parents' reports, especially since the main symptoms seem to have been respiratory," Morelli replied.

Quickly, they began to draw up a table with the dead children's names running down the side and a list of symptoms they had been told about across the top. The hospital where each child had been taken was given its own column along with the probable cause of death that Emily had gotten from the records. These ranged from "respiratory infection" to "seizure of unknown origin," suggesting that the doctors who attended the seven children had not investigated the cause of death but had reported what the situation seemed to be. Emily went back through her notes and read out the descriptions she had noted down as the parents talked about what had happened. Once that was done, she went back to the first child, Sam Jablonski, and read out his symptoms to Morelli who put an X in the boxes alongside the child's name for the symptoms he had had. She did the same thing for each of the other children in order: Jospeh Gutstein, Dorothy Rosenbaum, Hershel Dawidowicz, David Ojzerman, Pearl Varsaver, and Annie Bornstejn.

"Alright," said Morelli, "let's see what we can see."

"The one thing all the children seemed to have had was a cough," Emily said after studying the table for a moment. "Six of the seven had chest congestion. Their chest felt tight or they had trouble breathing. The parents phrased it in different ways."

"That fits for a chest cold, bronchitis, something of that kind," Morelli agreed. "Fatigue and fever can come with that as well but might not have been noticed by the parents. The main thing they would see would be the cough, especially since it would probably have kept the whole family from sleeping.

"Now, I'm looking at these other symptoms," Morelli continued, tapping the page with the eraser end of the pencil he had picked up from Emily's desk. "The stomach pains, confusion, difficulty standing and walking, and fits that the parents told you the children developed, even as they thought the cough and whatnot was getting better."

"Yes, it's almost as if they were suffering from a second disease," Emily said thoughtfully.

"Exactly. Now dizziness might go along with the chest infection, especially if the child had been in bed for a few days, but not the rest of it. Seizures could be caused by a high fever, but none of the children had much temperature." Morelli paused. "I think we need to concentrate on this group of symptoms and I think we ought to get expert advice."

"Advice? From whom?" Emily asked. "We could ask Director Kent. He is a pediatrician."

"As much as I admire Director Kent, I don't think he would have the expertise we need. He doesn't practice, which means he hasn't seen much illness in children in recent years, and we need someone who knows about disease in general, not just in individual patients."

"I see," said Emily. "Where do we find that kind of expertise?"

"Ah," said Morelli, smiling with his usually glee. "I happen to know someone who might be able to assist us. A big part of my job is knowing when help is needed and then knowing where to get it. In this case, we need someone who has the knowledge to look at what seems to be a random set of symptoms and determine what condition they go with."

Emily nodded. This was a new way of working for her.

"That must be extremely unusual. Who would have that knowledge?" she asked.

"Professor Harriet McIntosh at the Columbia School of Nursing," said Morelli happily. "She is a walking encyclopedia of human disease."

Emily could see that Morelli was proud to have a solution to offer at the impasse they had reached. For her part, she was relieved that he had a possible way out of the dead end they seemed to be stuck in.

"Is she a friend of yours?" Emily asked.

"I wouldn't exactly say she is a friend, but she has been very generous in helping me on a couple of occasions. If I'm honest, I'm a little afraid of her," Morelli admitted. "She can be very stern. You know what nurses are like."

Emily nodded. Nurses often had the task of keeping patients in line and making sure their well-meaning family members didn't undermine the treatment they needed to recover. That required a firmness few people could maintain. They also had to be able to handle people in serious pain and distress and somehow prevent them from becoming discouraged and giving up. It was a noble profession, Emily thought, but not one she herself would be suited to.

"We would have to go up to Columbia to talk to her," Morelli was saying. "She seems to spend most of her time there these days."

Columbia University had a campus in Morningside Heights on the Upper West Side of Manhattan. Emily knew it well having studied at Barnard, the women's college aligned with Columbia. In fact, she had taken a number of classes on the men's campus just across Broadway from the women's school. The university's move to its current location had taken place twenty-three years before when Emily was still a baby. The new campus was styled as an academic village with buildings modelled after those from the Italian Renaissance. But Columbia remained prominent in the consciousness of many New Yorkers as the shining example of the city's academic heritage. The institution itself had been founded by royal charter in 1754, before the revolution that had separated America from Great Britain, and it had prospered along with New York ever since. Emily was proud to be a part of the city's history in this way and thought of the prominent university with great pleasure and respect.

"It will be like coming home," she joked. "Do you think Professor McIntosh will be willing to see us?" Emily asked more seriously. She was wary of anything that might affect them completing the investigation.

"I'll try to telephone for an appointment," Morelli promised. "Can you leave the office tomorrow morning?"

"Oh, yes. I'll just leave a note for the director. He has given me permission to be in and out on this case," said Emily. "But what about you? And your other work?"

Morelli shrugged.

"I'll get back to it right now. My boss knows I'm working with you, so it'll be fine." He stood up abruptly and laid Emily's pencil down alongside the lined pad they had been using. "I'll let you know the plan by the end of the day," he said, pointing to the telephone on Emily's desk.

With little work to do, Emily spent most of the afternoon wondering first: Would Morelli be able to make an appointment to see Professor McIntosh on such short notice and would the professor be able to provide the help they hoped for, and second: whether there really was a solution to the strange cases of illness and death she had been charged with unravelling. By the time the telephone rang at four-fifteen, the only call of the afternoon, a third worry had materialized in Emily's thoughts: would Morelli really contact her as promised? So, it was with a sigh of relief that she picked up the receiver and heard his voice. They quickly decided to meet at eight-thirty the next morning in the lobby of the health department and go up to Morningside Heights together on the subway.

12

The ride uptown on the Broadway-Seventh Avenue IRT was disconcerting for Emily, who had rarely taken the subway and tended to avoid it when possible. Despite having lived in Manhattan for a number of years since college, she had never taken to the system of underground trains, which moved extremely fast along unseen tracks beneath the city's streets and buildings. It was only possible to tell where you were by the signs in each station, which were subterranean worlds of their own—some with multiple platforms at different levels, systems of turnstiles and stairways, ornate tiling and vaulted roofs, and even stores and kiosks. The cars themselves were like those of any other train, but Emily felt the constant rushing sound as the subway moved through the tunnels was strange, and she was unnerved by the long periods of complete darkness outside the windows alternating with brilliant illumination as the train came into a station. However, like most New Yorkers, Morelli seemed completely comfortable traveling underground, so Emily suppressed her wariness and followed his lead.

They emerged at 116th Street at the intersection of Broadway, just west of Columbia's main gates. Emily glanced wistfully toward Hewitt Hall, but quickly turned away to accompany Morelli onto Columbia's campus.

"Professor McIntosh has an office at the Presbyterian Hospital on East

70th Street," said Morelli as they walked across the quadrangle toward the administration building. "That was where I met her for the first time. She said she's working on something with some people from the medical school that requires she be on this campus."

Emily nodded. She was familiar with professors from her college days. They all seemed to be involved in mysterious research that had no end and no beginning but was always ongoing. This formed the material for a sheaf of articles and books each of them proudly authored and then required their own students to read. It all contributed to the progression of knowledge, Emily allowed, but the way in which this happened was a secret known only to these academic elites. Emily had seen enough to know an invisible hierarchy existed within this and probably every other university, as, she assumed, Morelli must have observed during his own college days. However, it would be necessary to spend many more years earning degrees and cultivating the right circle of contacts to be admitted into the rarefied world of the university. Emily's bachelor's degree did not entitle her to pass through that door. None of this engendered any bitterness in her though. She recalled her college days fondly.

"The professor said she'd meet us here," said Morelli, leading Emily up the steps into the massive and ornate building that housed the university library. As they passed between the columns and entered the foyer, he added, "We're to wait here and she'll come to us."

While waiting Emily looked around. It had been several years since she had been inside Columbia's library. As a student at Barnard most of what she needed for her classes had been available on her own campus, even though the libraries of both institutions were open to students at either college.

"It's rather formidable, isn't it?" she whispered to Morelli. The marble facades were intended to convey an impression of ancient Greece or Rome as an indication to library patrons of the stores of knowledge housed in the building. Despite a number of students and staff going about their business the library was supernaturally silent. A visitor would have no choice but to whisper.

"I was just thinking that," Morelli replied in a low voice. "Imagine having read all the books they keep in here!"

"You'd need more than one lifetime," Emily whispered back, with a silent laugh. She became serious immediately as she noticed a woman approaching them.

This was clearly Professor McIntosh. About sixty years old to Emily's eyes, the professor was dressed in a high-necked blouse and floor-length skirt that had long made up the uniform of the university woman, clothing that was completely resistant to changes in fashion and trend. Her hair was pinned up in a tight bun, and her ramrod straight posture gave away her training as a nurse. No other profession Emily knew of required this kind of decorum among its members. As she approached them Emily noticed the brooch Professor McIntosh had pinned to her blouse was actually a nurse's watch, whose face was suspended upside down from the fob that held the pin. Emily had seen timepieces of this kind before and knew they allowed the wearer to look down and see the time without having to pick up the watch.

"Edward," said Professor McIntosh loudly, "how nice to see you again. And this is the colleague you told me about?"

Emily felt everyone in the library must have heard the professor's greeting, but perhaps her rank and status permitted her to break the code of silence. She was a formidable presence. In fact, Professor McIntosh reminded Emily of the old photos of the Victorian ancestors she had seen in the albums her mother had inherited from her own grandmother.

"I'm Emily Lowe," said Emily. "I work at the Department of Health in the Bureau of Child Hygiene."

"I am well acquainted with Dr. Kent," said Professor McIntosh, holding out her hand for Emily to shake. Taken aback, Emily glanced at Morelli who was smiling and appeared to be perfectly calm.

"Professor McIntosh knows everyone," he said mildly.

"I understand you have a problem I might be able to help with. I have worked with Edward several times in the past," said the professor, indicating that they should get down to the business at hand.

"He told me that," said Emily, starting to overcome her reserve. "I am so pleased you have time to help with this case as well."

"Don't thank me until we see what I can do," Professor McIntosh told her. She led Emily and Morelli into one of the smaller reading rooms. All four of the walls were lined with shelves arranged in two stories. The upper story had to be reached by ladders that could be moved along a track. The room was furnished with a number of dark wood tables, some round and some oblong, each with its own set of matching captain's chairs. Professor McIntosh led them to one of the round tables and they all sat down. Emily felt very strongly that other library patrons must have left the room in response to some unknown signal because Professor McIntosh wished to use it, even though she knew this could not have been the case.

"As you may know, it has been some time since I have done any nursing, although we all had to help out during the influenza," said Professor McIntosh, in reference to the pandemic that had only died down a few months before. "I mainly teach these days," she went on.

"Do you teach nursing?" Emily asked politely.

"Not directly, although I do teach nursing students as well as any others who choose to take my course. I am a medical historian." The professor paused, waiting for a sign that Emily understood what this involved.

"I took a course in the history of science as part of my degree at Barnard," Emily said. "I didn't know the history of medicine was offered."

"That would have been Donaldson's course," Professor McIntosh stated, as if this were obvious and Donaldson was a badly behaved schoolboy, when in fact he was an eminent scholar and specialist on Darwin's theory of evolution. "He mostly discusses natural selection."

"That's right," said Emily with surprise.

Morelli laughed.

"See, the professor knows everyone," he said.

"Hardly that, Edward. I have been here a long time, and Miss Lowe attended Barnard College, which is really one and the same as Columbia."

Then, turning to Emily once more, Professor McIntosh went on, "I do a great deal of committee work now and have occasion to meet with a great many people. I am trying to fight the illiberal approach to liberal education that seems to prevail at this institution. As I tell anyone who will listen, students need to understand the history of their profession. How else can they be expected to avoid the mistakes of the past?" She looked hard at Emily for confirmation of this view.

"I agree completely," Emily replied quickly. She felt she was a student again, subject to evaluation, not just of her ideas and ability to express them, but of her whole person as someone worthy of obtaining a degree. "I wish I had known more about the history of public health before I began working at the health department."

"I'm sure Kent has brought you up to speed," said Professor McIntosh. Emily felt she had passed a test, the nature of which had been unexpected and covered material she was unfamiliar with.

"Now," said the professor, adjusting her long, full skirt and sitting up even straighter than before. "Tell me what the problem is."

Emily, assisted by Morelli, quickly explained what had occurred, everything they knew about the seven families involved, and what they had done over the past two and a half weeks to try to figure out what had caused the children's untimely deaths.

"It's been some time since I have done any nursing, but it seems to me that this is a very unusual situation. These patients have obvious respiratory symptoms but also what appears to be a second malady," said the professor thoughtfully.

"We came to that same conclusion," Morelli confirmed. "We were hoping you might be able to recognize something about that second illness."

"It strikes me that the second set of symptoms—the confusion, disturbance of vision, lack of coordination, even fits—relates to the nervous system. The body's organs behave in certain predictable ways, and these problems do not arise from bronchitis or a chest cold," the professor explained.

"Do you know what it might be?" Emily asked.

"An idea is starting to form, but I need to think about it further," Professor McIntosh told her. "What did the nurses say?" she asked.

"The nurses?" Emily said in surprise. "We haven't spoken to any nurses."

"Miss Lowe," said Professor McIntosh with the full force of her personality, "you must speak to the nurses. The doctors come in. They leave their instructions. That perhaps is as it should be. But the nurses are with the patients tweny-four hours a day. They are the ones who talk to the families, who attend the sick person. They see everything and know a great deal more than anyone about any given patient. You MUST talk to them!" the professor stressed.

Emily looked down at her hands. Now that Professor McIntosh had said it, it was obvious the hospital nurses who had cared for the sick children might have important information she and Morelli had missed. Where she had been fairly confident in talking to Professor McIntosh before, she now felt she had failed a test and would have to bear the consequences.

"I may be able to help you with that as well," said Professor McIntosh more kindly. "Needless to say, we have students and graduates at virtually every hospital in the city. "Two of your cases were taken to Bellevue. I am certain some of our nurses have been placed there and may be able to help you."

"Thank you so much," Emily stammered.

"Now, unfortunately, I do have to go. I have a meeting I must not be late for," said Professor McIntosh, ending the conversation. "Thank you, Edward, for allowing me to participate in this interesting case." Then, turning to Emily, she added, "You will hear from me directly once I have given this some thought."

On the trip back to Midtown Emily thought over everything that had happened. She hardly dared allow herself to hope that Professor McIntosh would have the key to the problem. At the same time, she was restless with anticipation and excitement. Surely a person of the professor's stature and experience would have insight unavailable to her and Morelli. For his part, Morelli seemed as calm and composed as ever. Emily realized his job involved carrying out investigations of this kind every day, and it made sense that he was used to the ups and downs of trying to solve these complex mysteries of human behavior and disease.

“I'd better get back to my other work,” he told Emily, unbuttoning his heavy coat as they entered the health department building. “Let me know if you hear anything,” Morelli added, looking seriously at Emily as if he feared he would now be excluded from the investigation.

“Of course,” Emily assured him. “If there's any news, the first thing I'll do is call you.”

As she made her way back to her office, Emily felt she was on the crest of a great wave. The question was whether she would be able to ride it easily in to shore or whether she would crash into a sea of despair and failure.

13

For the second time in as many weeks, Emily had a visitor. She was alone in the office after Director Kent had gone to one of the many meetings that seemed to make up an increasing portion of his duties. After the morning's discussion with Professor McIntosh, she had a great deal to think about. The routine activities of her job, like filing and tidying up the director's notes and papers did not require a great deal of concentration, and she found her thoughts returning to case. Relentlessly, she went over everything that had happened since she began her investigation, every word that she or anyone else had said, looking for a crack, no matter how small, that would help her break open the mystery of the seven children's deaths. Emily was aware that this feeling of puzzlement was becoming a constant state for her, but it gave her a kind of exhilaration, and she understood why Morelli enjoyed his work, which involved nothing but this kind of inquiry. The knock on the door startled her and she was shocked to see that the visitor was a young woman of about her own age, dressed in a heavy woolen cape and a starched white nurse's uniform and white cap. Behind her Emily caught a glimpse of her friend Julia, who had apparently escorted the visitor to the office.

Emily thought the young nurse looked tired, but before she could ask her to sit down the woman said, "I was told you wished to see me. Professor

Harriet McIntosh gave me your name. I came directly from the hospital. My name is Sally Malone."

Emily was shocked. She had certainly not asked to see anyone and had not expected Professor McIntosh to have represented her in this way. But she was aware the young woman might have important information, so she tried to hide her surprise and act as if she was used to summoning people in this way.

"Please sit down. If you don't mind, I will see if my colleague is available," said Emily. She picked up the telephone and asked the switchboard to connect her to Investigations. To her delight Morelli himself answered almost immediately. "A Miss Malone is here to speak with us," Emily told him, as if they had both been expecting the visit.

Morelli caught on immediately and demanded no explanation, which Emily would not have been able to give anyway. "I'll be there in thirty seconds," he said, his voice trailing off as he put down the phone before the end of the sentence.

Emily had no sooner smiled at the visitor and taken out her notebook when Morelli walked in the door. He must have run up the stairs, she thought, but he did not seem out of breath or unusual in any way. She waited while he introduced himself to Miss Malone and carried a second chair across the room to Emily's desk for himself.

"I was told you wished to see me," Miss Malone repeated. Emily watched as her expression changed from neutrality to concern. "Is something wrong? Have I made a mistake of some kind?" she asked, with worry in her voice.

"Absolutely not, Miss Malone," Morelli said quickly. He glanced at Emily, a signal to play along. "We very much appreciate your taking the time to stop in. We are interested in some children you might be familiar with. Which hospital do you work at?"

"I am so sorry, I should have mentioned that. I am at Bellevue in the pediatric ward," she answered, referring to the city's largest public hospital that was located on First Avenue some way to the north of the ghetto where the investigation had so far been centered. Now Emily understood why Professor McIntosh had referred this young nurse to her. Two of the children had been taken there when it became clear they were desperately ill.

"Do you recall a patient called Annie Bornstejn and another, David Ojzerman?" Emily asked, referring to her notes.

"Clearly, Miss Lowe."

"How do you happen to recall these two patients from the dozens you must treat?" Morelli asked. The question sounded casual, but Emily knew he must have a specific reason for asking. There were many aspects of conducting an investigation that she did not yet understand.

"Both patients were brought in a state of advanced illness. It was not clear what was wrong, and both died," said Miss Malone without apparent emotion.

"Surely deaths are not uncommon in the hospital, Miss Malone. Even among children," Morelli commented kindly.

"Sadly not. But we almost always know the cause. It is not common for anyone to suffer from an unknown disease, much less for two patients in short order to be afflicted in the same way," their visitor explained.

"This is exactly our concern," Emily put in. "These cases, as well as several others, came to our attention because it was uncertain what disease the children might have had. We are always alert to anything that may grow into an epidemic."

"Goodness gracious!" Miss Malone gasped. "Do you believe these children had a contagious illness? We put them in the general ward."

"It's looking less and less likely," Morelli assured her. "We know they originally fell ill with some sort of chest cold or bronchitis that had a lot of coughing. That was almost certainly contagious. By the time they were brought to the hospital, they seemed to have developed a different set of symptoms so it may have been something entirely different."

Miss Malone nodded.

"The little girl was brought in first and the older boy a few days later. They were both weak, confused, and complained of stomach pain. The girl could not stand. She seemed to be a very sickly child. Not robust in any way. The boy told us he couldn't see properly," she explained.

"What did you think was wrong?" Emily asked.

"I had not formed any clear idea. The doctor thought it was a kind of fatigue we sometimes see following a bout of serious illness. There was a great deal of sickness with symptoms of this kind among influenza patients," said Miss Malone. For most New Yorkers the recent epidemic served as a ready source of comparison and example when discussing health and illness.

"Did that seem likely to you?" Morelli wanted to know. Emily was impressed at how he adapted his tone of voice to make questions that under other circumstances might have seemed insulting, sound completely reasonable and ordinary. It was an ability Emily very much admired.

"Not really," said Miss Malone after thinking for a moment. "But it was not my place to comment. We nursed them as best we could, but they both took a turn for the worse and sadly died."

Emily reflected that it was a sad story. She had witnessed the distress and bewilderment of each of the families and had seen firsthand the pain of not knowing what had happened to their children.

"Did the parents tell you anything about the children's illnesses?" Emily asked.

"No more than what you mentioned before. They had been sick, coughing, fatigued, but it had not seemed serious. When they did not recover and seemed to be getting worse, they were brought to us. I did think the little girl's mother looked ill herself, but she kept her head the whole time."

"Was there anything unusual that you can recall about either child?" Morelli asked.

"It's hard to say. I had the impression there was a faint odor on the little girl's breath, but it was almost nothing."

"What sort of odor?" Morelli wanted to know. Emily saw his eyes light up. Perhaps this was the clue they had been searching for.

"I can't really say. It reminded me of a laboratory, but it may have been nothing. People work in all sorts of places and carry it home on their clothes," the young nurse told them. The reference was clear in its implication. The city's poor did dirty and unpleasant work that those who were better off would shun out of hand and bore the traces of those jobs often without knowing it.

"Were any blood or tissue samples taken from the children, would you know?" Morelli asked.

"There was no reason to when they were brought in," Miss Malone explained. "The two children seemed to be suffering from an obvious respiratory illness. The parents would not allow anything to be done postmortem," she went on. "I was on duty at the time. One of them stayed with the body every second. Then some members of their own religion came and helped them take the deceased away for burial."

"I see," said Emily, looking to Morelli for confirmation. When she saw him nod slightly, she continued, "Thank you so much for coming, Miss Malone. We appreciate your time and effort enormously."

"I owe a great deal to Professor McIntosh. She asked me to come, so of course I did."

"Well, thank you again," Morelli said. "I am sure your information will help us greatly."

Miss Malone smiled slightly and left, escorted by Morelli to the lobby of the building. Emily looked at the clock and saw it was after five. She turned to Morelli who had quickly returned.

"Will any of that information really help us?" she asked without prelude.

"It's hard to say. You have to take a crumb here and a crumb there and build up a picture of what happened. The smallest detail may be useful in filling in the outline once you have a general idea of what happened," Morelli explained.

"We don't even have that outline," Emily sighed.

"Actually, we do. We know the whole sequence of events and we have a lot of information from different people about what those events meant. We now need to sort through it and figure out what is fact."

"I guess I've been hoping for the one clue that will solve it all," Emily admitted. "Like in a murder mystery."

Morelli laughed.

"We may have that clue and not even know it. Why don't we get something to eat and try to puzzle it out."

Emily was only too happy to agree. She had not been looking forward to yet another restless night, her mind flying in circles as she went over what they knew again and again. The chance to talk about it all with Morelli would be a welcome change and might lead to the breakthrough she had been looking for. In addition, he was a good companion, and Emily enjoyed all the time they had spent together on the investigation. She would have liked some of that time to have been more personal, and this seemed to be a step in the right direction.

Neither Emily nor Morelli spoke much on the short walk to a nearby Horn & Hardart. Despite being early evening, it was already dark and very cold. The days were still short at the end of February, and the city had not yet begun to feel a taste of spring air. They waited while the cashier made change and passed them a handful of nickels. The first of these waiter-less automats had appeared before the war and had taken off immediately. Emily had loved the automat from the first time she had eaten there, which had been with her parents soon after the restaurant first opened. The novelty of choosing something to eat, inserting the requisite number of nickels into a slot, and opening the little glass door to remove the dish had never worn off.

They carried the bowls of tomato soup and ham sandwiches they had both chosen to one of the marble-topped tables and sat down opposite each other to discuss the case.

"Let's go back to the beginning," Morelli suggested.

As they began to eat, Emily recited everything that had happened, beginning from the minimal information she had received from Director Kent at the very beginning of the case. In chronological order from that point, she repeated everything she could recall from her encounters with each person involved either directly or indirectly. Morelli asked a number of questions, which she tried to answer. When she reached the point in the story where he had taken an active role in the investigation, Morelli took a turn sharing his impressions and recollections of what had happened. Emily marvelled at how much had taken place in less than three weeks and how fast the investigation had moved, even though in her mind, it had not resulted in anything of much use. It was hard to believe that it was only earlier that same day that she and Morelli had spoken to two important informants: Professor McIntosh and nurse Malone. There was so much to try to make sense of and no guide to which details might be the crucial ones.

After a while the discussion died down, and both of them took a moment to think. They had finished eating, and Morelli lit a cigarette.

"I'm thinking of having a piece of pie," he said.

Emily nodded. The automat was famous for its several varieties of pie. A thought entered her mind and, independent of her conscious control, formed itself into words.

"What if someone did this to them?" she blurted out.

"How do you mean, Em?" Morelli asked calmly.

"Well, we noticed the second set of symptoms didn't fit the original illness reported in each of the children. Professor McIntosh thought as much as well. Maybe it wasn't a disease at all."

"You mean like someone murdered them? Like in a mystery novel?"

That was what Emily had meant, but it sounded ridiculous even to her, now that Morelli had said it aloud.

"I guess I did have something like that in mind," she acknowledged. "But, of course, that's crazy."

"It would be nice if real life were like literature," Morelli laughed. "But it isn't crazy. I wouldn't go so far as to think someone murdered these children—there are too many of them for that and there aren't really many connections between them. But you may be right that the second illness was not a disease in the way we've been thinking. That would explain why there were seven cases and no more. The last child died three weeks ago, and there has been nothing similar since. If there had been, your director would have let you know immediately," Morelli went on.

"How can we figure it out then? We've been looking for a disease," Emily said.

"In a way, this possibility makes things easier, but it also makes them harder. It's easier because we would only need to find one thing that all the children were exposed to that could cause the illness that we've been told about. The hard part, though, is finding out how that exposure could have happened."

"Have you had a case like this before?"

"Once or twice. You can appreciate, we mostly look into cases of infectious disease, but every so often something like this comes up. There was an accidental poisoning a few years ago that we traced to a place the victims worked. That was a clear connection we could follow up. Other than living in the same neighborhood, these families don't seem to have known each other. The children were different ages, went to different schools, but they all died from the same cause," Morelli explained. "At least it looks that way," he added.

"Do you mean you think maybe they didn't?" Emily was alarmed at this possible complication she had not anticipated.

"No, I actually do, but nothing is out of the question." Morelli stubbed out his cigarette. "Maybe we need to sleep on it and start fresh in the morning," he said. "I'll see you home . . . if you'll allow it," he added.

"With pleasure," Emily replied. She stood up to put on her coat and hat before going back out into the cold.

14

Emily awoke the next morning after a restless night of dreams. They combined elements of the ongoing investigation with events she had recently read in a popular novel called *The Circular Staircase* that she had come across in the reading room of her hotel. Her dream had taken place in a mysterious mansion in the country, and the events surrounding the children's deaths had been entwined with the characters in the novel. As in the story, a murder soon took place in her dream. Emily awoke as tired as she had been when she went to bed and with no further insight into what had happened to the sick children.

Arriving at the office, Emily was greeted by Director Kent who was on his way out to take part in a conference being held at City Hall on child health and welfare. He had no time to talk and no instructions for her, except that she was to take care of the routine business of the office and then continue on with what she was doing. He stressed the importance of a resolution but had neither suggestions nor criticisms. The director left carrying a briefcase full of files, presumably related to the topics that would be discussed at the event he was attending, and Emily contemplated how she would fill the day. The prospect of eight long hours alone with her thoughts was not appealing. She found she was unable to break out of the circular thinking that trapped her.

She would have liked to talk to Morelli again but knew he had other work to do and she shouldn't bother him without something more concrete to discuss.

She spent almost an hour going over her notes yet again and making a summary on a pad of lined paper. She tried to write down anything that might be an indication as to what had happened but finally concluded she simply did not have the knowledge and experience to spot the vital clue. At that point, however, the day's mail arrived, creating something for her to do that would occupy at least a few minutes.

As usual, there were a number of official letters for Director Kent, two public health journals he subscribed to, and an internal health department bulletin that was sent out on a weekly basis that Emily would generally read when she had time. Much to her amazement, however, there was also a letter addressed to her in small, old-fashioned handwriting. Turning over the envelope, she saw the sender was Harriet McIntosh, PhD. Professor McIntosh had promised to let them know the result of her research, but Emily had been afraid the professor was just being polite. She certainly had not expected to hear anything immediately. For the letter to have reached Emily that morning, Professor McIntosh must have mailed it within a few hours of their meeting the day before. Without thinking she reached for a letter opener and slit open the heavy cream-colored envelope. A sheet of matching paper, folded in half, slid out onto the desk and Emily carefully picked it up and read the brief message in the same neat handwriting:

Dear Miss Lowe,

Thank you for allowing me to participate in your interesting case. Having thought it over, I can come to only a single conclusion that I fear will not take your investigation much farther. I do not know how it can be the case as your victims were all children, but the symptoms you describe suggest poisoning by methyl alcohol. I refer you to the excellent work by Dr. Chapman entitled A Manual of Medical Jurisprudence and Toxicology. It is available in the University Library.

Cordially yours,
Harriet McIntosh

This was not at all what Emily had expected. When Morelli told her about Professor McIntosh's expertise, she had expected the professor would at best be able to suggest a number of possibilities. This definitive answer with one specific cause was an enormous step forward in the case. But at the same time, Emily was confused. As the professor had said, how could seven young children be the victims of chemical poisoning? Under what circumstances could such a thing have occurred? This was at least as mysterious as the events of the crime novels she had read, but those books had not prepared her to solve this problem in real life.

Emily hoped Morelli would know what to do. As she reached for the telephone, it occurred to her that she should have called him as soon as she realized the letter was from the professor. He had earned a place as a full partner on the case with the help he had given her. In fact, Emily felt he was really the senior partner but he had never tried to take over or deny her the credit for what they had managed to do so far. Morelli came to the telephone having been summoned by a colleague who had answered Emily's call to the Investigations room.

"There's a letter from Professor McIntosh," she told him in an excited reply to his greeting.

"Excellent!" said Morelli. "Let's hope she has something for us. Can you read it aloud?"

"With pleasure," Emily replied, not letting on that she already knew the content of the letter. She rustled the paper loudly, as if she were just opening the envelope, and read the professor's note to Morelli.

"That puts a whole different light on things," Morelli said with uncontained glee. "Can you talk now? I'll come up."

"Yes, of course," Emily told him. "Come up now."

Within moments, Morelli was walking in the door, and, like before, Emily wondered if he had run up the stairs.

"Methyl alcohol poisoning," said Morelli without prelude. "So, you may have been right, Em, that someone did something to these children. But I don't think it was intentional," he added.

"Do you mean to say there is no way this could have happened by accident? It couldn't have been a coincidence?" Emily asked.

"Assuming the professor is correct—and I believe that she is—no, it could not have been a coincidence," said Morelli. "How much do you know about chemistry?"

"Nothing at all."

"I'll give you a crash course," Morelli said with his customary enthusiasm. "The alcohol we drink in wine, spirits, and liquor of all kinds is ethyl alcohol. It's formed by the fermentation of sugar by yeast and can be distilled to increase its potency. A person would have to drink an enormous amount of liquor to show signs of poisoning. But there is another kind of alcohol, methyl alcohol—or wood alcohol, as it's sometimes called." Morelli paused, as if waiting for Emily' confirmation.

Emily nodded. "I've heard that term, but what exactly is wood alcohol?" she asked.

"It's actually a simpler form of alcohol that can be produced by distilling wood, hence the name. The problem is, it is quite poisonous," Morelli went on.

"But where would it have come from?" Emily asked. "And how would the children have gotten it?"

"That's the question," Morelli agreed. "Wood alcohol can be used for cleaning, and it's important in several industrial processes, so it might have come from one of the parent's workplaces. The problem with that is that you found the parents mostly worked in the garment industry, and why would they have given the children wood alcohol anyway?"

Emily thought this over. Morelli was right that no parent would knowingly give a child wood alcohol, even if they did not specifically know it was poisonous. It would be clear to anyone that a substance of this kind would not be safe to drink, and Emily did not believe any of the parents she had spoken to were negligent or lacking in care and concern for their children.

"What if they didn't know?" she said finally.

"You mean, what if they thought whatever they were giving the children was alright, but it turned out it wasn't?" Morelli asked.

"Yes, exactly," said Emily. "What if they thought they were giving the children something that would help them, but the medicine was adulterated?"

"I think you're onto something, Em!" Morelli exclaimed. "We did hear about something like that—the brandy Mrs. Jablonski bought from the peddler. She was looking for something strong enough to treat the boy's cough."

"That's right—I'd forgotten," Emily said. "None of the other parents mentioned anything like that though."

"They probably thought it wasn't important. We're going to have to ask them about it."

"I don't think they will be very happy to see me again," Emily said ruefully.

"Perhaps not," Morelli agreed. "But they'll have to. There are one or two questions we need each of them to answer, but first, I think we need to know more about methyl alcohol and where it might come from."

"Do you have another expert we can talk to?" Emily wanted to know.

"As it happens, I do," Morelli told her confidently. "In-house this time. I think we need to pay a visit to Bill Waters in the lab. We've known each other for years. He's using all those chemistry classes we took together."

"Oh, he was a classmate of yours. And he works here in the health department?"

"Yup." Morelli smiled, obviously pleased with himself. "But we'll have to go over to the lab. Bill doesn't get out much."

"I'll get my coat," said Emily, once again grateful that the answer to one of her problems had presented itself in a handily simple form.

Barely able to contain their excitement at this new phase of the case, they almost forgot to stop at the Investigations room for Morelli to get his hat and coat before they set off across town to the Public Health Laboratory on First Avenue near the Bellevue Hospital.

15

"So, you're interested in wood alcohol? Are you thinking of doing some bootlegging?" Bill Waters asked.

Emily and Morelli were sitting in the forensic laboratory of the Department of Health where Waters worked. The room was large and light, an impression strengthened by the winter sun that streamed through a row of windows set high in one wall. Waters's work area—really just a section of lab bench—was opposite this row of windows and benefited not just from the added light, but also the extra warmth. It must have been very hot in summer, Emily thought, but at the moment the effect of the sun on the glass was pleasant.

A number of other technicians in white lab coats were working at their own stations. Emily couldn't tell what they were doing but the array of flasks, retorts, and other glassware lined up on all of the benches was a clear indication of the kind of work done in the lab. Visitors were not normally allowed inside, Morelli had told her, and this was confirmed by signs throughout the building. But Waters was the manager of the laboratory and was able to take some liberties, especially when the visitors were from inside the health department.

"That's more your line than ours," Morelli said and went on to explain the salient points of the investigation. Waters appeared to listen carefully, his eyes on the row of jars and vials on the bench in front of him. In terms of appearance, he was as unlike Morelli as it was possible to be but when it came to personality, the two men seemed very similar.

Morelli finished his summary and waited for Waters to comment. Waters ran his hand through his dark, curly hair and nodded thoughtfully.

"It sounds like a difficult problem. This is a forensic lab and we see this kind of thing all the time. Someone gets ahold of some homemade hooch. It seems okay until they drink it, and then the trouble starts. They don't call it 'blind drunk' for nothing, you know," he added, smiling.

"What do you mean?" Emily asked, somewhat embarrassed. She was having trouble following what the two men were discussing.

"I'm so sorry," said Waters with genuine concern. "Ed here did say this was your first investigation. Liquor is expensive. It always has been, but alcohol is cheap. Now, not all alcohol can be consumed, but people don't know this. They figure it's all the same stuff. So, maybe they're making their own at home and don't get the distillation quite right or maybe they buy some legitimate product and mix in a little extra alcohol to give it more kick. Or maybe they just can't find or afford what they really want, so they drink whatever is on hand. The problem is, the alcohol we drink is ethyl alcohol. It's probably not that good for you, but the body can handle it. Wood or methyl alcohol is a poison. It can cause a lot of problems, including blindness, and death of course."

"Some of the families told you the child complained of not being able to see properly," Morelli said to Emily. "That was the clue Professor McIntosh saw."

"But where do people get this wood alcohol?" Emily wanted to know. "The whole thing sounds incredible," she added.

"It's all over," Waters explained. "It's got plenty of legitimate uses, but human consumption is not one of them. The most common source is people trying to make their own liquor. It is quite difficult to separate ethyl alcohol that we can drink and methyl alcohol, which is poison. This has been a problem for centuries—people want to drink—but it's only going to get worse with Prohibition."

"Of course," Morelli said. "That explains a lot. There's been no liquor to buy for more than a month now. Someone must have become desperate."

"Are you suggesting the parents gave the children wood alcohol because they couldn't get real spirits?" Emily asked. This suggestion shocked her.

"I actually don't think so, Em. It's more like what Bill said. They bought a product that had been purposely adulterated to make it go further or that someone made themselves and was careless with. I'm sure they had no idea anything was wrong with it."

Emily thought this over for a moment.

"Were you thinking of the peddler the Jablonskis mentioned?" she asked.

"That's possible. But it seems more likely it came from whoever he bought the brandy from. Someone who deals in spirits might have the wherewithal to refill empty bottles with homemade hooch, seal them and sell them," said Morelli. He looked thoughtful. "Bill, how hard is it to make your own spirits?"

"Not very hard. You could look it up in a chemistry textbook and set up the distillation right at home," Waters said readily. "The trick would be to separate the methyl alcohol from the rest of the batch."

"How would that be done?" Emily asked. She was becoming quite interested in this.

"Distillation is just a process of boiling and condensing liquid," Waters began. "Once it boils to produce vapor, you feed the vapor through a series of tubes or pipes at a lower temperature, and the vapor condenses to form liquid again. When you're talking about liquor, the distillation process concentrates the alcohol, so you have to start with a liquid that is alcoholic in the first place. This liquid, or wash as they call it, is usually made by fermenting grain or fruit. The fermentation produces ethyl alcohol that you want but also other substances you don't want. The trick is the separation."

"So, you could end up with methyl alcohol in the fermented liquid that was going to be distilled?" Emily asked to confirm her understanding.

"You could indeed," Waters said. "Methyl alcohol boils at a slightly lower temperature than ethyl alcohol, so you could just discard the first part of every batch. This is what commercial manufacturers do. You would have to calculate, though, how much you had to throw out," Waters told her.

"It sounds like most people would not be able to do that," Morelli commented.

"Of course not. Most don't even know the risk," Waters agreed. "But you can avoid it completely by making a sugar wine with just sugar and yeast. It's the fruit pectin that allows for the formation of methyl alcohol."

"Pectin!" Emily exclaimed. "You need pectin to make jam. Are you saying it's dangerous?"

Waters laughed.

"No, of course not. In jam and jelly, the pectin causes the mixture to thicken. It's found naturally in most fruits. When it's boiled, it bonds together and thickens the jam. There is no chemical reaction. When you have fermentation, the pectin contributes to the formation of methyl alcohol," Waters said.

"So, for example, you might have unwanted methanol in homemade cherry brandy," Morelli suggested. Emily had forgotten about the investigation for a few minutes, absorbed as she was in this practical chemistry lesson.

"You might," Waters confirmed. "Cherries don't have as much pectin themselves as some other fruit, but it's there."

"So, it isn't impossible someone tried to produce their own cherry brandy and ended up making something poisonous?" Emily asked.

"Not at all," Waters confirmed. "Plenty of people know how to do it safely, even at home, but more don't. Now that you can't buy any liquor, we're bound to see more of this."

"You know a lot about it, Bill," Morelli commented, laughing. "Maybe you've missed your calling."

"Now you two do as well. If you want to go into business, give me a call," Waters suggested with a smile.

Bundled up against the cold, Emily and Morelli left the lab and, as if by agreement, began to walk slowly up First Avenue in the thin sunlight. Neither of them was in a hurry to get back to the health department, and they had to decide what to do next.

As they were passing a cafeteria, Morelli stopped.

"Let's duck in here. I could use a cup of coffee, and we can plan our next move," he said.

They picked up their coffee from the serving table and paid the cashier. Morelli casually waved away her offer of a tray, and they carried the cups to an empty table near the back of the restaurant.

"It seems we've broken the case," said Emily, with a mixture of delight and disappointment. She was happy that she would be able to report success to Director Kent, but at the same time she was sorry the investigation seemed to be drawing to a close. It had been much more exciting than her work in the office and she was thoroughly enjoying talking to people all over the city and trying to puzzle out what had happened. She would miss working with Morelli and had even been wondering whether there were any women investigators and whether it might be possible to move to that kind of work.

"Almost," said Morelli. He lit a cigarette and inhaled deeply. "We can't get ahead of ourselves. We need to be able to show that some kind of spirit was given to each of the children. Otherwise, we can't be sure the Jablonski boy wasn't just a coincidence. We then need to show that whatever each of the families gave to the children was contaminated with methyl alcohol. Ideally, we'd have samples from the children that could be analyzed."

"Unfortunately, we don't. None of the families permitted any kind of postmortem examination," Emily said. Inside she was secretly elated that the investigation was not over. She wondered if Morelli could sense her feelings and perhaps even felt the same way. He certainly seemed to be enjoying the case.

"Maybe some of the families have some of the stuff left. That could prove exposure. But really we need something that links the children. We need to find out what they were given," Morelli said thoughtfully.

"What do we do?" Emily wanted to know.

"I think we need to talk to the families again. Well, probably the Jablonskis have told us everything there is to tell, but the rest of them may know more."

"Right," Emily agreed. "When?"

"How about now?" Morelli suggested. "The more time that passes the more likely it is that people will forget details or rewrite what happened in their head. After a certain point, there's no way to know whether anything they say is accurate."

Emily considered this. It sounded like Morelli had been misled by people's statements in the past, something which was probably to be expected in his line of work. She also realized she had been taking his continued participation for granted because it was what she hoped for.

"You'll come with me, won't you?" she asked, recalling the mistakes she had made in her first visit to the remaining families before Morelli had joined the investigation. She had decided there was no point in being subtle about her desire to have Morelli there. She was very much aware that they had come this far because of his expertise, something she would not be able to match.

"Of course, if you want me to," Morelli said. Emily noted how he was still careful not to insinuate himself into the investigation that still officially belonged to the Bureau of Child Hygiene under her director.

"You know I do," Emily told him happily. "I wouldn't know what to ask."

Once again, they put on their winter clothes and prepared to venture out into the street. This time, they turned south toward the ghetto and walked slowly toward the streetcar that would take them back to Orchard Street.

16

Emily sat anxiously at her desk waiting for Director Kent to summon her and for Morelli to arrive. She had been told that there would be an important meeting today that she must attend. It would take place after a series of other meetings involving the Director, the Head of Investigations who was Morelli's immediate boss, and a number of even higher-ranking officials whom Emily did not know. She had subsequently learned that Morelli had been instructed to attend the meeting as well and fervently hoped he would arrive before she was called to enter the director's private office, tentatively scheduled to take place at two o'clock.

This series of mysterious and highly unusual meetings seemed to have been triggered by Emily's report to Director Kent about the deaths of the seven children. She had given him a brief oral summary before handing over a typewritten document she had prepared from her notes, supplemented by discussion with Morelli, who had given her some advice about how best to structure the narrative. Emily had been satisfied with the result, especially once Morelli approved it, and had confidently turned it over to Kent. Perhaps naively, she had not imagined that the content might lead to further action on the part of the bureau or department. In fact, she had never really thought about why anyone beyond her director might be interested in the case.

The report outlined everything Emily had found and everyone she had spoken to, including the second visit to the families that she had made with Morelli. Those visits had provided a few tantalizing details and confirmed what they had begun to suspect on the way to the ghetto, namely that the peddler was the missing link between the affected families. And in fact, each of the families confirmed having bought some kind of cherry brandy from such a man.

At the Bornstejn residence—the first they visited—they learned that the family, like virtually all of their neighbors, frequently bought various items from peddlers, street vendors, and other informal salesmen. The convenience these sellers offered in small amounts, extending even to single cigarettes, was an important way to economize and Mrs. Bornstejn had seen nothing wrong in purchasing a small bottle of cherry brandy to treat her little daughter's cough. Emily, at a sign from Morelli, made no comment but noted down everything the woman told them. When asked by Morelli if any of the brandy was left, Mrs. Bornstejn just shook her head. There had not been much to begin with and the whole family had been sick. On the way to the next address Morelli explained that there was no reason to let on that something may have been wrong with the brandy. It would only add to the guilt and unhappiness the families already felt. Emily nodded regretfully. The families all seemed to be suffering greatly, not just from the loss of a child but from a hard life, and she wondered whether Morelli met such people in all of the investigations he was involved in.

Mrs. Varsaver told a similar story. She was aware that it had become impossible to buy alcoholic beverages in the usual locations, so she had simply bought something she needed from an available source. She could not remember if she had ever done business with the peddler in question before this and commented that such men were all similar. She could not say whether he had a usual route or where he might be found at the present time. She, too, was unable to give them a sample of the cherry spirits and no longer had the bottle. Her husband, fearing the Prohibition law, had disposed of the bottle as soon as it was empty.

At the Ojzermans', the next family on their list, Morelli tried a different tactic. Implying that they already knew all about what had happened—which Emily felt in all likelihood they did—he forcefully but cheerfully opened the conversation with a demand to know all about the man who sold them the cherry brandy. Neither Mr. nor Mrs. Ojzerman could offer much information except that the peddler was much like all the other sellers who could be seen in the city. They couldn't say what he had looked like, nothing in his actions had stood out to them, and he had offered a reasonable price for something they needed. Emily's discouragement was building as they left the tenement building where the family lived, but Morelli was as optimistic as ever, certain that someone would be able to provide them with a clue to the man's identity, if not his whereabouts.

Mr. Dawidowicz similarly had little to say on the matter of the peddler, whom he readily acknowledged having spoken to. All he could add was that the man was "a *Galitzianer*."

"What is that?" Morelli asked.

Dawidowicz shrugged.

"You're an American," he said. "He's a *Galitzianer*."

Despite their confusion as to why Emily and Morelli wanted to see the brandy bottle and anything remaining in it, both the Dawidowiczes affirmed that the spirits had been finished and the bottle thrown away with the rest of the household rubbish.

"*Galitzianer* must be his nationality," Emily suggested when they were out on the street again.

"Maybe," Morelli agreed. "Or at least the place he comes from." Morelli explained that his parents were the same way. They identified other Italians they met by the regional accent they spoke with or by some behavior they associated with a certain city or part of the country. "This is probably the same," he added. "We couldn't tell the difference, but to these people it's obvious."

Unlike the others, Mrs. Gutstein related that she had made the purchase of cherry brandy from the peddler on Hester Street, a few blocks from her home. The street contained one of several informal "pushcart markets" where anything and everything could be bought cheaply from itinerant sellers who transported their wares on handcarts or their back. Emily made a special note of this; it might be a good place to start if they had to trace the man. Like the other families, Mrs. Gutstein no longer had the brandy bottle.

Mrs. Rosenbaum had had a similar experience but had encountered the peddler when she was shopping on Essex Street. She had been unable to buy any kind of spirits at several shops she had visited. Another shopper, who had overheard her explaining that she needed brandy for a sick child, had suggested she try the peddlers who thronged the street. There was plenty of demand but not much supply. Nonetheless, she had found what she wanted fairly quickly by asking around and bought a small bottle of cherry spirits from a nondescript man with a pushcart. The brandy had not lasted long nor gone far in treating the children's coughs, and she had no idea where the empty bottle now was.

"Are we any farther ahead?" Emily asked Morelli as they left the last address.

"I think so," he said cautiously. "We know each family bought the spirits from a peddler. It seems almost certain to have been the same man. If more than one person was peddling contaminated drink, there would have to be more people sick or dead. I think we can assume all of these families bought the brandy from the same man."

Emily ran through all of this yet again as she waited for Morelli and for the meeting to begin. The hands of the clock on the wall crept closer to two. At one minute before the hour, the door finally opened and Morelli slipped in silently and sat down in the chair opposite Emily's desk. He was flushed but not visibly flustered.

"I was out on another case," he said in a low voice. "I had to run to make it back on time."

Emily nodded.

"They've been in there some time," she said, gesturing toward the door to Director Kent's office that was closed tight. "Do you think we're in trouble."

Morelli smiled.

“I can’t see how we could be in trouble,” he said. “We haven’t done anything, except what we were told to do. This might be bigger than we know, though.”

“What do you mean?” Emily asked.

“Well, we have been thinking about these seven children and have seen this as a public health problem. But public health sometimes involves other considerations, legal ones or political ones. This could involve things bigger than a few sick children and some bad medicine,” Morelli said.

Despite this reassurance, Emily could not help feeling like she was back in school and was waiting to see the principal for some infraction of the many written and unwritten rules that govern a child’s world. She hoped Morelli was right but so much of what went on at the Department of Health was beyond her experience and outside her need to know. It seemed like it would be easy to make a serious mistake and she wondered what the penalty might be if that was what she had done.

She gasped when the door to Kent’s office suddenly opened, and the director gestured for them to enter.

17

Director Kent's private office was roughly the same size and shape as the outer office where Emily did most of her work. It was furnished in a more impressive manner, but the furniture was still standard issue for a bureaucrat of his rank. One whole wall behind the large desk was lined with shelves. These shelves were currently almost full, and it was Emily's job to place new reports in the appropriate file box as well as to keep track of the journals and textbooks that Kent needed to refer to for his work. He had said to her on several occasions that it was about time they sent some of this material to the archives, but beyond that he had made no attempt to create space for the new journals and documents that appeared relentlessly on a daily, weekly, and monthly basis. A bank of similarly overfull filing cabinets stood against the wall next to the large window that looked out onto the street. Emily had spent a great deal of time, not just filing forms and correspondence in those drawers, but also reading through old cases and reports of programs that had been concluded, as her boss believed this was the best way for her to familiarize herself with the business of public health.

The rest of the floor space was taken up by a small conference table capable of seating six people. This was where she and Morelli were directed to sit by a subdued-looking Director Kent. Already at the table was Andrew Wetherill, the Director of Investigations and Morelli's supervisor. Wetherill was a well-known figure in the health department, having come up through the ranks to his current position from a lowly start as an inspector when the department was just beginning to carry out evaluations of restaurants, manufacturers, and the like. He was known to be an intelligent man and also a shrewd administrator. Unlike Director Kent who had begun his career as a practicing physician, Wetherill had always worked for the department and had an encyclopedic knowledge of city ordinances and procedures.

"First, I want you to understand that everything said in this meeting is confidential and must not be discussed with anyone other than the people in this room," Kent began the moment Emily and Morelli were seated. He had remained standing and seemed, to Emily at least, troubled or perhaps upset. "If you do need to discuss it, you can talk to me or Director Wetherill and if you discuss the case among yourselves," Kent added, looking sharply first at Emily and then Morelli, "make sure to do so outside of the hearing of others."

Emily was startled by her boss's formality as well as by the realization that the case she and Morelli had been working on seemed to have become some sort of problem. She wondered again whether they had made a serious mistake and if they were going to be disciplined as a result of it, but she rejected this idea immediately. Neither Kent nor Wetherill seemed angry at them and she trusted that Morelli knew how to deal with members of the public in accordance with the department's rules.

"Was there something wrong with my report?" she asked timidly when Kent paused for breath.

"Your report was excellent," Wetherill answered. "Both of you are to be commended, but it has opened up the proverbial can of worms."

"Exactly," Kent agreed, finally taking a seat at the table. He tapped on its surface with a pen, betraying the internal anxiety he must have felt. "Your work in determining the cause of illness and death of the seven children was exemplary. Ordinarily, we could chalk this up to an unfortunate accident and file it. However, things are different now," Kent went on. "In fact, it has been necessary for Director Wetherill and myself to take advice directly from the commissioner."

Wetherill nodded in confirmation.

This confused Emily more. She glanced at Morelli but his face was impassive and showed no hint of what he might make of all this.

"It's Volstead," Kent explained, perhaps seeing that Emily had failed to grasp the significance of the situation.

"No one is supposed to be able to buy alcohol," Morelli put in.

"And no one is supposed to be selling it," Kent added.

"You may be aware," Wetherill began, "that since the Volstead Act was enacted, there have been numerous violations, some involving violent crime. The first one occurred less than an hour after the law came into effect."

"I remember seeing that in the newspaper," Emily said. "There was a robbery in Chicago, if I recall."

"That's right. Some men robbed a train carrying a large amount of whiskey," said Morelli. "The police thought it was an organized gang."

"Needless to say, the authorities all over the country are committed to cracking down on this kind of thing. Especially if there is an indication people are making their own liquor," said Kent.

"And if organized crime is involved," Wetherill put in.

"Surely, the man who sold the children's parents the brandy was not involved in organized crime," Emily cried.

"That would be highly unlikely," Kent agreed. "And we are not so much interested in him. But he did buy the tainted spirits from someone, and we want to know who that person is."

"Shouldn't this be a matter for the police, sir," said Morelli respectfully. Emily had been thinking the same thing.

"Ordinarily, yes, it would be," Wetherill told them. "But nothing is ordinary when it comes to Prohibition. The whole scene has changed and now we have to think about policing as part of the public's health." He paused. "You noted that you spoke to several individuals about this investigation," he went on.

"That's right, sir," Morelli told him. "We needed expert input on several technical matters."

"I appreciate that. How much do these people know?"

Emily considered this. She thought back over everything they had discussed with Professor McIntosh and with Bill Waters in the department's own lab. She went over in her mind their conversations with the families themselves. Looking at Morelli for support, she said, "Several people know that there were a number of unexplained deaths among immigrant families and that we were investigating in case there was an unknown infectious disease spreading among the public. No one knows the results of the investigation, except you two of course. Were we wrong to ask for help?"

"Not at all," Wetherill said. "There would have been no way to solve the problem if you hadn't. But we need to maintain control of the situation and limit knowledge of what really happened. That is the commissioner's directive."

"I'm not sure I understand what this is all about," Emily admitted. "Why is such secrecy necessary?" she asked, turning to look at Kent.

Kent looked at Wetherill and then back to Emily. "It's the Jews," he said finally. "If anyone else had been involved, it would have been much easier to deal with. The people involved were all Jews. The sickness and death of children is always sensitive, but this is much worse. People will see it as if they had been poisoned. To make sure it doesn't happen again we need to find the peddler and speak to him, get him to tell us where he got the stuff. He's undoubtedly a Jew, too. The minute any of this gets out, the community will start screaming persecution, and then there'll be trouble."

"The Jews are very powerful in this city," Wetherill said. "They make up almost thirty percent of the population. They're not all poor immigrants like the people you spoke to. They own businesses, they're prominent socially. Many of them have been good friends of the health department. They've raised money for various causes through their organizations and have supported our work against disease. But, if it looks like we're targeting the part of the community whose situation is already difficult, they'll turn against us just like that.

On top of that, any reaction will become one more grievance the public has against immigrants."

"Where does that leave us?" Morelli asked.

"We want you two to continue the investigation," Wetherill told him. "With the utmost care and sensitivity of course. You are to find the peddler, identify the source of the tainted liquor, all confidentially of course. It will then be decided whether a prosecution is in order."

"Are we permitted to offer the man immunity from the law?" Morelli asked. "If we find him, that is."

"You will find him," Kent decreed. "But the answer is 'no.' You must not promise anything. However, you can strongly imply that no action will be taken against him if he cooperates."

"How can we find this man?" Emily broke in. She was confused and was having trouble taking in all this information about things she had never thought about before. "We don't know his name, where he lives, what he looks like or anything."

Wetherill smiled slightly, and Kent looked down at the tabletop.

"We leave that to your ingenuity and that of Mr. Morelli," Wetherill said after a moment's pause.

"What is the timeframe for this?" asked Morelli lightly. Emily had been wondering this as well and feared they would be given an impossibly short period in which to find the peddler.

"Obviously, we want this resolved as soon as possible. But there have been no more reports of illness associated with alcohol poisoning that could be linked to this same man, so perhaps we have some leeway there," Kent told them. "The sooner the better, of course."

Morelli nodded and turned to Emily with a smile.

"Looks like we're going to be working together for a while longer," he said cheerfully.

Emily smiled back. Inside she was very pleased about this one aspect of the assignment. She hoped Morelli would have some ideas about what to do.

She could not see a way forward herself.

"If only these families had taken the children to the doctor," she said wistfully.

Kent nodded in agreement. Emily had known her boss would share this sentiment.

"We can only hope to one day educate all mothers to recognize the signs of serious illness and seek expert advice," he began. "But that costs money, and many people in this city simply cannot afford to see a doctor, especially if the situation does not seem dire. Many children and adults die needlessly among the immigrant groups."

"The irony of it is that Volstead has exemptions," Wetherill commented. "Doctors can prescribe alcohol for their patients for various complaints. Pharmacies will then dispense spirits as required."

"That's correct," Kent confirmed.

"But surely no doctor would prescribe alcohol to children," Emily said in surprise.

"You never know, Em," Morelli told her. "If the parents believed that was what was needed, a doctor might feel it couldn't hurt. Cough syrups usually contain alcohol anyway, don't they?" he asked, directing the question to Kent.

"Yes, they do. Alcohol suppresses the cough reflex," said Kent, nodding. "Perhaps these people didn't know they could have asked a doctor."

"I wonder," said Emily. "Some of them might have known, but I didn't know that myself until you mentioned it now. Still, they seemed well informed. I saw newspapers in most of the homes."

"Then they should also have known they could have asked their rabbi for help," Wetherill went on. "Volstead has another exemption for clergy who can use spirits in their religious activities."

"Like a lot of people, I think they probably didn't realize the situation was serious until it was too late," Morelli said. "Immigrants usually feel they have to be self-reliant. They were probably just trying to solve their own problem, and the peddler happened to have the answer it seemed."

"I'm sure you're right," Kent told him. "But it was a poor solution that you two now have to clean up. We have to make sure nothing like this happens again."

Later that afternoon as she left the health department to return to her lodgings, Emily wondered how she and Morelli were going to complete what seemed like an impossible task—find a nameless, faceless man among the millions of people in the largest city in the world. Her original assignment to interview the families about the deaths of their children now seemed simple in retrospect. She had known who they were and where they lived. It had not been easy to speak with the grieving parents, but she had persisted and succeeded—once Morelli joined her in the investigation. His connections had proven invaluable in getting the technical information they needed. This new assignment seemed infinitely harder and less certain. Emily had no idea how they would begin, but she and Morelli had agreed to meet first thing the next morning to work out what to do. She felt like she was standing on a cliff above a featureless sea that stretched out in every direction. Without something more to go on, she could not imagine how they would ever find this man in a city where everyone seemed to be selling something and could be the person they sought.

18

They met the next morning at nine a.m. inside a coffee shop near the health department. Emily had eagerly accepted Morelli's suggestion that they discuss how to proceed outside the office. The requirement that the whole case be kept secret made it difficult to talk anywhere on the premises because staff were always around, and even Emily's office was not sufficiently private as people constantly came in and out to speak with Director Kent. He had happily released her to "get on with it," after once again hoping out loud for a swift resolution, and Morelli never spent much time in his office anyway.

Having stopped in to say good morning to her boss and check that he had the files he would need for an afternoon meeting, Emily slowly walked the half block to the restaurant where she and Morelli had agreed to meet. There was something springlike in the air, although the temperature was still quite low. Nonetheless, Emily opened the top button of her coat and loosened her scarf. After a bitter winter even a temperature only slightly above freezing seemed balmy and pleasant.

As she walked she reflected on how much time she and her friends seemed to spend in coffee shops and restaurants. This was a habit she had developed in her college days, imitating the social practices of the other women in her dormitory and classes. New York had become a city of restaurants after the war and dining out was quickly becoming an important pastime. It was not unusual for people to do all their socializing in restaurants, diners, and even the automat. Emily smiled to herself to think that for her and Morelli a coffee shop was an extension of the office.

Looking through the plate glass, Emily saw Morelli had already arrived and was seated at one of the small tables. He had a file folder open in front of him and had hung his overcoat on the back of his chair. He looked up as Emily approached and smiled as he tried to make room for her. The papers he had been reading took up most of the table.

"I was just looking over my notes," he said by way of explanation. "I haven't ordered anything. I was waiting for you," he added.

"You could have gone ahead," Emily told him. "You didn't need to wait."

"What will you have? I didn't eat breakfast and that crumb cake on the counter looks mighty tempting." Morelli indicated a cake blanketed in powdered sugar on a glass stand behind them.

"I might just have coffee," Emily said. "That looks very sweet for my taste."

Morelli gave their order to the waitress as she passed and said nothing more until she had returned almost immediately with two cups of coffee and a large piece of cake. When no one was in earshot Morelli put his papers on his lap and leaned closer to Emily to speak confidentially. Emily felt like a spy and was enjoying the excitement.

"The question is," Morelli began, "how to find a man we know almost nothing about in a city of six million."

"It is daunting," Emily agreed, lowering her voice to match Morelli's. "How do you normally find the people you're investigating?" she asked.

"That's just it. We almost always have a name, an address, or a workplace or even all three. We're dealing now with a man whose name no one knows, with no known address, and who works anywhere and everywhere." He paused to put a forkful of cake in his mouth. "The few things we know about him don't give us a clue as to how to find him. They're not distinctive enough."

Emily thought this over for a moment. The families they had spoken to had been able to provide a few details about the man's background and confirmed that he sold his wares in several of the street markets of the ghetto. That could describe thousands of people. They had to find something about this man that made him stand out.

"We know so little about these people," Emily said at last. "There is nothing to grasp onto. I can't imagine what sort of background this man comes from and what he does all day. Everyone in this case seems very strange to me," she admitted. "They're not like us." Emily stopped. Even to her own ears what she had said sounded horrible. The people she had met as part of this case had suffered terrible losses as they tried to make a life in the biggest city in the world, which happened to be located in a country that was foreign to them and their ways.

"I know what you mean," Morelli said kindly. "Because we don't have much in common with the people involved it's hard to think about what would be important to them and what they would likely do."

"Yes, that's it exactly. When I try to think, if I were a peddler in this city where would I go? I come up blank," Emily told him.

"We know he's been seen in two markets, Hester Street and Essex. But there are hundreds of people who sell things in those places, and we have no idea whether he's there regularly, once in a while, or if the times we know about were the only times he's ever been there," Morelli said.

When the problem was outlined in this way, it seemed to Emily to become more complex and less possible to solve.

"What we need," Morelli said, finishing the last bite of cake, "is inside information."

"What do you mean?" Emily wanted to know.

"Well, when we needed to know about symptoms, we went to Professor McIntosh who is an expert in that area. When we needed information about alcohol production, we went to Bill Waters in the lab. Now we need someone who knows the ghetto and how people there think."

"Do you know anyone like that?" Emily asked.

"That's what I am trying to think about. No one comes to mind immediately, but I might be able to get a contact from one of the other investigators. I wouldn't tell them what it was for, of course." Morelli said. It did not sound to Emily like he was confident this approach would be the best option.

At that moment, Emily had an idea that had come to her in a flash.

"I may know just the person," she said with excitement. "The rabbi's wife."

"You know a rabbi's wife?" asked Morelli with visible interest.

Emily at once felt proud and embarrassed. She had not included her meeting with Mrs. Miriam Kandel, the self-named rabbi's wife, in her notes or report on the case. She had justified this to herself by the fact that woman was not directly involved, despite knowing several of the families who were, and she was not an expert whose opinion and insight might have helped them solve the case, until now that is. However, if she cared to admit it, Emily knew the reason she had not mentioned Mrs. Kandel either officially or to Morelli was because the rabbi's wife had confused her, and she had found the strange story about the prophet and the rabbi to be disconcerting and difficult to understand.

To make up for this now, Emily quickly explained to Morelli how Mrs. Kandel had appeared in her office one day shortly after Emily had interviewed the families for the first time. She left out none of the details, including the tale she had been told and its moral. The relief she felt at no longer feeling she was hiding something related to this investigation was immediate, and Emily realized she must have been worrying about her omission without being aware of it.

Morelli said nothing for a long time, obviously thinking hard. Just as Emily began to wonder if he was angry that she had kept something back, he spoke.

"This rabbi's wife sounds like just the person we are looking for," he said. "I was just wondering how to get the information we need without explaining why we want to know."

"I'm not sure we would be able to get away without giving her some kind of explanation," Emily said. Apparently, Morelli had made the same assessment she had of how Mrs. Kandel would react to their inquiries. She ran her finger around the rim of her empty coffee cup. "She's very sharp."

"She sounds it. We may just have to strongly imply it is for a case, not this case of course, but some case, and leave it at that. People do have an idea a lot of official work is confidential," Morelli said with what sounded to Emily like misplaced confidence. Still, she allowed he might be right.

"This is your line of work," she said smiling. "I'm sure you'll know how to put it."

"I hope so," Morelli told her. He stood up and began to put on his coat. "Let's get going then. There's no time like the present."

The coffee shop, which had been nearly empty when they arrived shortly after nine o'clock, was now full as midday approached, and the first early lunchers had begun to arrive. As they stepped out onto the sidewalk and headed back downtown to the ghetto, Emily had a very strong feeling that this next part of the investigation was going to be much more difficult than the beginning had been.

19

Hester Street, where Miriam Kandel had a store, was bustling as it always seemed to be. There, too, the signs of spring were in the air, and the red brick facades looked bright in the sunlight, belying the decades of dirt and grime produced by the city's teeming millions. At street level the shopfronts were packed, with every possible kind of transaction taking place at the same time. Much of this activity had spilled over from the sidewalks to the street itself, reducing the space vehicles and even pedestrians could pass with ease.

Emily and Morelli picked their way carefully down the street. They had no idea where the store they were looking for might be located.

"We need to do this systematically," Morelli said. "Really, you could take one side of the street and I could take the other, but in this crush, we might lose each other and waste a lot of time, even if one of us found the place right away. So, we'd better stick together."

"Why don't we ask someone?" Emily wanted to know. Her head was reeling. She had never seen a place quite like this. Even Orchard Street, which she had visited several times as part of the case, seemed quiet by comparison. There were colors, sounds, and movement in a constantly shifting mix generated by the sea of people, each intent on their own business of buying or selling. Peddlers with their pushcarts were everywhere, and she realized they might have walked right past the man they were looking for.

"That's usually not a good idea, if you can help it," Morelli explained as he scanned the shops on both sides of the street. "Word gets around quickly, and it's often better if the person you're looking for doesn't know you're coming."

"Why is that?" Emily asked. His response had taken her by surprise.

"Well, people don't like to talk to the government. Even when they have nothing to fear really, they worry about what we want and what the repercussions will be to them, so they'd rather avoid the whole thing by avoiding us."

Emily thought back to the reactions she had experienced when trying to talk to the families the first time. She knew she meant no harm and was only trying to do a job, but they had reacted as if she were an enemy who had to be repelled. It was one more example of how differently people could see things. She wondered how Morelli and the other investigators managed to face the public's hostility day after day in the name of public health—a very broad and amorphous concept at the best of times. Suddenly, a narrow shop a few yards from where they stood caught her eye.

"I think that's it," she cried, pointing to indicate to Morelli where she was looking.

The plate glass had been carefully stencilled and read: M. Kandel, Fine Fabrics, Notions. Some additional text that may have meant the same thing followed in the Hebrew alphabet, which Emily couldn't read but she knew must have been Yiddish. As they watched the door opened, affording a glimpse of the store's interior, and an older woman wearing a heavy coat and fashionable cloche hat in light brown wool, emerged carrying a paper-wrapped parcel. She squeezed past Emily with a murmured, "Pardon me," and disappeared into the crowd.

Pushing the door to the shop open, Emily entered followed closely by Morelli. They found themselves in a small room lined with shelves full of bolts of fabric. Much of the floor space was taken up by several glass cases that contained buttons, hooks and eyes, packages of pins, needles, a small display of emery bags, and every other conceivable item required for dressmaking and tailoring. A girl of about sixteen sat behind the counter deftly arranging spools of thread in a rack. Her fingers flew as she transferred the colors in order of shade from a cardboard carton to the display. This suggested to Emily she had a great deal of experience working in the store, just as her appearance indicated she must have been Mrs. Kandel's daughter. The girl was a younger version of her mother in her movements as well as looks. However, the bright blue dress she had on was very much unlike the somber clothing Mrs. Kandel had been wearing when she visited Emily's office. Emily noted the same blue fabric was for sale at fifty cents a yard. The girl looked up as they entered and was about to speak to them when her mother emerged from the back room.

"Miss Lowe, how nice to see you again," said Mrs. Kandel with obvious pleasure. "Are you looking for something special? Material for a big occasion, perhaps?" she asked with a pointed look at Morelli.

Emily watched with a mixture of horror and amusement as Morelli blushed from his collar to his hairline at this comment. She had forgotten to mention how outspoken the rabbi's wife could be.

"Actually, Mrs. Kandel, we were hoping you might be able to help us with some information," Emily said with forced seriousness.

"I would be delighted if I can." Mrs. Kandel came around the counter where her daughter was still sitting, taking in every word of the conversation. Mrs. Kandel wore a woolen dress in a deep chocolate brown. Emily guessed a bolt of the same the material was in the store but didn't see it. Her hair was completely covered by a thin scarf that matched the dress and came down low over her hairline, concealing her ears. Only the lobes with their garnet earrings were visible. "What can I do for you?" she asked.

"We're looking for a peddler," Morelli said. He had regained his composure as well as his customary good humor.

Mrs. Kandel shrugged. "Take your pick," she said expansively, gesturing toward the street outside. "They're a dime a dozen around here."

"Not just any peddler," Emily clarified. "A specific one."

"There's a peddler who eats at Dora's," said Mrs. Kandel's daughter quietly.

“Hush, Ruthie. No one is interested in Dora or what goes on at her house.” Turning to Emily and Morelli, Mrs. Kandel added, “Dora is Ruthie’s friend. Her mother sells meals.” She stopped abruptly.

“Don’t worry,” Morelli told her. “We aren’t interested in that. That comes under the sanitary code.” Emily was aware he was referring to a regulation passed three years before that required restaurants of any kind to obtain a permit and allow inspections by officers from the Board of Health. The new regulation was mentioned quite often in the newspapers. In addition, many New Yorkers were aware of the strange story of Mary Mallon, an Irish woman who had worked as a cook for a number of families whom she had inadvertently infected with typhoid fever, despite suffering no symptoms or illness herself. She was currently in enforced quarantine, having violated the conditions of her parole from an earlier period of isolation, and was widely referred to as “Typhoid Mary” by the press and public alike. The rules were intended to protect the public from people like her who might pose a risk.

“So, it’s a specific peddler you’re looking for?” Mrs. Kandel seemed confused.

“Yes, it’s part of an investigation we’re involved in,” Morelli told her. “Unfortunately, we don’t know much about the man.”

“What’s his name?” Mrs. Kandel asked.

“We don’t know,” Emily said.

“What does he sell?”

“Again, we aren’t sure,” Morelli told her.

“I see,” said Mrs. Kandel. “You don’t have much to go on. I suppose you know where he peddles?”

“This area,” said Morelli. “As well as Essex Street. Maybe other places as well.”

Mrs. Kandel nodded. She appeared to be thinking.

“There’s a peddler who eats at Dora’s,” said Ruthie again. She had been following the conversation with obvious interest and was clearly anxious to contribute.

Recognizing this and recalling how it felt to be old enough to understand adult conversation but not old enough to be included, Emily took out her notebook and a pencil. She opened the book to a clean page and wrote down what Ruthie had said.

"Where does Dora live?" she asked, addressing Ruthie.

"Just down the street. Number 50," the girl said with a wide smile.

"Do you know the peddler's name?" Emily asked.

"No," said Ruthie, some of her elation vanishing. "I just know what Dora said. That one of the customers is a peddler."

Emily made a note of all this. Appeased, the girl began to arrange the spools of thread again.

"Alright," said Mrs. Kandel to her daughter. "You've had your say. So, what do you two know about this peddler?" she asked.

"He might be a *Galitzianer*," said Morelli with confidence.

Emily smiled to herself. She knew that the term was just a word to Morelli as it was to her. Neither of them had any real idea what this referred to, so they had to trust what had been told to them.

"That doesn't narrow it down much," said Mrs. Kandel, with a tone that suggested they had set her an impossible problem. "I think we'd better ask my husband. He may have an idea how to get at this. Ruthie, go get your father."

The girl dutifully stood up and went into the back room from which Mrs. Kandel had emerged. Presumably the family's living quarters were located behind the shop. In a moment she returned followed by a tall man dressed in shirtsleeves and vest with a worn fedora on his head. He had apparently been reading and still held the book, closed over his index finger to mark the page. He looked curiously first at Emily, then at Morelli, and finally at his own wife.

"My husband, Rabbi Daniel Kandel," Mrs. Kandel told them.

"What can I do for you good people?" the rabbi asked.

"They're looking for a peddler," his wife explained and quickly summarized everything Emily and Morelli had said.

"So, we know almost nothing about this man," Rabbi Kandel said. He waited for an indication of agreement from Emily and Morelli. "Is he a Jew?"

"I think so," Morelli said. "It seems most likely."

"Then he'll go to *shul*," the rabbi concluded.

Before Emily or Morelli could speak, Mrs. Kandel said, "They can't look for him there. They can't go around to synagogues. You could, but not them," she admonished.

"I suppose not," the rabbi agreed. "Peddlers must sell their wares somewhere. Maybe he's known at the pushcart markets."

"Of course, that makes sense," Emily said. The pushcart markets had been greatly expanded by the city government during the war years. At the same time there had been a crackdown on itinerant peddlers. Chances were the man they were looking for made his living in various city markets, at least some of the time. "But where would we start looking?" she asked.

"That's more my wife's department than mine," said the rabbi. Mrs. Kandel smiled at the compliment.

"In my experience," she began, "people keep to their own neighborhood, so I think you'll find him around here. If you know he's been working on Essex Street, he may go to Orchard Street as well. Or he could be right outside. It would help if you knew what the man sells. Most of them sell some kind of food," she added hopefully.

"We're not sure what he sells or whether he specializes in one type of merchandise," Morelli said.

Mrs. Kandel nodded knowingly.

"Well, you said he's a *Galitzianer*," she said. "He probably sells anything he can get his hands on."

"That is beneath you, Miriam," said the rabbi gently. "Everyone needs to make a living."

"Everyone knows what I am saying is true," Mrs. Kandel retorted. "People are what they are. You can't change it or say they aren't," she added petulantly.

Emily was becoming frustrated by this conversation that seemed to hinge on knowledge that members of the community had but that she and Morelli lacked. She had been tactful about this up to this point but now felt they had to finally find out what this cryptic comment about the man they were looking for really meant.

"What exactly is a *Galitzianer*?" she asked. As she spoke, she noted a mixture of alarm, curiosity, and relief on Morelli's face. Apparently he wanted to know as well but, like her, was concerned about offending the Kandels.

"The word just means a person from Galicia. That was part of the Austrian Empire," the rabbi explained. "Until a few years ago, of course," he added, referring to the Great War that had only recently ended and that had changed the face of Europe in ways that defied longstanding orientations of nationality and language.

"So, he's Austrian," Morelli summarized.

Mrs. Kandel laughed. "I'm sure he would say he is," she said. "The *Galitzianer*s, they're old fashioned. Unsophisticated. And they're ashamed of it."

Emily considered this. Mrs. Kandel herself was very sophisticated by any measure, so this might stand out to her. But, on the other hand, almost anyone would seem provincial by comparison, so the characterization might not be very meaningful.

"Are there things about him we might be able to recognize?" she asked.

"He's probably a religious man," the rabbi ventured. A sharp look from his wife silenced him. She had already established that Emily and Morelli would not be able to pursue the man within the religious environment.

"These *Galitzianer*s are always on the make," Mrs. Kandel explained. "They'll buy and sell anything, and they're shrewd operators. We can recognize them by how they talk, but that won't help you," she added insightfully. Then, seeing a lack of comprehension in her audience of two, she went on, "It's like with the war stamps," she said, pausing for a reaction.

War stamps were a recent memory and, Emily recalled, had been very popular as a way for people with few resources to support the nation's war effort and invest at the same time. The stamps were sold for twenty-five cents each, compared to five dollars for the cheapest war bond, and could be collected and redeemed when the holder had the twenty that made up the full value of a bond. The opportunity to invest in instalments had appealed to many people with little or irregular income.

Mrs. Kandel looked from Emily to Morelli with an expression of dismay. "You must have read about the peddlers' rally at the Liberty Loan Office on Delancey Street," she said. "It was in all the papers."

"Yes, I did see that," said Morelli. "How does that relate to the man we're looking for?"

"A lot of the peddlers are *Galitzianer*s. It's in their blood. There was one of them who invested all his own profits in the war stamps he was selling and cashed them in for a thousand-dollar bond!" Mrs. Kandel explained in a tone of exasperation.

"That seems like a smart move," Morelli commented with a laugh. Ignoring the affronted look Mrs. Kandel gave him, he went on, "So, you're saying we should be looking for someone with a keen sense for business, who is willing to buy and sell anything, and who may be quite provincial in outlook?"

This did seem to make sense, Emily thought. If it were possible to characterize people from a certain place based on common practices or social behavior, the description provided by the rabbi's wife did seem likely. The man they were looking for had sold tainted brandy to desperate women looking for medicine for a sick child. She wondered whether the peddler had known what the brandy was for or if he had simply seen a way to make a little profit.

Mrs. Kandel smiled, her ruffled feathers forgotten. "Just look for the most aggressive seller on the street," she said.

Morelli thanked them all graciously, including Ruthie, who beamed at having been recognized in this way. The rabbi replied with an equally cordial response and wished them luck before returning to the back room with his book. As Emily was about to follow Morelli out onto the street, which was even busier now than when they had entered the shop, Mrs. Kandel called out to her.

"Come back when you need that special dress, Miss Lowe."

As the door closed behind her, Emily heard Mrs. Kandel start to give a long list of instructions to Ruthie as she got back to the business of running her store. Emily marveled at the woman's insight but, at the same time wondered about the extent to which her assessments might be accurate. And, once again as she had so many times in the course of the investigation, Emily found herself hoping Morelli had made more of this unusual encounter than she had.

20

The din on the street had been somewhat obscured inside the Kandels' shop and took Emily by surprise when she stepped out onto the sidewalk behind Morelli. He turned to her and smiled.

"They're quite the characters," he commented with a laugh.

"You can certainly say that again!" Emily agreed. "But are we any farther along?"

"Yes, I think so," Morelli said after a moment. "Let's find a place to sit down and consider the situation."

Morelli scanned both sides of the street and quickly located what he was looking for. Moving around the crowds of shoppers and vendors, he led Emily down the block where a large sign advertised a dairy restaurant.

"They'll have coffee," he said confidently.

The restaurant was surprisingly bright and spacious compared to what Emily had been expecting based on its appearance. They sat down at a small table at the front and a waiter immediately appeared to take their order. The menu, which was printed on a card at the table, seemed to Emily to be mostly vegetarian dishes, some fish, and a number of things whose names meant nothing to her. This was of some interest to Emily, as her mother had long been a proponent of vegetarianism as a health regime and liked to talk about it with her.

“Are you having something to eat?” she asked Morelli, remembering his fondness for cake. “It says they have cheesecake.”

“I was considering it, but maybe not today,” Morelli decided. He asked the waiter for two cups of coffee and waited a moment until the man disappeared behind the counter.

“I feel even more lost,” Emily began. “Mrs. Kandel told us a hundred different things. I have pages of notes. But what does it all mean? Did we learn anything important?” she asked.

“In my experience, everything is useful,” Morelli told her. “But we did get some important facts. First, we learned that the Jewish peddlers stick to their own territory. Second, we learned that even women like Mrs. Kandel who really understand the community, don’t know much about them and how they work. Third, we have reason to suspect the man we’re looking for will take any opportunity to make some money and will probably continue to sell bootleg liquor if he can get it.”

Emily nodded. All that seemed obvious from their conversation with the Kandels, but she didn’t see how it helped them.

“What does it all mean?” she asked.

“Well, if we know the man was seen on Essex Street and the surrounding area, chances are he works there regularly. We don’t need to go looking across the bridge in Brooklyn or uptown somewhere. The ghetto is a large area with a lot of people, but it’s much more likely we’ll find the man if he stays around here,” Morelli explained. “Since people who are part of the community manage to find the peddlers who sell the things they want to buy with no special knowledge, that means that we can, too.”

“Can we?” Emily interrupted. “Everyone seems to speak a strange language and understand things we know nothing about,” she added, thinking about the torrent of information they received when they asked about the term *Galitzianer*.

“Of course,” said Morelli with absolute certainty. “Have we met anyone so far who didn’t speak English at least to some extent?”

Emily was forced to agree. In fact, she had been surprised by how well some of the people she had spoken to had mastered English. Even the ones whose language was not as good had no trouble making themselves understood. She realized it was more her own lack of knowledge about their way of life that made her feel it might be difficult to communicate with the people they might meet. More importantly, she knew this feeling derived from her own apprehension, not anything she had experienced.

"Finally, we are interested in this man because he was selling a product that used to be legal and has now become illegal. It happened to be tainted as well. If Mrs. Kandel is correct about these *Galitzianer*s' attitude to business, then he probably hasn't stopped. In fact, he might be known in this area because people haven't stopped wanting to buy liquor just because it is no longer allowed," Morelli was saying.

"All of that is true," Emily allowed. "But how does it help us find him? He won't have a sign like the fruit and vegetable men or the ones selling shoes, will he?"

"Of course not. But the families we spoke to found him. So, what drew them to this one man, as opposed to all the others? They were looking for something to treat a sick child. They had reason to think this peddler might have what they wanted. The man probably sells patent medicine, among other things," Morelli said at length.

"That's an excellent deduction," said Emily. She was genuinely impressed. Morelli's explanation was logical and probable, at least it seemed so to her.

"Well, I did spend my childhood reading *Sherlock Holmes*," Morelli admitted. "And I always wanted to be a great detective. Now, assuming all this is right, there can't be many peddlers who fit the bill since he has to be from Galicia and has to have sold illegal liquor, not just medicine."

"How do we go about finding him?" Emily asked, hoping for another revelation that would allow them to solve the case.

"We ask. It's as easy as that."

True to his words, a few minutes later when the waiter returned to see if they wanted to order anything else, Morelli asked, "Suppose I need to buy something for a bad cough. Is there anyone around here who might be able to help me?"

"Goldberger's Drugs, just up the street," the waiter replied instantly.

"Is there anything less expensive?"

The waiter looked at Morelli quizzically. "Out there, you mean?" he asked gesturing toward the crowd of sellers on the street outside.

Morelli nodded.

"You can try the carts. There ain't nothing those guys don't have."

"Do you know anyone like that?" Morelli asked. Emily could see he was trying not to seem too eager or give the waiter reason to suspect there was more to these questions than met the eye.

The waiter thought this over. "There's one guy I've seen around. You could try up the other end of the street."

Morelli thanked him and paid their bill. A moment later they were back on the sidewalk making their way through the crowds of shoppers in the direction the waiter had indicated. Emily scrutinized every pushcart and street vendor they passed, but they all seemed to be selling the same few types of merchandise. Not surprising to her, much of the trade of this kind involved food. Others of the sellers peddled clothing and household items, while a few sold pots and pans, brooms, and tableware. A significant number of these traders were offering a service, and Emily saw men waiting for customers who needed knives and scissors sharpened, watches repaired, and shoes re-soled. The street was a whole world in miniature and exactly the place that—with a little luck—they would find the one peddler they sought.

21

"I'm thinking we should come clean," Morelli was saying as they made their way down Hester Street, scanning the storefronts and street vendors for anyone who seemed like he might be the man they sought. Emily had not been paying attention. Her feet hurt, and she was contemplating her mother's constant warnings that sitting in an office all day was not good for her. Her mother would have preferred Emily get plenty of exercise in the form of keeping house and running around after her own small children, but different shoes better suited to walking were more Emily's idea of a solution. The narrow-toed boots she wore were a stylish and fitting choice for work but were not practical for the trek they were on. Emily marveled at Morelli's energy and enthusiasm. He did not seem either tired or discouraged, even though she felt both.

"What?" she asked, snapping back to the present moment.

"I meant we probably have to tell anyone we speak with who we are and, if they ask, what we are investigating," Morelli explained, apparently thinking Emily had not understood the reference. "It doesn't seem like anyone is going to be prosecuted," he went on, "and probably not even fined, but you can get into a lot of trouble if you present yourself under false pretences. The public has a right to know who they're talking to."

"I see," Emily said. She had not considered this aspect of their assignment.

They had been instructed not to discuss the details of the case, but that did not mean they could conceal their own identity and intentions. "Will people be willing to talk to us, do you think?" she asked.

"I hope so," said Morelli honestly. "They aren't required to, and a lot of them would rather not!"

Emily nodded. She realized this was the reality of the situation, even though she and Morelli meant no harm and there really was no risk to anyone who assisted them.

"I think that's someone we should speak with," Morelli said suddenly.

Following his gaze, Emily saw a very tall man standing by a large, solid-looking handcart. He was thin to the point of being emaciated and wore a tweed apple cap that sagged over his narrow forehead. A sign attached to the body of his pushcart read "Authorized Agent for Haber & Haber." Emily knew this could not be the peddler they were looking for because there was no way anyone who had dealt with the man could have failed to notice his unusual height and mention it as a distinguishing feature. But he was selling patent medicine and might have knowledge of the man they were looking for.

Walking up to the man with Emily a step behind him, Morelli positioned himself directly in front of him in a way that would make it difficult for the peddler to avoid speaking to them.

"I'm Edward Morelli and this is my associate, Miss Lowe. We're from the City Health Department," he began.

"I have a permit," the peddler countered instantly, before Morelli could say another word.

"We're not interested in that," Morelli told him. "We're looking for someone."

The man eyed them warily but said nothing.

"We're looking for a peddler like yourself who may sell patent medicines," Morelli explained. "We think he might be able to give us some information."

"I sell only Haber & Haber," the peddler said, referring to a small pharmaceutical company located in the city. Emily had seen some of their products, including something called Salutophin that was supposed to be a universal remedy for anything that ailed you.

"I see. Is that usual?" Morelli asked.

"How do you mean?" the man asked.

Emily realized another peddler—a shorter, sturdier-looking individual—had silently approached them and was listening to the conversation. Apparently, they were attracting attention even though most of the people around seemed oblivious to anything except their own transactions.

"Would most people selling medicine be associated with one company like you or would they sell different products from different makers?" Morelli clarified.

"Most sell anything they can get their hands on."

"Do you know others who sell medicine?"

"What is this about?" the shorter man who had been following the conversation with interest suddenly interjected.

"We're looking for a man, a peddler like yourselves," Morelli told him. "We believe he may trade in patent medicines."

"What's he done?"

"Possibly nothing. We believe he sold a treatment to several people and we'd like some information about it," Morelli said. It was obvious to Emily he was trying to tell the truth but offer as little information as possible.

"What's the man's name?" the interloper enquired.

Emily saw he had his own pushcart, a smaller, much less substantial vehicle, loaded with all kinds of miscellaneous items, among which she could see some books, a few items of cheap children's clothing, a cardboard box containing a number of brown glass bottles labeled "Thompson's Vinegar Bitters," and some small boxes of dyspepsia pills. Apparently, this man also sold patent medicine.

"We don't know," Emily answered truthfully.

"How you gonna find him?" asked the newcomer. Emily saw a look of relief on the face of the tall, thin peddler now that someone else had become the focus of their attention.

"That's a good question," Morelli admitted. "Maybe you can help us."

"Maybe," the man said pleasantly. He leaned back against his cart. "What's he look like."

Emily thought back to their interviews. No one had been able to give them any definite information about the man's appearance. When neither she nor Morelli answered, the man said, "So, you don't know his name or what he looks like. What do you know?"

"We know he's from Galicia," Morelli said hopefully.

"So are half the guys on this street," the man told them.

"We know . . ." Morelli glanced at Emily for confirmation and then turned back to the peddler. "He may have sold some people some brandy."

The peddler looked at the tall man who had been the original target of the questions. Both men seemed to realize the matter had just become serious, if Emily judged their expressions correctly. Everyone knew about the Volstead Act and that the ban on the sale of liquor was being enforced aggressively by the authorities. These efforts filled the newspapers every day.

"He's in trouble then," said the peddler, standing up straight.

"No, he isn't," Morelli assured him. "We just want to talk to him."

"For that, you gotta find him," the man quipped.

Emily noticed the tall, thin peddler had quietly moved a few feet away and was now talking to a woman who seemed interested in one of his products. Emily wondered whether Morelli had noticed, but of course it didn't really matter. The tall man was clearly not the one they were looking for, and his colleague seemed much more inclined to talk to them.

"How would you go about that?" Morelli asked suddenly, eyeing the man intently.

"Well," said the man pushing back his flat cap. "I think I might ask the union. You know, we peddlers have an organization. There's more than one in fact. Maybe they know or can find the guy you want."

"That is a very good idea," Morelli agreed. "What's your name?"

"Dan Wolf," the man said without hesitation. "I trade in anything and everything. If you want it, I can get it for you."

Emily had to laugh at this self-confident proclamation. It was true the man was in business for himself and possibly successful, although his clothes and merchandise did not seem to indicate that. It was hard for her to believe he would have the resources to get anything someone might want. She wrote down the name and a brief note of the conversation in her notebook.

"Where can we find you again?" Morelli asked. "Are you here every day?"

"Me? No. The law says you gotta move along every thirty minutes, unless you've got an in with someone. I'm not gonna pay for a prime spot. Not like some people I know." The peddler gestured with his head toward the Haber & Haber pushcart of his colleague.

"So, how do we find you?" Emily pressed. She found the man amusing and quite liked his brashness.

"Just ask around. I'll hear and come to you."

With this, the peddler lifted his cart and trudged away at the slow pace required to move the heavy barrow through the crowd of shoppers.

Emily and Morelli spent the rest of the afternoon walking through the marketplaces of the ghetto slowly scanning the streets for any sign of a peddler who might be the man they were looking for. They spoke to eight or ten likely individuals but quickly ruled them out. None of these men had any idea who their quarry might be or where to find him. Exhausted and somewhat dejected when she and Morelli parted for the night, Emily returned to her room and collapsed into bed too tired to think any more about the case till morning.

22

Emily wished Morelli was with her as she approached the headquarters of the United Peddlers Association of Greater New York. However, he had to work on another investigation as their ordinary duties at the department had not been suspended, despite the pressing nature of the case they shared.

"Just see what they have to say," he had advised her. "You'll do fine. Look at all the practice you've had interviewing people already," he added, confident as always. That attitude must have been infectious, Emily thought, because she was feeling more capable and less nervous, even though it would have been even better had she not been alone.

Following the suggestion of the peddler, Dan Wolf, Emily had found out about the peddlers' union by contacting various city offices until she finally located someone who was able to advise her about the organizations that served this profession. It had also been Morelli's suggestion to proceed in this way. He was a great believer in turning to people who were experts in their own field for information that would otherwise be very difficult and time consuming, or even impossible, to get. As they had been told by the peddler, there were in fact, a number of unions that had been formed by various groups of peddlers in different parts of the New York. The United Peddlers' Association was the largest in terms of membership and was centered on the lower east side of the city with the ghetto at its heart. It had seemed to be the most likely of the peddlers' unions, and hence Emily had once again made her way to Orchard Street.

The address had turned out to be a large and somewhat dingy shopfront that seemed to be home to something more like a warehouse than a retail business. A small sign confirmed that the place was the location of the union office she was looking for, so she carefully opened the door and went inside.

The room she found herself in was full of cardboard boxes, some sealed and some open. The contents seemed varied and included a range of household items, like scrub brushes and whisk brooms, and also dishes, articles of clothing, inexpensive umbrellas, and fancy hairbrush sets. There were numerous closed boxes that gave no indication of what they might hold. The items she could see did not appear to be arranged in any identifiable way, and Emily wondered how the proprietor could possibly do business in these conditions.

"Can I help you, lady?" a man called from the back of the store. He was sitting at a desk with several ledgers in a pile in front of him, smoking a cigarette.

Emily approached the man as quickly as she could in the cluttered environment, stepping carefully around the obstacles in her path.

"I'm looking for someone associated with the peddler's organization," she began.

"That's me," the man said affably but with a note of surprise.

"My name is Emily Lowe. I'm from the health department."

Emily noted that if this surprised the man in any way, he gave no sign of it.

"I hope you can help me locate a specific peddler," she explained.

"What's his name?"

"That's the problem," Emily said. "We don't know his name or anything very much about him. We know he is a *Galitzianer* and we're interested in some things he sold to members of the public."

"That could be hundreds or thousands of men," the man said, seeming to be completely unaffected by the information Emily had given him. But perhaps, she reflected, the police or other authorities were frequently looking for peddlers who had violated the city's numerous regulations. The newspapers were always writing about the disorderly conduct of these traders, even though it was acknowledged they performed an essential service used by a large number of city residents, especially in poorer neighborhoods. "It could even be me," he added, smiling.

"Are you a peddler?" Emily asked with a start.

"I used to be," the man told her. "Now I run this store and manage the organization," he went on.

"What kind of a store is this?" Emily could not resist asking. She had never been a place with so little order or observable purpose.

"You call this a supply store," the man said. "The peddlers come in here to get their merchandise. It saves going to the wholesale markets, and I can buy more cheaply in bulk than they can as individuals."

"I see," Emily said. "Can anyone come in here and buy whatever they want to sell?"

"Yes, of course. Whether they've got a permit or not is their own business. But we only run tabs for union members," the man explained.

Emily nodded and wrote this down in her notebook.

"A lot of the peddlers sell fresh food. You don't supply that, do you?"

"No. Other places do though. Even with fresh food, it's cheaper for the men to pool their money and have someone like me buy in bulk than go to the markets themselves. Keeping down costs is the key to this business."

Emily contemplated this. She realized she was straying from her mission, but the explanation of how the peddlers worked was interesting and had never been explained in the newspaper stories that she had read.

"Might you be able to help me identify this man?" she asked.

"If you knew his name, there would be a good chance he'd be in one of those," the man told her, gesturing to the ledgers on his desk. "Without a name, there's no place to look."

"Is there a listing of peddlers by what they sell?"

"No, it's not that kind of business. Most of the general merchandise men sell whatever they can get or whatever they think customers want to buy. It's different with fruit or vegetables, of course, but a lot don't specialize."

"Well, thank you anyway," said Emily. This had been another dead end. They were going to need a more effective way of finding the man they sought.

The man touched the brim of his hat and nodded. As she made her way out of the supply store, Emily tried to think of another way they might be able to find the man who had sold the brandy.

The glare of the early spring sun surprised her as she stepped from the gloom of the store onto the street. All around her people were going about their daily affairs oblivious to her problem. She could not help feeling that somewhere among the crowds, maybe even within her field of vision right now, the man they were looking for was plying his trade. There had been no more reports of alcohol poisoning that she knew of, but that had been improbable anyway. She and Morelli agreed that it was unlikely the peddler had known there was anything wrong with his merchandise. From what they had learned during their investigation, it was much more likely that someone who was producing bootleg liquor and selling it to others for illicit sale had made a mistake and produced a batch containing too much methanol.

As she stood on the sidewalk and contemplated what to do next, Emily suddenly caught sight of a familiar face.

"Mr. Wolf," she called, recognizing the outspoken peddler she and Morelli had spoken to the day before. "What are you doing here?" Emily realized the absurdity of the question as soon as it was out of her mouth.

"I'm a businessman," the peddler said. "I go where the business is. What are you doing here?"

"I'm trying to get a line on the man we're looking for," Emily told him.

"No luck with the union?" Wolf asked, gesturing toward the storefront behind Emily.

"No. Not without the man's name. Perhaps you have another idea," she suggested. "You've been very helpful."

That was true, and Emily did appreciate the peddler's willingness to talk to them. She hoped he was still prepared to assist her. Any idea would be a help as she had none of her own at that moment.

"That's tough," the man agreed. He appeared to think for a moment. "Maybe you need to get word out on the street. Let people find him for you."

"You mean use the grapevine?" Emily asked, laughing. It was simple and might work.

"People like to talk. There are connections among us peddlers, but you need the buyers, people on the street, to be on the lookout for your guy, too. If he's working this neighborhood someone knows him," Wolf explained.

"Could you help us put the word out?"

"Maybe. What do you know about this guy?" The peddler asked. "I mean besides that you don't know his name or anything about him."

Emily explained as best she could, without divulging too much information, what they had found out. There was no harm in telling Wolf where the man was known to have done business, that he had been selling a kind of brandy referred to as *palinka* by one of the families, and that this brandy, sold as medicine, was the focus of their interest.

"What'll happen to him when you do find him?" Wolf asked conversationally.

"I'm not sure," Emily replied truthfully. "Most likely nothing. We are quite sure he didn't know there was anything wrong with the brandy he was selling. We are only concerned about where it came from and keeping anything like that away from the public."

"So, he's got nothing to fear," the man asked in confirmation of what Emily had said.

"I don't think so," Emily agreed. "He would be doing a public service by coming forward."

"Okay, lady. I'll help you if I can," said Wolf. He turned, picked up his cart and began to walk slowly away in the direction he had been going.

"Mr. Wolf," Emily called after him. "Thank you!"

The peddler raised a hand in acknowledgement but did not turn or alter his gait. Emily stood there for a moment before making a decision that she would need to speak to the rabbi's wife once again.

23

Emily walked the few blocks to Miriam Kandel's Hester Street shop. She was beginning to feel more at home on the crowded streets of the ghetto where everything seemed to be in motion at once, forming an ever-changing panorama of people and objects. The relative stability of the buildings that lined every inch of the streets with no discernible space between them provided a brick-colored backdrop that stood in sharp contrast to the shifting waves of human activity. Emily wondered whether it was ever quiet, like the streets of New Rochelle and other small towns that had not been touched by the tides of immigration and hordes of newcomers they brought.

The Kandels' sewing shop was busy when Emily arrived. Several women were waiting their turn to be attended to by Mrs. Kandel and her daughter Ruthie. Mrs. Kandel looked up when Emily opened the door. Seeing who the visitor was, she thrust her customer's paper-wrapped parcel into the woman's waiting hands and hurried around the counter to where Emily stood.

"You're alone today, Miss Lowe," she said with obvious pleasure. "Where is your young man?"

Unsure whether it would be best to correct Mrs. Kandel's impression of her relationship with Morelli or to let it go, Emily opted for the latter.

"Good day, Mrs. Kandel," she said. "I am hoping to impose on you again for some help."

"Anytime, Miss Lowe. I am always happy to help," said the rabbi's wife. "Have you found your peddler?"

"No," Emily told her. "And that is what I hope you can help me with."

"I'm not sure I can," said Mrs. Kandel. "I told you what I know."

"I know and we are very grateful for your help," Emily said. This was true. She and Morelli had agreed that the rabbi and his wife had been very generous with their time and the information they provided. A lot of the understanding they now had about how the public viewed the occupation of peddling had come from them. "I am wondering whether you can help us make it known that we are looking for this man and that he can come forward without fear."

"What do you mean, Miss Lowe?"

"You yourself told me you know a lot of people from different backgrounds," Emily began. Mrs. Kandel smiled and nodded, apparently taking this statement as a compliment. "If you could tell some of your acquaintances about the man we are trying to find, some of them might buy from peddlers or shop in the pushcart markets."

"Yes, they might do that. Almost everyone in this neighborhood does," Mrs. Kandel agreed.

"Someone might recognize the man and be able to give us a lead. Or they might mention it to some of the peddlers when they are doing their shopping, and the man might come to us of his own accord," Emily went on.

"I don't doubt you, Miss Lowe," Mrs. Kandel said calmly. "But I would have to know what this is all about before I agree to help you in this way."

Emily had expected something like this. She knew the rabbi's wife had very strong principles, which she had observed the first time they met when Mrs. Kandel came to see her at the health department. She had resolved to tell Mrs. Kandel the whole story and ask her to keep as much of it as possible in confidence. However, she would have liked to consult with Morelli about this plan before carrying it out. She could have easily called his office from one of the many pay telephones located on street corners throughout the city, but Emily knew she would be unlikely to catch him, and there was nowhere he could call her back. On top of that, she did not want to wait. The sooner they could take some kind of action, the sooner they might find the peddler.

"I will ask you to take what I am going to tell you as confidential to the utmost degree," Emily said. Seeing the rabbi's wife nod in agreement and her jovial expression change to one of seriousness, Emily told Mrs. Kandel all about the seven families and the tainted brandy they had bought in a futile attempt to treat their children's cough. By the time she finished, the shop was empty. Ruthie had attended to all the customers, who had left one by one while Emily and Mrs. Kandel were talking. Ruthie herself had disappeared into the back, where presumably the rabbi was immersed in one of his books.

"This is a very bad situation, Miss Lowe," Mrs. Kandel said when Emily had finished. "The man must be found, if only to protect others who may be tempted to buy from him."

"But we are sure the man is not at fault," Emily stressed. "We do not think he knew the brandy had anything wrong with it."

"I am sure you are right. But there is a market for such things, especially now that they cannot be bought legally," Mrs. Kandel said. Emily had noted that virtually everyone she had spoken to as part of this case, even those who—unlike the rabbi's wife—seemed very foreign and spoke English poorly, seemed to know all about the changes to the law of the land. "This man has found a market for this brandy, and I am sure the price he can demand is high. He may be tempted to continue to sell it, assuming he can get more."

Emily realized that Mrs. Kandel was undoubtedly right, and this was the same concern Director Kent and his colleague Director Wetherill had expressed when Emily and Morelli met with them and received their current assignment to find the peddler involved.

"I will help you," Mrs. Kandel was saying. "And if you give me permission to speak to my husband about this, he may be able to help as well. As you can imagine, my acquaintances are women. They are the shoppers and undoubtedly deal with peddlers from time to time. My husband, however, deals with men. It is possible some of his connections are even peddlers themselves, but certainly there may be peddlers among his congregation or those of other rabbis he knows."

"Yes, of course, tell your husband," Emily confirmed. "But please do not let this get out beyond the two of you. My superiors are very anxious that the public should not panic or get the idea the department is trying to persecute anyone."

"I think I understand, Miss Lowe. Leave it with me, and I will try to help you as best I can."

Emily thanked Mrs. Kandel and gathered her handbag and notebook to leave the store. As she was about to step out onto the street once again, the rabbi's wife called after her.

"One more thing, Miss Lowe."

"Yes?"

"The families involved. Did you tell them their children were killed by poisoned brandy?"

"No. We thought it was not necessary to burden them further with that knowledge. They have all suffered greatly," Emily explained formally.

"Thank you, Miss Lowe. On behalf of all of us, I am very grateful for that small mercy."

Emily wondered, as she made her way back uptown to her office, who "all of us" referred to and why this act of omission seemed to have special meaning to the rabbi's wife.

24

"That was smart thinking, Em," Morelli said.

Emily had just finished explaining everything she had done that day to start spreading the word among residents of the ghetto that they were hoping to speak to one specific peddler among the thousands who worked on the streets and in the marketplaces. She had tried to explain her thought process as clearly as possible so that Morelli would understand why she had decided to take Mrs. Kandel into their confidence and that she had seen no other way to proceed. Emily felt strongly that the rabbi's wife was a person who could be trusted in a serious situation like the one they faced, but she did not know if Morelli felt the same way about a woman he had only met once. Emily had expected that Morelli might be annoyed or even angry, but he seemed as calm and thoughtful as usual.

The voices of other patrons in the coffee shop where they were talking provided a backdrop for their council of war. Both Emily and Morelli had been questioned about their progress by their respective directors, and every passing day made the situation more urgent. Kent had explained to Emily that there was obviously considerable profit to be made in selling liquor, even if it was bootlegged. The more time that passed, the more likely it was that the peddler would assume his actions had gone unnoticed. This, in turn, might embolden him to get more supply from wherever the tainted brandy had come from, a situation that could lead to more illness and death. Morelli, as he had explained to Emily first thing that morning, had been warned by Director Wetherill that more delay in finding the man could lead to an embarrassing situation for the department if it became known that they were aware bad liquor was circulating in the city and had not acted on it, either through the health department itself or through the police.

Morelli still had not spoken again. Emily carefully aligned her cup and saucer on the table and placed her teaspoon alongside. What he might say when he did speak weighed on her, and she feared she had made a serious error in judgement. But, when she looked up, Morelli was smiling.

"I was just trying to think of a way we might be able to make things go faster," he began. "The public has a lot of knowledge, and it would be great if we can get it, but it might take some time for our interest to get to the right person and for that person to come forward. It isn't clear how they should contact us either. I am just not sure what we can do."

"Why don't you put an ad in the paper."

Emily was startled. Her hand brushed the coffee cup, which rattled loudly against the saucer. A flash of anger crossed Morelli's face as he whipped around to see who had spoken. The voice had clearly come from the table right behind him where a middle-aged man with dark hair and glasses was sitting with a cup of coffee and a sandwich in front of him.

"No offense," the stranger said mildly, "but I couldn't help overhearing you talking about your problem. The best way to find someone is to put an ad in the paper," he reiterated.

Emily saw Morelli's expression soften to one more wary than angry.

"Well, that may be a good idea, but who are you?" Morelli asked the man, who continued to eat his lunch.

"Stanley Meyer." He stood up and offered his hand formally first to Morelli and then to Emily by reaching across the table. "Your problem is not that uncommon, you know."

"Perhaps not," said Morelli, "but there are at least a dozen newspapers in this city."

"So there are," said Meyer. "That's why you need to choose the right one."

Emily was following the conversation with interest. She had the impression that Morelli wanted to hear what Meyer had to say, despite their need to be as careful as possible about the details of the case.

"You seem to have a lot of ideas about all this, Mr. Meyer," Morelli went on. "What would you do in our position?"

"Like I said, I'd put an ad in the paper, say who I was looking for, and let him know where I'd be and when, so he could find me," Meyer explained casually, as if it were the simplest matter imaginable.

"You heard quite a bit of our problem," Morelli noted. "What paper would you choose?"

"I got the impression you are looking for a street peddler of the Jewish variety." Meyer looked first at Morelli then at Emily for confirmation. Morelli looked impassive, but Emily nodded in affirmation.

"*The Forward* would be your best bet," Meyer told them.

"*The Forward*?" Emily asked. She had not heard of this newspaper before.

"It's a Yiddish paper. Your guy is almost certain to read it. They all do."

"That is a very good idea, Mr. Meyer," Morelli said. "We are very grateful to you for your help."

"You just need to know your public. The sort of man you're looking for is one of the workers. He's probably a socialist. They all are." Emily wondered exactly who "they" referred to: the city's peddlers, the Jews who lived in the ghetto, or the population at large. Meyer might have meant any of these, she thought, and everyone was a worker of some kind, even herself, Morelli, and presumably Meyer. "Do you know *The Forward*?" Meyer was asking.

"The paper, no," Morelli told him. "I've passed the building many times."

"Pretty impressive, huh? They're a major paper, very influential among their own readers," Meyer told them.

"How do you know so much about it?" Morelli asked suspiciously. Emily also began to suspect Meyer might have more of an interest in their problem than he was letting on.

"I work for *The Sun*. We're one of the competition. You've got to know what you're up against."

"Mr. Meyer," Morelli began, speaking in a commanding tone that Emily had not heard before. "What you overheard is confidential information. If any of this gets out, much less appears in print, our superiors are likely to take a very hard line." Emily wondered whether this were, in fact, the case. Morelli sounded like he had had to give this warning before in other situations.

Meyer shrugged and stood up to pull on his coat.

"No one will hear anything from me," he said. "I know enough to protect a source. But," he added hopefully, "if something is going to come out, I hope you'll think of me." He reached into his coat pocket and pulled out a couple of business cards, which he proffered in their direction.

Emily took the one offered to her. It read: Stanley Meyer, Reporter, *The Sun*, and "It shines for all," followed by a telephone number. She put the card carefully into her handbag and noted that Morelli had placed Meyer's card in his jacket pocket. He also seemed to think it could be useful to know a reporter at one of the city's more serious newspapers.

When Meyer had gone, Morelli turned to Emily and smiled.

"I guess we know where we have to go now," he said.

"To *The Forward*?" Emily asked with a laugh.

"Of course," Morelli confirmed. "A good idea is a good idea, no matter the source. They're on East Broadway. I know the building."

25

Emily and Morelli once again made their way downtown, this time to East Broadway, where the Jewish *Daily Forward* had its offices. The paper was located in a new building specially built to house its operations. It had an elaborate facade with bas-relief columns topped by medallions picturing the stern faces of men Emily didn't recognize.

"Who are they?" she asked Morelli as they climbed the steep steps that led to the lobby.

"I only recognize those two, Karl Marx and Friedrich Engels," Morelli told her. "I'm not sure about the other portraits or the two figures with the torch."

Once Morelli said it, Emily realized that she too recognized these well-known figures. She would not have thought of their names herself, however, as to her they were only characters in a textbook. She saw that *The Forward* was a socialist newspaper, perhaps focused on the rights of workers as this political movement seemed to be. That was probably why their acquaintance from *The Sun* thought it would be the best vehicle to reach someone who knew the man they sought or perhaps the peddler himself. The Bolshevik overthrow of the Romanovs in Russia and the founding of the Soviet Union in 1917 had brought to light, at least to some observers, the existence of an international proletariat that needed to be defended from capitalism and pushed the concept of socialist government into the mind of the public. *The Forward* seemed to see itself as part of this defense.

They climbed the steps and passed under an arch above which the name "Forward Building" was carved in the classical style. The lobby was busy with people coming and going. Some were looking at a series of bulletin boards that displayed what Emily assumed was the day's newspaper. She glanced at the Yiddish type, which imparted no information to her, and noted this was one of the newspapers she had seen in the homes of some of the families she had spoken to about the case. Signs in Yiddish and English directed visitors to various sections of the company. They made their way down the hall toward the advertising section.

The advertising section was located in a large room divided by a wooden counter that separated the public area from a space where several employees sat at their desks typing and taking telephone calls. There was a short line of people waiting to place ads. Emily and Morelli took up a position at the end of the line to wait their turn. A single young woman in a dark dress was working the counter and did not seem to be in a hurry to deal with the customers.

"Have you got the ad?" Morelli asked.

"Right here," Emily replied. They had composed the text on their way to the paper. Emily had noted down their ideas as they talked about it on the streetcar. Then she had quickly written out a clean copy of the final wording they had decided on. It was a straightforward ad asking anyone with information about the man they were looking for to contact them through the paper. They were assuming *The Forward* operated in much the same way as other newspapers did and would serve as an accommodation address for any replies.

Their turn came at last after what seemed to Emily to be a very long time. Morelli handed over their text and explained that they wanted to place an ad in the paper. The woman studied the page with care.

"This is a Yiddish newspaper. We can't publish something in English," she said finally.

"Can you translate it for us?" Emily asked. This was a possibility she and Morelli had considered.

"Wait," the woman told them.

Emily and Morelli looked at each other. Morelli smiled hopefully. A moment later, the woman returned with a middle-aged man wearing a suit. His white shirt was buttoned to the top but he had no tie.

"These people want to place an ad. They're looking for someone," the women explained to the man, who seemed to Emily to be her superior. "But it's English and they want us to translate it."

The man took a pair of glasses out of his pocket, put them on, and considered the text of their ad with as much concern as the woman had.

"Let's see," he began. "Information wanted. . . . That's fine, nothing unusual in that. . . . Peddler known to work Essex-Hester Street area. . . . hmm. . . . Thought to be from Galicia . . . well. . . . May be selling medicinal spirits." The man frowned and looked up at Morelli and then Emily. "If you are this man or know him, please contact care of this paper." The man removed his glasses, folded them, and placed them back in his pocket. "Who are you exactly?" he asked.

"We're from the Department of Health," Morelli explained. "We want to speak to this man about a matter of public health."

The man looked at them cautiously. Emily felt his expression contained a deep note of skepticism and perhaps distrust.

"Public health how?" the man asked, an expectant look on his face.

"Some people have become ill from tainted liquor," Morelli told him gravely. "We need to find out where it came from." They had discussed the possibility they would have to explain why they were looking for the peddler and had settled on this abbreviated explanation.

"Is this man in trouble? Are you planning to arrest him?"

"No," Morelli confirmed. "We don't have that authority," he added truthfully. "We just want to know where the sprits came from. How did he come to be selling them? We know it was not intentional."

The man seemed to be thinking this over.

"We'll run this on my authority," he said to the woman who had been waiting patiently for instructions. Then turning to Morelli and Emily, he added,

"I will translate this for you myself. Let's just add something that says the man is not in trouble."

"Gladly," Morelli agreed. He turned to Emily.

"That's a fine idea," she said. "We're very grateful for your advice and your help."

"We are a major newspaper, Miss," the man told her. "And we can't have people being poisoned by accident or any other way. Miss Schwartz will help you."

Miss Schwarz took out a form and began to fill it in. In a noticeably friendlier tone she asked the name the ad should be placed under and how long they wanted it to run. Morelli gave his name and then hesitated.

"How long should we give him, Em?" he asked.

"I don't know," Emily said. "What do you think, Miss Schwartz?"

"I wouldn't recommend longer than a week. If you haven't gotten the information you need by then, you aren't going to."

"A week then," said Morelli.

"That's done then. This will run from tomorrow. You can come in to pick up your replies any day during business hours," Miss Schwarz told them, placing the text of the ad and the form together in a wooden tray, presumably to be acted on by another employee.

"It will be April in a week," Emily reminded Morelli as they were leaving. "I don't know how much longer Director Kent will keep us on this case."

"That's a good point," Morelli agreed. "At least we have something to tell him in today's report."

Morelli was referring to the written reports Emily typed up every afternoon to keep Directors Kent and Wetherill up to date on the investigation. For the past several days, those reports had been dismally lacking in progress, and Emily had struggled to portray their efforts hopefully. Today, at least there were some concrete developments that might lead to a successful conclusion of the investigation. The one consolation in all this, Emily thought, was that there still had been no further illness or deaths due to tainted liquor, but that could change at any time, which was the situation they were struggling to avoid.

26

"Look, Em. Isn't that Dan Wolf?" Morelli said suddenly. They had left *The Forward* building and were walking slowly down East Broadway toward Pike Street where they would be able to turn and cut back to Orchard Street, the heart of the pushcart markets. While waiting for a response to their ad, there was no alternative but to return to combing the neighborhood, hoping to find a needle in a haystack.

"It is, Ed," Emily cried in surprise. "What can he be doing here?"

The outspoken peddler Emily had now met twice on the streets of the ghetto was leaning against a telegraph pole watching the people coming in and out of *The Forward* and the neighboring buildings. There was no sign of his pushcart, and Wolf was not wearing the cap Emily had seen him in both times they had met. Today he had a battered fedora on his head and had traded his bulky Mackinaw coat for a worn ulster overcoat that reached his knees. The wide cuffs of the coat, which would have fit a much taller man, covered most of his hands, exposing only his bare fingers.

"Not working today, Mr. Wolf?" Morelli asked as they came up to the peddler.

Wolf shrugged.

"Everyone gets a day off now and then," he said, smiling.

"You're like that bad penny, Mr. Wolf," said Emily, joking.

"I don't follow you."

"It's a saying," Emily explained, suddenly embarrassed. "A bad penny always turns up."

"Got it," Wolf replied. "Well, it is a coincidence, always running into you, Miss Lowe. And you too, Mr. . . . ," he trailed off.

"Morelli," Morelli supplied. "What are you doing here?"

"I've come to see my benefactor," Wolf replied conversationally. "He's got an office in The Forward Building."

"That is coincidental," Morelli said. His tone was light, but Emily could tell her colleague had suddenly gone on the alert. "In that case, you must know we're just coming from The Forward Building."

The peddler seemed unaffected by this lightly veiled accusation. It occurred to Emily that Morelli suspected Wolf was following them around the ghetto or perhaps trying to spy on them. She wondered why the peddler would want to do that. But, she told herself, it could be no more than curiosity and might not even be related to the case.

"I did happen to see you come out," Wolf was saying. "And I did wonder what business you had there."

Morelli ignored this.

"Who is your benefactor, Mr. Wolf?" he asked instead.

"Sam Goldberg of Goldberg & Son. He's the son," Wolf answered immediately.

"Why do you need a benefactor?" Emily asked. The hidden world of the city's peddlers fascinated her, and Wolf had been surprisingly forthcoming about details that could only be had from someone who did this kind of work for a living.

"I want to move to the country and open a general store. Maybe upstate somewhere or even Canada. I hear a man like me can make something of himself that way. But you need capital," Wolf explained.

"So, Goldberg is going to stake you so you can open a store somewhere?"

Morelli said, reiterating what the peddler had told them.

"It's a partnership," Wolf clarified. "Who knows? Maybe after a few years I can buy him out."

"What is Goldberg's part of the partnership?" Emily asked.

"Supply. The merchandise will come from him."

Emily thought this over. This might be a very good business opportunity if Wolf could pull it off. She remembered the excitement in New Rochelle when the first larger stores began to open on Main Street when she was child. Many of the small towns farther upstate lacked any kind of establishments that sold city goods, yet the public was always anxious to buy the latest items.

"Don't you like the city?" Morelli asked. To Emily, he seemed visibly more relaxed now. Wolf's story did make sense, and the peddler had spoken easily and without hesitation.

"It's too crowded and too noisy. I like the woods, the open air," Wolf said. "When I was a boy I was always out in the fields."

"Where are you from, Mr. Wolf?" Emily wanted to know.

"Belz."

"Where is that?" Morelli asked.

"Hungary, Poland, Austria, maybe Russia," Wolf replied. "Who knows nowadays?" he added in a more subdued tone.

Emily knew Wolf was referring to the collapse of the old order in Europe following the Great War that had only ended a couple of years before. The geography Emily had learned in school no longer applied, and she had not followed closely the maps and diagrams that had been published in the newspapers after the war ended. She did know that the negotiations between governments following the conflict had resulted in national borders being shifted such that whole regions were now in different countries than they had been just a few years before, and the people who lived there had suddenly found themselves to be citizens of what to them was a foreign state.

"When are you planning to leave the city?" Morelli was asking.

"Summer maybe. I have to seal the deal with Goldberg and decide where to go. But that part is really up to him," Wolf replied.

"You have no idea?" Emily asked in surprise.

"I have plenty of ideas," Wolf told her. "I took a little scouting trip upstate last fall, before the snow came. I got as far as Binghamton."

"Binghamton!" Morelli exclaimed. "Why there?"

"I started walking and that's where I ended up," Wolf explained.

"But that's almost two hundred miles!" Emily put in.

"It was nothing. It's my profession. I keep to the backroads. In every village people want to buy or sell or trade. They've got no stores in these places. Where can they get what they need if not from a peddler like me?"

"That's true," Emily agreed, thinking back to her own experiences. "In New Rochelle, where I come from, we used to wait for the peddlers to come through. It was terribly exciting to see what they would bring."

"New Rochelle, I've been there," said Wolf. "I went up through the Putnam Valley and headed west though the Catskill Mountains." Wolf paused, assessing his audience. "There's all sorts up there. Germans, Austrians, Hungarians, even those Deutschers who have no machines. But everybody needs something and if they have no cash, they've got something to trade," he continued.

"It sounds like a hard life," said Emily, with sudden compassion for the peddler.

"Not really. There are always people willing to give a peddler a bed for the night and a hot meal in exchange for something they want," Wolf went on. "Someone gives me some homemade jam in trade for a book of needles. In the next town, someone else wants to buy that jam or trade for some eggs. Someone else is out of eggs. Or if not, well, I gotta eat, too."

Emily was impressed by the peddler's enterprising nature and his apparent acceptance of what really must have been a very difficult lot in life.

"So, are you thinking you'll move out there?" Morelli asked.

"It depends on my benefactor. He seems to think there are better prospects farther north, up by the Canadian border," Wolf said.

"What does your family think?" Morelli pressed. Apparently, he too was taken by the peddler's story, Emily thought.

"Haven't got any. Not here anyway. They're all back in the old country. Maybe one day I'll be able to bring them here." Wolf smiled sadly. "For now, it's just me here in what we call *Di Goldeneh Medineh*."

"What does that mean, Mr. Wolf?" Emily asked seriously. It seemed to her the peddler was speaking from the heart.

"The Golden Country," said Wolf. "Twelve years I've been here. No, almost thirteen." He paused for a moment then added, "I better get going. I don't want to miss my appointment."

"We'll see you around, Mr. Wolf," Morelli said as the peddler walked slowly away.

Emily suddenly realized how late it had gotten. The afternoon had worn on without her realizing it, and the workday was almost over. On the way back uptown, she and Morelli said little, but what did pass between them related to Dan Wolf. His story, to the extent they now understood it, opened a window into the life of the ghetto. Even Morelli, whose own parents had come to America from Europe, seemed sobered by what he had heard. Emily wanted to ask him whether his family viewed their life in the way Wolf did, but she didn't dare. It was the heartbreaking hope that lay just beneath the surface of Wolf's story that had brought so many to the city. This must have made the loss of the children that were the subject of their investigation so much more bitter for their families, Emily thought. Those youngsters must have symbolized a future, now tarnished beyond recognition in a strange land.

27

Emily stood outside the courthouse on Essex Street wondering what to do next. Accompanied by Morelli when he was available, she had spent the last three days systematically scanning the streets for any sign of a peddler who might be the man they sought. They had spoken now to hundreds of people who had surprisingly little to say. Apparently, no one paid attention to the men who provided the goods and services they needed to keep on living in the constant crush of movement and activity that characterized the ghetto. People saw only the role, the peddler as a seller of items they might wish to buy, but never noticed the men who did this job, Emily reflected. They really seemed to have no information to give. Many spoke little English and were very difficult to understand. Some seemed frightened to be approached by an obvious outsider to the neighborhood and hurried away before Emily even had a chance to explain who she was. One or two were angry, and she and Morelli had been told in no uncertain terms by a young woman guiding a much older one, perhaps her grandmother, through the market to go "help" someone who wanted their assistance. Emily had realized very quickly that there was little trust in authorities of any kind, and that was how she and Morelli were seen by the people they approached. There was equally little respect for the Department of Health or the city government as a whole, a very different perception than Emily was used to from the people she knew.

Every afternoon, she—and Morelli if he had the time—would drop by The Forward Building and make their way to the advertising bureau where the taciturn Miss Schwarz would be working behind the counter. Standing in the doorway a little way from the ever-present line of customers seeking to place or respond to ads, they would wait to receive the day's tally of responses to their ad. On each of the first three days, Miss Schwarz had just slowly shaken her head to indicate nothing had come in and turned immediately back to the next person in line. On the fourth day, they had been rewarded as Miss Schwarz raised two fingers. Elated, Emily, who had been alone that day, took her place at the end of the line to wait her turn to stand at the counter.

The atmosphere of The Forward's offices fascinated Emily. As she waited, she tried to catch some of the conversations going on around her. The place was almost as noisy as the street outside. People were constantly talking, many in the foreign tongue which she knew to be Yiddish, the unfamiliar, guttural sounds punctuated quite frequently by English words or phrases she could sometimes grasp, despite the speakers' accents and rapid speech. Employees rushed around, dropping off and picking up sheets of paper that Emily assumed contained the text of ads to be published in the next edition. The place seemed to run with an efficiency and speed she had rarely seen anywhere else and that suggested a single goal shared by everyone on the premises to get the newspaper out on time. This eminently capitalist mechanism was a sharp contrast to the paper's political stance, Emily thought.

When her turn had finally arrived, Emily eagerly reached for the two envelopes Miss Schwarz pushed across the counter but pulled back in shock when she saw an alien scribble on the front of the top one.

"That's not in English!" she cried.

Miss Schwarz looked at her with a humorless smile.

"Of course not. This is a Yiddish paper. It's Yiddish. Didn't the boss tell you that the other day?" she said.

"Yes, of course," said Emily. "And I knew that. I just didn't think about the replies to our ad."

Miss Schwarz made a noise that might have been a laugh.

"Do you want me to translate?" she asked.

This generous offer surprised Emily even more than the fact that the correspondence was in the language of the newspaper. Miss Schwarz had struck her as a cold, rather rigid person, but now she realized that might have been an unfair judgement. The woman may have simply been nervous around them, perhaps viewing Emily and Morelli the way so many people on the street did, as representatives of the government whose presence could not possibly be associated with anything good.

"Would you?" Emily asked. "I would be very grateful."

Miss Schwarz nodded and gestured for Emily to open the first envelope. It contained a letter written on a sheet of cheap paper torn from a child's school tablet.

"*The man you want moved away two months ago. He went to California for the sunshine*," Miss Schwarz read out. "That's all it says," she added.

Emily nodded and wrote down verbatim what she had been told. She could see the letter did contain only one short sentence. She said nothing but was aware this writer could not be referring to the man they were looking for. The timing was wrong. Their man had to have been in the city more recently than two months ago. She picked up the second envelope and removed a similar sheet of paper, which she handed to Miss Schwarz.

"It says something impolite."

"No information at all?" Emily asked.

"No. It's from someone who obviously doesn't like you," Miss Schwarz replied conversationally. She handed both letters back to Emily and prepared to return to her regular duties.

"Thank you again, Miss Schwarz," said Emily. "We very much appreciate all your help."

"The boss said to help you, so I'm helping."

Emily understood she was being dismissed and had left the office after carefully replacing the two letters in their envelopes and securing them inside the cover of her notebook. Later, back at the office, she and Morelli had discussed the contents briefly. The serious reply to their ad was reason for optimism, Morelli had said. It was possible, he had added, that they would receive other letters with information that they could follow up. It would be difficult but not impossible, if they were sent a real clue. Emily had been encouraged by this and was still hoping for another response that contained usable information. There was no point in returning to The Forward until later in the day, however, so now it was a matter of deciding what route to walk in her increasingly fruitless attempt to find the peddler by chance.

Emily stood for a moment in front of the courthouse enjoying the mild weather. It had been a long, cold winter, and the spring air was a welcome change, even though she knew the hot, humid summer the city was prone to could not be far behind. She suddenly realized it was April 1. She had been working on the case for more than six weeks; the season had changed, and they had collected a huge amount of information but were still surprisingly far from a solution, Emily thought. Suddenly, as had happened before, she saw a familiar figure emerge from the courthouse and turn in her direction.

"Good morning, Miss Lowe," Dan Wolf greeted her. His coat was open, exposing a worn but clean shirt that was fraying at the collar. The cap Emily had seen him in before was on his head.

"Mr. Wolf," Emily said. "I am beginning to think you are following me."

"This is my territory," said the peddler and shrugged.

That, Emily knew, was true. Nonetheless, it seemed very strange to her that the man kept crossing paths with her and Morelli. At the same time, she was curious as to why Wolf had been in the courthouse.

"What are you doing here?" Emily asked, even though she knew the question was abrupt and the answer was none of her business.

"Here? At the court you mean?" Wolf replied. "I was helping out a friend."

Emily wondered if there really was a friend or if Wolf was the actual subject of whatever proceedings were involved. But the man seemed perfectly willing to talk about his business there, so she pressed further.

"Is your friend in trouble?" Emily asked.

"He was caught peddling without a license. They hauled him into court to pay a fine. I was translating. My friend doesn't speak much English," the peddler explained.

"That sounds serious," Emily said gravely.

"Not really. It happens all the time. My friend's a greenhorn. He doesn't know how to handle the *polizei*," Wolf went on.

Emily took all this in. Wolf's insights into the life of a peddler had opened her eyes to a kind of existence that was both difficult to imagine and yet easy to believe, now that she was more familiar with the city's huge immigrant population all struggling to make a living in the ghetto.

Abruptly and without prelude, Wolf turned and began to walk quickly away.

"Be seeing you, Miss Lowe," he called, disappearing into the crowd before Emily had a chance to say a word.

28

"Hold up there, miss!"

Emily turned to the source of the voice and found herself face to face with a large man in a rumpled suit. He had apparently come from the courthouse while she was speaking with the peddler and had approached them from behind. Emily knew Wolf must have seen the man and decided to leave immediately.

The man took a leather folder from his pocket and held it open just long enough for Emily to see he was a police officer assigned to the Seventh Precinct. She had not had time to read his name and suspected this had been intentional. Nonetheless, Emily had been brought up to respect the law and its agents and immediately began to wonder if she had done something wrong.

"Are you the woman from the health department?"

"Yes," Emily admitted. She was confused as to how this police officer could have known who she was and why. "Why do you ask?"

"We've been hearing about you and your partner rousting the peddlers, asking questions, and looking for people," the policeman said.

"We're investigating a case of serious illness among children. We're just trying to find a man who might have information about it," Emily explained. The officer did not seem sympathetic to this, so she went on. "We don't mean to upset anyone. We are just looking for anyone who can help us find the man."

"Well, you're upsetting everyone. The whole place knows about you and what you're looking for. Liquor is a police matter now. You should keep your nose out of it."

Emily was taken aback by the man's abrupt manner and rude tone.

"I've done nothing wrong," she protested. "I have a job to do."

"So do we," the officer told her. "And you're making it harder." His expression softened slightly. "Maybe you didn't realize," he added.

"I most certainly did not," Emily said in self-defense. She hadn't thought about it before, but of course she really had no authority as an investigator. Morelli did, but he was not here today. Maybe she had violated some rule or had even broken the law.

"This is a tough neighborhood, miss," the policeman was saying. "We have enough trouble with the peddlers as it is. They're all anarchists, and anything sets them off."

Emily was well aware of the danger posed by the anarchist movement, having read about it in the newspapers, whose coverage had included the sensational deportation of more than two hundred individuals from the United States the previous December. This mass removal of people believed to represent a danger to the nation because of their radical views and actions had included the famous Emma Goldman and her companion, Alexander Berkman. The pair had been heavily discussed in the press due to their stance against the Great War and President Wilson's Selective Service Act that required young men to register for the draft. Goldman and Berkman had even founded a "No Conscription League" and had been prosecuted for encouraging non-registration. Along with other members of the movement who were intent on overthrowing government and abolishing the state, Goldman and Berkman had been transported by ship to Hanko, Finland, and taken to the Russian border under a flag of truce. Despite the dangerous and erratic behavior of such people, Emily found it hard to accept that all or even some of the city's peddlers supported such things, much less identified themselves as anarchists.

"Look, miss," the police officer was saying. "Whoever you're looking for, just leave them be. It's for your own good."

Emily noticed that the officer's change in tone and approach was intended to appeal to her sense of self-preservation. Oddly, this caused her to relax somewhat, although she was still wary of the policeman's true motive.

"What do you mean?" Emily asked.

"These people you're talking to, they're troublemakers. They fight among themselves. They make factions. They set themselves up in front of legitimate stores and businesses, block the sidewalk, and interfere with trade. We get called to move them along, but the next day they're back in greater numbers."

"I am sure you have a very hard job," Emily said. "But none of that has anything to do with me."

"I think you'll find that it does, if you mix in. We've got things under control here, but it's a delicate balance. Just see that you don't upset the applecart, if you know what I'm saying," the officer told her and—like Wolf had done a few minutes before—turned abruptly and walked away from Emily as if they had never spoken.

Emily sensed the policeman had been referring to something quite different from either her safety or the fact that she had been asking questions among the peddlers, but she did not know what he was really talking about, and the conversation had made her feel confused and apprehensive. She wondered if the applecart metaphor was ironic or if the policeman had meant something specific by it. A large number of the peddlers did sell fruit and vegetables. Perhaps Morelli would know, Emily thought. He would be familiar with the balance of power in the city's streets and had probably dealt with the police before. While she would be able to talk to Morelli about this later back at the office, Emily would have also liked to ask Dan Wolf about what the policeman had said. She had no idea how to find the peddler though. The best she could do was to hope that he somehow found her again as she walked the streets and markets.

Emily did not run into Wolf again that day, and she learned nothing from anyone she spoke to. Arriving once more at The Forward, she walked quickly to the advertising bureau, desperately hoping for another reply to their ad. As she entered the room Miss Schwarz looked up and slowly raised one finger to indicate that there was indeed a letter.

The wait was almost intolerable. Emily shifted from one foot to the other as Miss Schwarz slowly and deliberately dealt with each of the four customers in front of Emily in line. By the time her turn finally arrived Emily felt like screaming, but she greeted Miss Schwarz as calmly as she could and waited for what seemed like minutes for the young woman to retrieve a wrinkled envelope from beneath the counter and pass it across to her waiting hand. Emily opened the envelope and without a glance handed the letter inside back to Miss Schwarz.

"I'll have to impose on you again to translate," Emily said apologetically.

"It's fine," Miss Schwarz told her. She looked at the sheet of paper thoughtfully. "The writing is hard to read," she concluded after a moment. "It says: *There is a man you ought to talk to who rents a room on Hester Street, corner Ludlow.*"

Emily wrote this down in her notebook. Could it be that they had a real clue at last? she wondered. This sounded like something that could be checked. If the writer of the letter was correct, this would reduce their search to four buildings. Even if each housed a hundred people, it would be far better than continuing to search the whole of the ghetto that was home to many thousands. That was assuming the man the letter referred to was in fact the one they wanted, Emily reminded herself.

Emily thanked Miss Schwarz once again and as she was leaving, Miss Schwarz reminded her that this was the last day their ad would run, unless they chose to extend it. There was a lot she wanted to tell Morelli about, and she was anxious to get his view on the things that had happened that day. Despite the odds against the letter being the key to the puzzle, Emily felt a thrill of excitement that had been building all day but had reached a peak when she learned what its content was. Her instinct told her this was important and may have been the breakthrough they so badly needed.

29

Emily and Morelli were once again conferring at Emily's desk. They had spent the last hour and a half bringing their respective directors up-to-date with their case and discussing the next step. Wetherill and Morelli, both of whom were much more familiar with investigations, were wary of reading too much into the letter advising them to look for a man who lived at the corner of Hester and Ludlow Streets. Not only did that encompass four buildings, each of which housed numerous people, but there was no reason to think the person the letter referred to was their man. Nonetheless, the address was in the right neighborhood and might be the focus of what they would do next. For the first time, however, Director Wetherill had asked the group how long the search was going to continue. This was really a question for Kent, of course, but he framed it as a matter for consensus among all of them.

"I understand the pressure you're under, Andy," Kent had said. "And I do appreciate you giving us Morelli here much of the time. But we have to make absolutely certain that this is over and there is no more tainted liquor floating around."

Wetherill nodded gravely.

"Is it time to bring in reinforcements?" he asked.

"You're thinking the police?" Kent confirmed.

"It may be the only way," Wetherill said. "They have resources way beyond what we can muster."

"I think Miss Lowe's encounter tells us that will not result in success," said Kent, effectively putting an end to the idea of involving the police force.

To Emily's very great surprise, when she told the three men about the conversation she had had with the policeman outside the Essex Market Courthouse, all of them had exactly the same understanding, which Wetherill had explained to her in some detail.

"As employees of the Department of Health, we come in contact with other city workers from time to time," he began. "There are many situations we look into that overlap with the duties of other offices, and most frequently that is the police department."

Wetherill had looked first to Kent and then to Morelli for confirmation.

"The police have a hard job in this city," he went on. "And there are a lot of opportunities for wrongdoing on all sides. The peddlers present a special problem in law enforcement. As you have now seen," he said, turning to Emily directly, "they set themselves up anyplace that seems likely and go to work. Many times, that is on the sidewalk in front of some other establishment that is also competing to draw customers.

"If that happens, which it does many times a day, the owner of the building or the person leasing the ground floor has the right to call a policeman to remove the offenders who are blocking the entrance to the building. This happens from time to time, but mostly the shopkeepers see it as a chance to demand large sums of money from the peddlers in exchange for allowing them to operate in front of the place. This is extortion, but the police look the other way. Even worse, some of them are on the take and have their own arrangements with the shopkeepers and peddlers."

Wetherill paused.

"So, that policeman was warning me to stay away from the peddlers in case I found out this was going on?" Emily asked.

"I think he probably thought you knew exactly what was going on," Morelli said. "It's an open secret. More likely he was afraid that some of the people you were talking to might have given you names and amounts, information that could be turned over to the police commissioner's office."

"But wouldn't he stand to get in trouble for bullying me?" Emily pressed.

"Of course," Morelli told her. "That was why he made sure you didn't see his name and he didn't identify himself, as the law requires. He was very cagey. If you did report what happened, he could claim he was referring to your safety in a bad neighborhood."

Emily could do no more than shake her head in amazement. This did not fit with the way she viewed police officers nor with the respect for the law that she had been brought up with.

"How do you avoid stepping on toes?" she asked Morelli.

"With great difficulty," he answered, laughing. Director Wetherill smiled, but Director Kent looked grave. Perhaps his expectations were more similar to hers, Emily thought. Ultimately, though, they had decided to continue the investigation for another week and then reassess the situation.

Now Emily and Morelli were trying to figure out what to do, seeing as none of their previous attempts had yielded much information. The excitement Emily had felt was fading, as if it had been crushed by the weight of the practical considerations that had not occurred to her the day before.

"Miss Lowe, are you here?" The voice came from the partially open door to the hallway. Emily and Morelli looked up in unison to see Mrs. Kandel, the rabbi's wife, peering around the doorjamb.

"How did you get here, Mrs. Kandel?" Emily cried.

"What do you mean? I walked in," the rabbi's wife said indignantly. She entered the office and waited while Morelli hurriedly stood up and brought another chair across the room to Emily's desk.

"You are supposed to stop at the reception desk so someone can bring you to this section," Emily protested.

"I've been here before. There was no need to bother anyone," said Mrs. Kandel with a dismissive gesture.

"What can we do for you, Mrs. Kandel?" Morelli asked. Emily could hear he was stifling a laugh. The woman was very sure of herself.

"You've placed me in a difficult moral position, Miss Lowe, Mr. Morelli," she said. "My husband said I must do what I know to be right, so I am here. But now I'm having second thoughts."

"Can you explain what you're talking about?" Morelli asked in a voice that exuded calm.

The rabbi's wife shifted on her chair and pulled the cloth coat she wore more tightly around her. Her fingers toyed with the clasp on the large leather handbag she held on her lap.

"I saw your ad," Mrs. Kandel said in an almost accusatory tone. "Everyone did. I knew it was you who must have placed it because you told me what this is all about."

Emily nodded in confirmation.

"Please go on, Mrs. Kandel," Morelli said. Emily turned to a clean page of the pad in front of her and began to take notes.

"The families deserve some kind of justice," the rabbi's wife continued. "But what's done is done. Nothing will bring the children back, so maybe it would be better to leave well enough alone. There are a lot of people who could be hurt if I am wrong," she added.

"Mrs. Kandel," said Emily trying not to show the exasperation she felt, "we don't know what you're talking about."

The rabbi's wife looked at Emily sharply and then let her gaze travel to Morelli. He was waiting patiently for whatever might come.

"I may know who the peddler you are looking for is," said the rabbi's wife, as if this should have been obvious to Emily and Morelli.

Emily felt a new surge of excitement that overrode the deflated sensation their earlier meeting with the directors had left her with.

"Please go on," said Morelli after a moment.

"Ruthie's friend, Dora, she mentioned her when you came to the shop, said something that made me think a man who eats with them might be the one you want. But I can't be sure," Mrs. Kandel qualified. "Girls like Dora are always trying to make themselves important."

"What makes you think this man is the one we're looking for, Mrs. Kandel?" Emily asked.

"Like I said, everyone saw your ad and is talking about it. Dora and her mother were, too. I think I told you, Dora's mother sells meals. She's a widow and has trouble making ends meet. Anyway, Dora and her mother were talking and this man who eats there, a peddler, told them it wasn't so hard to get liquor, even with the Prohibition. This is according to Dora. He even offered to try to get some schnapps for Dora's mother."

Mrs. Kandel stopped. She looked around as if she were expecting to see someone else in the room.

"We are not looking to prosecute this man," Morelli reassured her. "We just want to know where the tainted brandy came from. So we can stop any more reaching the public."

"I may believe that, Mr. Morelli, but other people will not. If you talk to this man, it won't matter to people what the real story is. They will view him as a criminal, as someone who has shamed and endangered the whole community. You can't stop people talking. It will affect Dora, her mother, and everyone else associated with this, maybe even the families who lost a child because of this," Mrs. Kandel said in a low voice.

"Then, what's the answer, Mrs. Kandel?" Morelli asked in a somber tone that matched that of the rabbi's wife.

"I would have to have some assurances from you before I tell you more," Mrs. Kandel said suddenly.

"If we can," Emily said. She could see the moral dilemma the woman felt was very real to her and perhaps she was exactly right about what would happen if she and Morelli showed up to speak to this man. A visit of this kind in New Rochelle would start a chain of gossip that would be hard to break, and Emily felt she could understand the risk the woman was talking about.

"First, you would have to promise me the police would not be involved.

You would talk to this man yourselves," Mrs. Kandel said.

"We have no intention of involving the police," Morelli told her. "Just this morning we had a meeting with our superiors where that was ruled out."

"Second, you would ignore anything not related to what happened to the children." Seeing the look of confusion on their faces, Mrs. Kandel continued, "People's lives are very hard. A lot of them do things they shouldn't or that are not allowed."

"Are you talking about Dora's mother selling meals?" Morelli asked. "I assure you we have no interest in that."

Mrs. Kandel sighed.

"Dora is a nice girl. Her father was killed in a street accident two years ago. It has not been easy for her and her mother."

"Is there anything else?" Emily asked. So far, Mrs. Kandel's demands seemed very reasonable to Emily. The rabbi's wife was very protective of the people she knew, as Emily had seen at their first meeting.

"Yes. I know you are very anxious to find this man and have been searching for him for a long time, but you must promise not to desecrate the sabbath. You can't do anything till Sunday."

"Agreed," Morelli said quickly. Emily realized that any action that could be perceived to violate the religious customs of the community could become a major issue of exactly the kind Director Kent wished to avoid.

"Alright then. Dora's mother, her name is Hedda Friedenthal, lives at 50 Hester Street, just down from us."

Emily looked at Morelli.

"The letter," she whispered. Morelli nodded and gestured for her to say nothing.

"This man, Mr. Wolf . . ." Mrs. Kandel was saying.

"Wolf?!" Morelli exclaimed. Emily gasped and tried to hold her pencil steady. Was it really possible, she wondered, that Dan Wolf, the peddler who kept appearing everywhere she went, could be the man they had been searching the city for? Had the solution to the puzzle been right in front of them all this time? Wolf was a common name, but that another man with the same last name might be involved was too great a coincidence.

"Yes, I don't know his first name," Mrs. Kandel went on, looking curiously from one to the other of them. "He eats his midday meal there most days." She paused. "Do you know this man?" she demanded.

"We may," Emily admitted. Once again, she was amazed at the reasoning ability of the rabbi's wife and her astute appraisal of people and situations. "But we didn't know he might be involved in the case."

"What you just told us brings him into the picture," Morelli added.

"That reassures me," said Mrs. Kandel. "If you already know this man, it is likely he really is involved. But you must still keep your promises." She looked sternly first at Emily and then at Morelli.

Seeing the expression on Morelli's face, Emily knew there would be no possibility other than doing exactly what they had said they would. The rigid morality of the rabbi's wife did not allow for anything other than the right thing. But, for the first time, Emily began to wonder what the right thing really was, and if perhaps the action Directors Kent and Wetherill believed to be correct might in fact be the exact wrong thing to do in this case.

30

Friday afternoon passed in a flurry of activity. Morelli escorted Mrs. Kandel to the lobby, as required by department policy. Members of the public were not permitted to visit the offices of health department personnel unaccompanied, despite the fact that the rabbi's wife had made her way in alone. During the few minutes that took, Emily made urgent calls to Directors Kent and Wetherill. Wetherill had been in his office, but Kent was in a meeting in another part of the building. It had taken Emily some time to reach him. She had to phone the assistant of the man Kent was meeting with and ask her to interrupt the meeting to tell Kent that Emily needed to speak with him urgently. By the time he reached the telephone, both Wetherill and Morelli were waiting in Emily's office. Hearing what had transpired since they last spoke, Kent said he would return immediately and join them very shortly.

"How sure are you about all this?" Kent asked as he sat down at the conference table in his office where the others were already waiting.

"All the evidence is circumstantial," Morelli explained. "But it fits together and comes from different sources."

"And this man has figured in your investigation?" Kent asked.

"Yes, sir," said Emily. "What I mean is, we didn't realize he might be involved directly until today, but we have spoken to him several times and he has told us quite a bit about himself and what it's like to be a peddler."

"Did you tell him what you were investigating?" asked Wetherill.

"Yes, sir," Emily confirmed, turning from Kent to the other director. "We told him exactly what we told everyone we spoke to."

Wetherill thought this over.

"In your opinion, does he realize he is the man you are looking for?" he asked Morelli. "Does he understand that his actions may have had serious consequences?"

"Wolf may be a peddler, sir, but he is highly intelligent. In my opinion, he cannot not know he is the man we are looking for," Morelli replied.

"I had a feeling our meetings weren't coincidental," Emily said. "Now I realize he may have wanted to know what we were doing."

"And whether we were onto him," Morelli put in.

"It sounds to me like that is exactly what was going on," said Kent in a tone of certainty. "In retrospect, I mean."

Emily knew Kent was referring to the fact that all of them had been aware of the meetings with Wolf because they were recorded in the daily summaries of the investigation she provided to both directors. No one had recognized his importance in the case because it was the rabbi's wife who had finally made that clear by providing the one piece of information that connected Wolf to the events that had occurred. Nonetheless, Emily recalled a detail that now took on special significance. Ruthie Kandel had told them about the peddler who ate at her friend Dora's house weeks ago. The conversation was recorded in Emily's notes, but she had only written it down to make Ruthie happy. They had come to talk to Mrs. Kandel, and she had not considered that what seemed to be an offhand comment by her daughter might be very important. In fact, Emily had felt Ruthie was just making herself important in the same fashion Mrs. Kandel ascribed to Dora. If they had followed up that lead at the time, the case might have been solved long ago. Emily decided to say nothing to the directors about this oversight and hoped neither Kent nor Wetherill would remember the missed opportunity.

"We need a plan," Kent was saying. "This is where we have to defer to you, Andy," he continued, addressing Wetherill. "We can't have rules being broken and mistakes being made."

The next hour was spent discussing every possible approach to the problem of how Dan Wolf could be interviewed in a way that would produce the information they needed while minimizing public exposure. This related directly to the promise they had to Mrs. Kandel, which, to Emily's surprise, the two directors accepted immediately.

The need to preserve the privacy of members of the public came up frequently in the department's investigative work. Wetherill, as head of the investigations section, and Morelli, as an experienced investigator, were well aware of what could happen if neighbors, co-workers, and sometimes even family members learned someone had been paid a visit by the health department. People always assumed the worst, and the stigma of disease frequently cost jobs, relationships, and peace of mind. In this case, deaths had occurred and the law had been broken. If generally known, the consequences imposed on Dan Wolf by his friends and neighbors would be severe, even though it was highly unlikely he knew anything was wrong with the spirits he had sold, and there would be no legal proceedings. People would brand him a criminal, even a murderer, and it would be extremely difficult to restore his name.

At the same time, while many people would welcome harsh treatment for a Jewish peddler involved in any sort of scandal, there were others who would see the health department's effort to question Wolf as a form of persecution. Anti-Jewish sentiment had been growing since the end of the war. The Jews were too numerous, too successful, a destabilizing element in American society in the eyes of many. But on the other side, the more established and acculturated Jewish community inevitably took badly to anything that seemed to single out or disadvantage the newer arrivals. Even though their background was not identical, these well-connected and often well-to-do Jews had great sympathy for the newcomers when they came up against the wider community and especially the government. They might despise them privately and look down on their attachment to old country ways and customs, but these established Jews had considerable financial and political power they would not hesitate to use in the interest of those they felt were helpless.

After a great deal of discussion about possible alternatives, it was finally decided that the best way to approach Wolf would be at Hedda Friedenthal's house where he was known to eat lunch almost every day. They did not know where he lived, except for the fact that it was in the vicinity of the Friedenthals' home, and they could not count on running into him on the street. If they missed Wolf they could try again the next day, assuming no one realized they were waiting for him. This was the key to the operation, Wetherill stressed. They were not to approach the place or speak to anyone in the household, unless they were absolutely certain Wolf was inside. They were to knock on the door and ask to speak to the man by name. That would be unusual but would not give anyone listening an indication of the purpose of their visit.

"I know you have played a key role in all this, Miss Lowe, but Morelli will have to take the lead from now on," Wetherill apologized. "He holds an official position as an investigator, and we need this done by the book."

Emily smiled.

"Of course," she said. "I understand completely."

"I do think the two of you should be present, however," Wetherill went on, speaking directly to Emily. "You've done a great deal of work on all this, and this man, Wolf, seems to like you. Perhaps he trusts you as well."

Emily nodded. She hoped Wolf trusted her, but there was no way to be sure. In fact, she had never thought that she would be in charge of this phase of the investigation for exactly the reason Wetherill had alluded to. She had learned from Morelli that there were numerous rules and regulations about how formal investigations were to be conducted. Any deviation from these rules might invalidate any information the investigator obtained and nullify the evidence collected. This might prevent a case being made, especially in a situation where the law had been broken or members of the public had been exposed to risk.

"What's your view on this, Morelli?" Kent asked after a moment. "You must have some experience with matters like this."

"Well, I've never handled anything exactly like this," Morelli confessed. "But I think the thing to do is move as quickly as possible. We don't want Wolf to suddenly pick up and leave town."

"Do you think that's likely?" Wetherill asked.

"Not really, sir," Morelli replied. "But he told us himself he has plans to move upstate. If he gets the idea we're after him, he might simply go."

Emily thought this over. She recalled how simple it seemed to have been for Wolf to travel some two hundred miles on foot just to scout out the prospects in the western part of the state.

"I think we can rely on Mrs. Kandel," she said, more to Morelli than to the two directors. "I don't believe she would say anything to her friend, and she doesn't know Wolf."

"I agree," Morelli confirmed. "Nonetheless, I think we ought to try to catch him on Sunday. We promised not to violate the Jewish sabbath," he added, referring to another of the conditions the rabbi's wife had placed on them.

"I can't order you to do that," said Wetherill. "This investigation is off the record, so there can't be any overtime recorded. I can let you have a day off during the week, but it will all have to be by agreement."

Emily knew some health department employees sometimes worked on weekends. This included members of the Investigations section and workers directly involved in healthcare, like the visiting nurses. Even so, this only came up in some kind of emergency situation such as an outbreak of disease.

"I don't mind a Sunday on the job if you don't, Em," Morelli was saying.

"I'm happy to do whatever we need to," Emily confirmed. It happened she had no special plans for the weekend ahead, but she wouldn't have missed this part of the case for anything anyway.

"Alright then," said Kent. "You know what we want to know. Morelli will brief you on procedure, and you two can make your own plans. I am hoping we can wrap this up without adding to the problem."

Emily thought Kent seemed excited, despite his obvious concern for the seriousness of the situation. Wetherill, by contrast, seemed worried, Emily thought, and she realized he might suffer graver consequences if their attempt to talk to Wolf turned into a disaster. Emily figured the greatest risk would be if there was commotion among members of the public who were not involved because they misunderstood the purpose of a visit from the health department to the Friedenthal residence. This sort of thing had occurred a number of times that Emily knew of from Director Kent's files. The majority of the city's population did not welcome interference in their lives by officials no matter how well-meaning, and innocent initiatives on the part of the department could blow up at a moment's notice.

After a few more instructions from the two directors, Emily and Morelli retired to Emily's office to make plans for Sunday. There was a great deal to discuss, in terms of what they would do but also how it should be done. Emily wrote everything down out of habit, but hoped she would remember all the important details on the day. Luckily, she thought, she would have Saturday to re-read her notes and get everything clear in her mind. She and Morelli parted just before five o'clock with an agreement to meet outside the health department building at ten a.m. on Sunday.

31

Sunday morning was mild for the time of year, and Emily breathed deeply trying to imbibe the feeling of spring that was visible all around, even in the middle of the great city. At the same time she tried to suppress the feelings of excitement, nervousness, and concern that were making her stomach churn and her head spin. She tried to force herself to go over the plans she and Morelli had made as she waited for him to appear. Emily had been a few minutes early and Morelli, as it turned out, was a few minutes late. This brief period of waiting had almost sent her into a spiral of anxiety that she had somehow misunderstood what she was supposed to do, that it was not really today that they were meeting to try to intercept Wolf, and that Morelli was fruitlessly waiting for her in another location.

The moment Morelli turned the corner and Emily caught sight of him walking toward her smiling, all her misgivings vanished to be replaced by unmistakable excitement and anticipation. Morelli was casually dressed in a well-worn lumberjacket patterned in grey and blue plaid. Emily herself was wearing a hip length cardigan sweater over a plain blouse and narrow skirt. These were not garments she would normally have worn to work, but they had agreed as part of the plan that both of them would try to blend in by dressing more like the working-class residents who made up the bulk of the ghetto's population. Neither of them looked very much like they belonged in that neighborhood, Emily reflected, and apparently Morelli didn't think so either. It had been his idea to change their attire so as to generate as little notice as possible while they waited for Wolf to appear.

The plan was simple. They would watch the house where the Friedenthals lived beginning at eleven a.m. The crowds of shoppers on Hester Street would be a good cover if they could avoid attracting unwanted attention. Wolf was much more familiar with the streets than they were, but he had no real reason to suspect they were looking for him even he did happen to spot them, Morelli had reassured her. He was betting that Wolf would assume they were still trying to locate their man and would have no idea that they knew he was the one they wanted. Morelli was counting on the fact that they would be able to see Wolf climb the steps and enter the building, even if they could not spot him approaching. They knew from the rabbi's wife that Hedda Friedenthal lived on the ground floor in the apartment to the left of the entrance, so it would be simple to follow Wolf in once they were sure he had arrived.

"Are we just going to stand on the street?" Emily asked Morelli as they traveled downtown on the streetcar. "We could pretend to be shopping. I brought a string bag."

"That was good thinking, Em," Morelli told her. "But I scouted out the area on my way home on Friday and we won't have to. There is one of those dairy restaurants right across the street from the Freindenthals' building. If we can get a table by the window, we can watch the front of the house and see when Wolf arrives. It will be much easier to keep our heads down if we are having a cup of coffee than if we have to try to look like shoppers."

The restaurant Morelli had in mind was ideal to watch the Friedenthals' building. It was small but very busy. No one paid any attention to them as they sat down at the front and ordered coffee when the proprietor, who seemed to be the only one working in the place, approached them.

"If it gets to be a long wait, we'll just order lunch," Morelli said to Emily. "The important thing is, we stay here as long as we can and keep our eyes on those steps."

"How long will we wait?" Emily asked.

"Well, I'm guessing he'll be here before one. He's eating in someone's home. Mrs. Friedenthal is not going to have food available all day, even though she does this as a business," Morelli reflected.

The first half hour passed quickly. Morelli led her in a conversation about their jobs and family, and soon Emily forgot they were playing a role and were actually here to do an important job. Suddenly, she saw Morelli tense.

"I think that's him," Morelli said, gesturing toward the shifting crowd on the opposite side of the street.

Emily strained to look but saw no one who seemed familiar.

"I don't see him," she said.

"I don't either, now," Morelli agreed. "But I'm sure I did. Keep your eye on the door."

Emily did and in a few moments the now familiar figure of Dan Wolf emerged from the crowd and began to slowly climb the steps to the tenement entrance. The peddler, dressed uncharacteristically in a worn suit, opened the door and disappeared into the building.

"Come on," said Morelli. They had paid for their coffee when it was placed on the table so they would be able to leave the moment Wolf came into sight.

Morelli took Emily's arm and led her across the street between the ever-shifting waves of people and vehicles that threatened to block their way. When they reached the Friedenthals' building, Morelli slowed down and they climbed up the steps with as much decorum as possible and opened the door. There was no one inside, and the entryway was strangely quiet after the din on the street, which had now faded to a dull rumbling in the background. After stopping for a moment to catch his breath, Morelli glanced at his wristwatch and turned it so Emily could see.

"He's been inside for almost ten minutes," he whispered. "Let's go."

These words triggered a wave of apprehension that washed over Emily and gave her chills. What if they were wrong about Wolf and he wasn't the man they were looking for? What if the man they saw enter the building was not Wolf but someone else? What if this were the wrong place entirely and they were about to burst in on innocent people? Morelli turned to the door on the left and indicated a card pasted to the doorframe that read "Friedenthal." Seeing this Emily relaxed a little, but her heart was pounding, and she was glad it was Morelli, not her, who would have to do the talking.

Morelli knocked gently on the door. It was answered immediately by a middle-aged woman with a look of dismay on her face. Emily guessed that Hedda Friedenthal had been prepared by the rabbi's wife and had been expecting them, if not today than someday soon. Her hand gripped the edge of the door as if to prevent it from opening to them of its own accord.

"We'd like to speak to Mr. Wolf," Morelli said mildly, a smile on his face.

Mrs. Friedenthal stepped back and allowed them to enter. Emily saw they were in the front room of the apartment where almost the entire floorspace was taken up by a dining table and six chairs. Two of those chairs were occupied. Seeing them, one of the diners—a man Emily had never seen before—hurriedly stood up, picked up his coat and pushed past them into the foyer. Emily heard the outer door open and then close as the man escaped into the street.

"Mr. Wolf," Mrs. Friedenthal said in a hoarse whisper. "There are people here to see you." She hurried out of the room, closing the door behind her.

Wolf, a black skullcap on his head, sat at the table, his back to them. An empty plate lay in front of him from which he was mopping up remaining gravy with a piece of bread. A full cup of coffee, so far untouched, stood next to his plate. The fedora Emily had seen him wearing when they met outside The Forward had been placed on the seat of the chair next to him.

Wolf turned toward Emily and Morelli with a sad smile.

"So, you've found me," he said. "If you're going to arrest me, can it wait a few hours?"

"We have no intention of arresting you, Mr. Wolf," Morelli told him seriously. "I don't have that authority anyway. We just want to talk to you."

"If you're taking me away, can it wait till later?" the peddler asked again.

"We are not taking you anywhere, Mr. Wolf." Morelli said firmly. "What's wrong with talking to us now? After you finish eating of course," he added.

"Please," Wolf implored. "Can't it wait? I have a ticket to see Heifetz at Carnegie Hall at three o'clock."

"What?" Morelli asked, surprise in his voice. This had not been the response Emily had expected either. But she said nothing.

Wolf's benign expression changed instantly to one of anger.

"Are you implying I am too stupid to enjoy listening to the greatest musician of our time?" Wolf glared first at Morelli and then at Emily. "Or are you saying I am not good enough to mix with those robber barons from uptown?"

"Mr. Wolf!" Emily exclaimed in reproach.

"I'm an educated man," Wolf went on fiercely. "Just because I make my living as peddler . . ."

"We think no such thing, Mr. Wolf," Morelli cut him off. "We are simply amazed at your range of interests and knowledge. And I know you to be highly intelligent."

Despite this apology, which did reflect Emily's view of the peddler, Wolf had removed from his pocket an ancient leather wallet worn smooth from handling. Opening it, he took out his concert ticket and held it just out of Morelli's reach.

"That is indeed a ticket to see Heifetz at Carnegie Hall this very afternoon," Morelli confirmed, leaning forward slightly. "I never doubted you, Mr. Wolf."

"He's playing a solo partita by Bach and some minor pieces, accompanied by Chotzinoff," Wolf said, still apparently suspicious. He carefully put the ticket back in his wallet and waited to hear what Morelli would say next.

"I think you understand, Mr. Wolf," Morelli began, "that we are very concerned about a number of bottles of cherry brandy that were apparently tainted and led to serious illness in seven people who drank the contents."

Wolf paled as Emily watched. The shock he must have felt was genuine, she thought, as it occurred to her this was the first he was hearing about the harm caused by the tainted spirits. She realized that, up to now, he must have thought this was simply a matter of having violated the Volstead Act that might result in a fine. He now had serious illness among his customers on his conscience, and, without realizing it, the deaths of seven children. They had intentionally portrayed the situation as less serious than it actually was in deference to the families involved, but Emily suspected the peddler knew there was more to this matter than he had been told.

Wolf sat perfectly still except for a slight movement of his head in acknowledgement of what Morelli had said. He seemed to be waiting for his fate to be revealed. Emily herself hardly dared move. This was the moment their investigation had been building to. She turned her full attention to what Morelli was saying as a way of suppressing the rapid beating of her heart.

"We believe that you sold that brandy here in the city and that you have information about its origin and nature." Morelli looked very solemn, Emily thought. She had not heard him use this official tone of voice nor speak so formally.

The peddler nodded slightly.

"We hope you can assist us in clearing this matter up," Morelli went on. "I want to stress, you are not implicated in any way. We believe that you had no knowledge that the goods you sold were harmful."

Emily could see Wolf was waiting for the other shoe to drop. She realized he had no reason to believe what Morelli had told him, and a person in his position and with his experiences might well assume that any dealings with the authorities meant trouble. Many people Emily knew felt that way, and they had lived much less tumultuous lives than the peddler.

"What is it you want from me?" Wolf asked.

Now that his anger at being insulted had passed, the peddler was surprisingly calm, Emily thought, although she felt his voice held a note of sadness. Unlike Mrs. Friedenthal who was obviously frightened even though she was not involved directly, Wolf seemed alert and wary but not anxious. Perhaps he was resigned, Emily thought.

"We want to talk to you, to interview you, so we can find out what you know about the brandy you sold. Where it came from, for example, and how did you happen to be selling it," Morelli explained.

"So, you're taking me in," the peddler said, returning to his original assumption about their presence.

It occurred to Emily that Wolf seemed completely unconcerned about how they had identified him and knew where to find him as he was having his midday meal. Most people she felt, would have demanded that information from the outset. The peddler truly seemed to be worried about missing his concert.

"We are not taking you in, Mr. Wolf," Morelli repeated patiently. "We are asking that you come to the health department voluntarily so we can get a statement from you. We just want to know where the tainted spirits came from."

"Now?" the peddler asked again. His face fell, and Emily wondered at the apparent depth of his disappointment that something could interfere with his chance to see Heifetz perform. That seemed to outweigh any other concerns, including the impact of his actions. It could not have been easy to get a ticket, she reasoned, in terms of cost of course, but also demand. The newspapers, in their reviews of the violinist's appearances, always noted that every concert was sold out almost as soon as the tickets went on sale.

"Not now, Mr. Wolf, tomorrow. Monday morning. At the office of Miss Lowe's superior," Morelli explained. He held out a card to the peddler. "The address is on the card. We will expect you at ten a.m."

Wolf took the card Morelli handed him and studied it with care.

"What if I don't show?"

Morelli shrugged.

"Then you don't show. I told you repeatedly, we have no authority to have you arrested. We are asking for your help, nothing more," he said.

The peddler thought this over.

"I'll be there," he promised after a moment. "I have to get going now," he went on, picking up his hat and placing it on his head. "It's a long way to 57th Street."

Emily wondered if the peddler planned to walk all the way to Carnegie Hall. That might have been in character, she thought. As Wolf stood up to leave Emily had a sudden realization.

"Mr. Wolf," she called, just as the peddler made to step out the door. "You sent us a letter in response to our ad in The Forward, didn't you?"

Wolf threw back his head and laughed. It was sharp contrast to the demeanor that Emily had seen at their previous meetings.

"I wondered if you knew that," he said. "I thought you needed some help."

With that, the peddler slipped out of the apartment and disappeared onto the street.

"An interesting man," Morelli said as they too left the building. "It's only twelve thirty-five. He'll make the concert easily."

Emily could only agree.

32

For the tenth time that morning, Emily straightened the lined pads she had laid out on Director Kent's conference table for herself, Morelli, Kent, and Wetherill. She aligned the accompanying pencils and checked to see that they had not mysteriously lost their points. Coffee was ready in the pot on the hotplate in the utility area adjacent to the director's washroom, and she had a plate of sliced cake waiting as well. Director Kent often provided coffee and cake to visitors and attendees at meetings he hosted in his office, and it was one of Emily's duties to decide when refreshments of this kind were appropriate and to purchase them using the petty cash fund. The director relied on Emily's judgement of the relative importance of his visitors. In her view, Dan Wolf was one of the most important guests they were likely to have because of the seriousness of the events that had already taken place as well as the potential to gain important information the peddler might have.

Before she and Morelli had parted the day before, he to cross the bridge to Brooklyn and Emily to return to her midtown lodgings, they had discussed what the next day's interview with Wolf might reveal.

"He may know nothing at all," Morelli had cautioned.

"But he got the brandy somewhere," Emily had protested. "He must know that much."

"That's true," Morelli agreed. "But peddlers don't keep records and don't know their customers by name. He may simply not remember. You'd be surprised at the things people forget," he added.

Emily knew that was true, and Morelli's stories about his past cases just reinforced the fact. The brandy might have come into Wolf's hands months or years ago. He might very well have no idea where it came from. At the same time, Emily had reminded Morelli that Wolf was a very unusual man and might know a lot more than they imagined. Morelli was forced to agree. Everything they had so far learned about the peddler was surprising, and they said goodbye on a high note.

Once again, as she had many times during this investigation, Emily felt a rising anxiety that made her heart pound and her stomach churn. It had not occurred to her until now that Wolf might not come. He had seemed genuinely suspicious of their motives, even though Morelli had been completely honest about what their intentions were. If the interview did take place as expected, it would be one more completely new experience for Emily. She normally attended the director's meetings when he asked her to, which often involved her taking notes, when Kent thought that she could learn something by doing so. All of these occasions had involved other city officials, mostly employees of the health department, which was very large and encompassed many different but interrelated sections. She had never participated in a meeting that involved a member of the public and had never seen an official interview. Director Kent had said they would keep things informal because they were relying on the peddler's good will, but the interview would be official, and they might need to act on the information received.

At five minutes to ten, Emily, Morelli, Kent, and Wetherill were gathered in the outer office where Emily worked. The conference table, visible through the open door to Kent's private office, was ready and, Emily hoped, would impress Wolf. Morelli had tried to make small talk, but the two directors seemed as nervous as Emily felt. She realized they had the most at stake if the matter of the tainted brandy and the ensuing deaths of seven children could not be cleared up, especially as this would require guaranteeing there would be no repeat of the situation.

The hands of the clock on the wall moved slowly and unrelentingly forward. Ten o'clock passed. Emily began to fear that Wolf had changed his mind. She had almost convinced herself that this must be the case when the telephone on her desk rang, startling her badly. She moved to answer while the others watched.

"Wolf is in the lobby," she said, forcing her voice into its normal tone. The call had been from her friend Julia, whose job it was to escort visitors to the various offices in the building. Emily had asked her to let them know when the peddler arrived. As she spoke, Emily could feel the sense of relief that filled the room.

"Excellent!" said Director Kent, as if he had never doubted Wolf's arrival would take place on schedule. "Morelli, would you go down and bring the man up?"

"Of course, sir," Morelli replied and hurried out, although nothing had been said about a need for haste.

Within a few minutes, Morelli was back with Dan Wolf. The peddler was dressed in his work clothes and seemed out of place in the rigidly official environment of the director's office. Morelli introduced Kent and Wetherill as Wolf stood awkwardly in place. He made no move to sit down or to speak to any of them. The look in his eyes was one of fear and aggression, Emily thought.

Director Kent was running the meeting and Wetherill was responsible for the interview, Emily knew. But she was the one most acquainted with the peddler and felt she understood him better than the three men, including Morelli.

"Would you like some coffee, Mr. Wolf?" she asked before Kent had a chance to speak.

To her great satisfaction, Emily saw the peddler's expression soften.

"Plenty of sugar," Wolf said. "A little cake wouldn't hurt," he added, as Emily returned to the table with a cup of coffee on a saucer that she placed by one of the chairs.

"Please sit down," she told Wolf, as the others took their seats as well. She pushed the plate of cake toward Wolf, indicating he should help himself.

"How was your concert, Mr. Wolf?" Morelli asked.

The ice now broken, Wolf smiled, speaking as he selected a piece of cake.

"Perfection." The peddler looked around the room. "I guess you're really not going to arrest me," he said, taking a bite.

"There was never any possibility of that," Morelli told him with a smile.

"Mr. Wolf," Kent began. "I assume you know why you're here. We are trying to address the very distressing problem of some tainted brandy that injured a number of people who used it for medicinal purposes. It seems they got the spirits from you."

"You're talking about that *palinka*. I wish I had never gotten involved with that stuff," the peddler began. "It was a lot of trouble and now it turns out poison as well."

"Can you tell us how the spirits came into your possession?" Wetherill asked. "We understand there was no wrongdoing on your part, but we need to know as much as possible about this." He glanced at Emily to confirm she was ready to take notes. Emily nodded and Wetherill continued, "You will have a chance to review the notes of this interview to make sure they're accurate."

Wolf, who now seemed untroubled by the proceedings, took a large swallow from his cup and leaned back in his chair. Emily waited with the others, her pencil poised to start writing as Wolf settled himself more comfortably and cleared his throat to speak.

33

"As these two know," the peddler began, addressing himself specifically to the two directors. "I took a trip out of town last fall."

"To the western part of the state," Kent supplied. "Miss Lowe's report mentioned that. What was the purpose of the trip?"

"I was scouting. I am hoping to open a general store in some small town somewhere and was looking for a likely spot. There are lots of places where people need things but have nowhere to get them. My benefactor thinks it would be better to head up north," Wolf told him.

"Mr. Wolf has a business partner who is funding this undertaking," Morelli explained to the directors. This had also been in Emily's report but hadn't seemed significant to any of them at the time. He nodded to Wolf to continue.

"I went up to Monsey and then Spring Valley. I passed through Goshen and then turned west," the peddler explained. "There are a lot of villages along the river where people appreciate quality goods. I happened to bring my pack along and was doing business where I could," the peddler went on.

"You were on foot? Where were you planning to go?" Kent asked.

"Maybe as far as Binghamton. Maybe farther," the peddler said. "Depending on what the prospects were like."

"That's a very long way to walk," Wetherill put in, echoing Emily's own reaction when the peddler first told them about his travels.

Wolf shrugged.

"Could be worse," he said. "Somewhere near Peakville, a man stopped me wanting to know what merchandise I had. Ladies' shoes, dresses for a little girl, clothes for the whole family. He wanted it all. Like a lot of people, he didn't have cash, so I said, what are you trading?" Wolf spoke fluently once he got started and, Emily thought, was an engaging storyteller.

"So, he says, come back to the house and we'll talk," the peddler continued. "I thought, sure, why not? There might be a hot meal in it for me and I'm always looking for conversation. People interest me." He glanced around the room at his audience. Emily looked up from her notes and smiled at Wolf.

"It turns out he's a pig farmer. It wasn't much of a place, but his wife was very hospitable. She put out a plate of strudel while we negotiated. He tried to offer me vegetables, fruit, even sausages, but I don't deal in fresh food. It doesn't keep, and I didn't know where my next customer would be. So finally he says, what about *palinka*? I knew the Prohibition was coming and I figured people might want this, so I agreed."

"You said you regretted taking the brandy," Wetherill pressed. "Why was that?"

"The bottles are heavy. They can break. They took up a lot of space in my pack and had to be wrapped. But the guy wanted almost everything I had, so in the end, I agreed," Wolf told him. "I wasn't even sure where I could sell the stuff. But I took a gamble the market would open up when people realized they couldn't get liquor anymore."

Emily was impressed by this analysis. She was trying to note as many details of Wolf's story as she could as well as the questions asked by the others.

"I took eight bottles in total, wrapped them up and went on my way," the peddler was saying.

Emily saw Wetherill give a quick glance in Kent's direction. She knew this was the opening they had been hoping for. The department would be able to learn a lot more about the situation if a sample of the tainted brandy were available for analysis. To her surprise, however, Wetherill calmly changed the subject, turning to another line of questioning. This must have been intentional, Emily knew, but she could not guess what the director had in mind.

"Do you know the man's name?" Wetherill asked.

"Farkas," said the peddler. "The wife called him Joe, but he didn't tell me his first name."

Wetherill gestured for Emily to make a note of this. She knew that this was a crucial piece of information and hoped the peddler had a good memory.

"What kinds of bottles were these?" Wetherill asked.

"What do you mean? Just bottles," Wolf said. "About so big," he added, positioning his hands to suggest a container about six inches high.

"Were they labeled?" Morelli asked.

"Yes, of course," the peddler replied. "*Cseresznye Palinka*."

"What language is that?" Kent asked.

"Hungarian," Wolf replied, as if this fact should have been obvious.

"You speak that language?" Kent seemed surprised.

"Enough," the peddler told him cryptically.

Emily recalled the peddler was a *Galitzianer* and hailed from a region that had been part of Austria-Hungary. She wondered what it would be like to come from this tumultuous empire that had been one of the central powers in the recent Great War but was erased from the map when the fighting ended. Its reincarnation as the Kingdom of Hungary and the Republic of Austria left no place for the land where Wolf and so many others were born. Emily had read about all this in the newspapers. She could only imagine what this had meant for Wolf's family, left behind in a country that no longer existed.

"Was the brandy authentic?" Wetherill asked.

Emily knew this was another vital issue in the case. One of the points Directors Kent and Wetherill were most interested in clearing up was exactly where the spirits had come from and how had they been produced.

"The bottles said *Magyar Gyartmany. Budapesti*," Wolf replied.

"Please think very carefully, Mr. Wolf," Wetherill said, emphasizing every word. "Did you have the impression these bottles were commercially produced? Made in a factory?"

Wolf smiled again, more broadly this time.

"The bottles were. If you're asking, was the *palinka* homemade, then yes of course it was. But the bottles were genuine. I guessed Farkas had emptied them years ago."

"So, you knew this customer of yours had distilled the spirits himself?" Wetherill asked. Emily thought he seemed shocked.

"Of course," Wolf said again. "These Hungarians think the only real *palinka* is what they make themselves."

"You finished your trip and brought the brandy back to the city," Kent summarized. "How did you sell it?"

"From my pushcart," Wolf said simply.

"What I meant was, how did you let your customers know you had it for sale?" Kent said in clarification.

"I didn't," said the peddler. "People ask for what they need. There's a lot of sickness in wintertime. They're always asking for something for a cold, the grippe, croup, whatever. Cherry brandy is for coughs."

"So, you're saying people came to you and asked for brandy?" Wetherill asked.

"Yes."

Emily thought Wolf sounded somewhat defensive. Perhaps he thought he was going to be held responsible for what had happened after all.

"I see. And the *palinka* you had was what they wanted?" Wetherill went on.

"No one wanted it. But it was what I had and what they could get," the peddler said in a tone of reproach.

For a moment, no one spoke. With another sidelong glance at Kent, Wetherill asked cautiously, "You said you had eight bottles of the brandy, Mr. Wolf. Seven are accounted for. What happened to the eighth?" "I still have it," Wolf said evenly.

"You still have it?" Kent confirmed with barely concealed enthusiasm.

Wolf nodded.

"Would we be able to have that bottle for analysis?" Wetherill asked. To Emily, it was clear he was trying to not to let Wolf know how important a sample of the brandy was.

"I don't know," Wolf said slowly.

"Mr. Wolf," Morelli put in before one the directors could speak. "I am sure the department would purchase the remaining bottle from you. We would not want to cause you a loss."

"Of course," Kent agreed. "The department would like to purchase the remaining bottle. We should have made that clear."

Wolf appeared to think this over. Emily wondered whether he was still worried that he might be implicated in some way if he handed over the tainted spirits. This would mean the brandy could be linked to him under the law.

"It would be illegal for me to sell it," Wolf said. "Prohibition." He looked around the room, his gaze resting on each of them for a moment.

"You are correct, Mr. Wolf," Kent agreed. "It would be illegal for you to sell the brandy. But it is not illegal for us to compensate you for your time and trouble as well as for the potential loss of stock." The director paused. Emily knew the strategy Kent had just outlined was going to be the position taken in this matter. He was expecting Wolf to accept this way out of the problem and for the rest of them to support it. "Miss Lowe," Kent went on, turning to Emily. "Last fall, a comparable bottle of brandy sold for about a dollar fifty, wouldn't you say?"

Emily really had no idea whether this was accurate or not, but she knew she was supposed to agree with her boss.

"Yes, sir, that sounds about right," she said in a cheery voice.

"Does that sound right to you as well?" Kent asked, turning to Morelli and Wetherill who were sitting across the table.

"Yes, sir," Morelli said. Wetherill nodded, a slight smile on his face.

"Would you accept one dollar and fifty cents as compensation for your trouble, Mr. Wolf, with the understanding that the remaining bottle of brandy will be turned over to us?" Kent asked the peddler.

"That's fair," Wolf replied, relaxed again.

"Miss Lowe, please get the money from petty cash and make out a receipt for Mr. Wolf," Kent ordered.

Emily stood up to comply. The cash box was locked in the bottom drawer of her desk in the outer office. She knew it contained five or six dollars, so there would be no trouble paying the amount Director Kent had mentioned.

"Hold on a minute," Wolf said suddenly. "I don't have it with me. It's in my room with my stock."

Kent smiled.

"I didn't expect you would be able to produce it today, Mr. Wolf," he said. "Mr. Morelli will make an arrangement to pick it up from you at your convenience."

As Emily made her way to her desk to get the money and write out a receipt for Wolf to sign, she heard Morelli agree to meet the peddler at the corner of Hester and Mulberry Streets at four o'clock that afternoon. Wolf would hand over the bottle of brandy, and Morelli would give him the receipt, which he would sign before leaving the office that morning. This business concluded, Director Kent stood up abruptly and handed Wolf the envelope containing his payment that Emily had laid on the table at her boss's elbow. Kent then held out his hand to the peddler.

"Thank you, Mr. Wolf. You've been very helpful," he said. "Good luck with your venture."

The peddler shook Kent's hand gingerly.

"I have to live every day knowing I have caused harm," he said, before turning to follow Morelli out of the room, shoulders slumped and head down.

Emily stayed where she was, looking at the pages where she had taken down Wolf's story. Her thoughts ranged over the events the peddler related. She felt more clearly than ever that there were different worlds that intersected and overlapped, and it was not possible to be certain that the people you saw around you were living in the same reality you were. As Kent and Wetherill talked across the table about the practicalities of alerting the authorities in Delaware County to the Hungarian pig farmer who was distilling his own brandy, Emily was thinking about the strange and mysterious lives led by people like Dan Wolf and his customers and the risks and calculations such people made every day. She found she could not penetrate the surface of that existence to understand what they must think and feel. There were simply too many things she didn't know and could never experience.

Emily stood up and gathered her notes. Quickly, she cleared the table and put everything away. Kent and Wetherill were still talking but seemed as subdued as she felt. So, she slipped out and quietly closed the door. Taking her handbag with her, she left the outer office and went to find Morelli, who had not returned and must have gone back to his own desk. She longed for someone to talk to about all that had happened and to have it explained. Even if that were not possible, she knew Morelli's calm stability would ease the dull heartache she now felt.

34

As Emily had guessed, Morelli was at his desk in the inspectors' room. A wide shaft of sunlight from the large window behind him bathed the desk in warmth. Emily's office, by contrast, was always rather cold. Morelli looked up as she entered and smiled widely.

"I was thinking of going out for a sandwich," he said as she approached. "Join me?"

"Thank you. I think I'd like to get outside for a while," Emily said truthfully. The interview with Wolf had upset her, and she was not sure why.

"You look down, Em," Morelli said as they left the building and walked toward a coffee shop on the next block where many health department employees ate. "Is something the matter?"

"I'm not sure, Ed. Hearing Mr. Wolf tell his story, I don't know how I feel. It is all such a tragedy," she explained as best she could.

"Deaths are always tragic for those involved. You became involved with this, so you feel it more than if, say, you read about it in the paper. Certainly the loss of their children was tragic for the families," Morelli said. "But it was really just misadventure. There was no way Wolf or his customers or even the man who distilled the brandy could have known it was poison."

"Of course. You're right, Ed," Emily conceded. "But when I think about the hardship Mr. Wolf, his customers, and even the Hungarian farmer must have experienced, I can hardly bear it."

The sandwiches they had ordered were placed on the table, and Morelli bit into his as if nothing was wrong. Emily looked at her ham and cheese but didn't touch it.

"Eat your lunch, Em. I know it's hard. In the beginning, you can't quite separate yourself from the things we see in this job. The deaths, disease, children in trouble, coincidences that have terrible consequences like what happened here, it's all part of our work. We have to aim to make things safer and better for the rest of the public by learning from it. Unfortunately, before we can do that, there are often people who suffer," Morelli said. "I know you must feel terrible. You aren't used to it yet."

Emily picked up her sandwich and tentatively took a bite.

"Did you feel like this when you first started out?" she asked, swallowing hard.

"Of course. Everyone does, I think."

"How did you deal with it?"

"For a while, after every case, I would beat myself up. Could I have done more? Was there something I might have found out sooner that would have saved someone hardship? But then I realized I could only act on the information I had. I might be able to improve that as I gained more skill but I just had to do my best. And each case made it easier to reconcile my feelings," Morelli said.

Emily greatly appreciated this frankness. Morelli had seemed to be able to handle the most difficult aspects of the investigation with ease, and she had not known whether this was a talent or whether it came from years of practice.

"Do you think I could get used to it?" she asked.

"I think so. Having empathy for the people we work with is a good thing. You'll learn how to use that feeling without letting it hurt you. You'll come to understand their suffering rather than experience it yourself," Morelli told her.

"I was starting to think I wasn't cut out to be a public healthican," Emily said. She realized she had just told Morelli a private thought and felt herself blush.

"A what?" Morelli asked, laughing. "What's a public healthican? If you don't mind my asking," he added shyly.

Under other circumstances, Emily might have been too embarrassed to respond, but Morelli had a way of putting her at ease.

"It's a term I made up when someone asked me what I was doing when I worked on the case," Emily explained. "I realized I didn't have a status the way you can say you're an investigator, but I was working to protect the public's health. At least that's how I saw it in my mind. The term just came out."

"That's what we should be called. I have often had that exact problem. Someone asks, what do you do, and I have to explain because there is no name for our profession," Morelli agreed. "Maybe we can petition the department." He laughed.

Emily was forced to laugh at this as well. She took another bite of her sandwich. For a few moments, they ate in silence.

"The whole thing seems too simple somehow," Emily said. "Mr. Wolf's story was so straightforward. I guess I expected more."

"It's always like that," Morelli told her. "There are details we will never know. We found out what happened, in a general sense, and who was involved. Liquor is now a matter for the law, so the directors might turn this over to the Bureau of Prohibition or maybe just the local police. It's out of our hands in any case."

"What do you think will happen to Mr. Wolf?" she asked.

"Oh, I'm sure he will go upstate and open his store. He's bound to be successful," said Morelli cheerfully.

"He sounded truly upset about what happened," Emily said.

"I think he is. But he'll get over it. He has the kind of spirit that never accepts defeat."

"True, but . . ." Emily began.

"He doesn't know exactly what happened, Em," Morelli told her gently.

"This is one of the reasons we only give the public as much information as is necessary for us to investigate. We have to protect the privacy of the people who are directly involved but we also have to think about the feelings of people on the fringes of a case. People like Wolf. He knows that the tainted brandy injured people but not who they were, certainly not that there were children involved. He doesn't need to know that anyone died, how, or what happened afterward. I am sure he feels remorse, but he can tell himself that maybe what happened was not so bad."

"Do you think he is telling himself that what happened was not so bad?" Emily asked, recalling Wolf's parting words.

"No, I don't think he is," Morelli admitted. "He is a very smart man, and I think he knows this was extremely serious. I am afraid he will punish himself in some way."

"Life has already punished him," Emily reflected. "He lives from peddling. He is alone in this country. He even eats his meals in someone else's house."

"I don't think he feels any of that is punishment," Morelli told her. "People choose their own path. They try to make things come out the way they want them and, if they can't, a lot of them try even harder. Wolf is one of those. But most do enjoy what they have, and they try to be happy."

"Even the families of the children?"

"Yes, even them," Morelli went on. "Life in this city is still probably better than what they had in the old country. It was that way for my parents, and I think it is for the residents of the ghetto, too."

"But look what happened."

Morelli laughed.

"Bad things can happen anywhere," he said. "At least, we public healthicans are here to prevent anything like that from happening again."

They finished eating, and the conversation turned to other topics. Emily was feeling much better, almost normal in fact, but as she and Morelli talked and joked, she couldn't help wondering whether she would ever see Dan Wolf again and what would happen to the other people she had met in the course of their investigation. There was nothing to stop her from seeking them out, she knew, but she also realized that she would probably not do that. It was more comfortable to return to her own world, where she understood the rules and things operated in a way she could predict. Perhaps this is what Morelli meant when he suggested that it was necessary to separate herself from her perceptions about the case. Nonetheless, Emily harbored a faint hope that she might run into Wolf on the street or perhaps encounter Mrs. Kandel—who had been instrumental in them solving the case—somewhere in the city.

"Shall we go?" Morelli asked, offering Emily his arm, which she gratefully took. They stepped out onto the pavement where a narrow ray of springtime sunshine created a band of light on the pavement. "It's time for us public healthicans to get back to the office," he added, laughing.

35

A week later, Emily was still thinking about the case. She always referred to it in her mind in exactly that way. The Case. Even if she was called upon one day to take part in another investigation, her recent experiences would always stand out. They had opened her eyes to things she had not imagined and, in fact, could not have imagined even if she had tried. Her view that public health was important and that she was contributing to its noble goals in her own way had now become a conviction. She was aware that she used to say this to justify her choice of career, especially to her parents and friends who thought she should have chosen another path, but she hadn't really believed it. Now, however, she knew that this stance was not just a form of self-defense. She really did have role to play in protecting the public's health and welfare.

She found herself thinking a great deal about Dan Wolf and the peddler's life that she had seen through his eyes, as well as the other people she had met in the course of the investigation. She wondered whether the strange events of the case had changed their thinking and altered the patterns of their lives, as had happened to her. But, she reminded herself life goes on as the adage says, and she knew she should be concentrating on the duties Director Kent had set for her. Still, after the excitement of being out of the office, talking to people, looking for information, her routine tasks seemed flat and uninteresting. She recognized that they were a vital part of the work the department did but she could no longer rouse up much enthusiasm for filing and recordkeeping.

Most of all, Emily missed collaborating with Morelli. She had learned an enormous amount from him during the time they had worked together, not the least of which was the importance of optimism. It was not that she had not seen the investigator over the past week; in fact, they had spoken at least briefly most workdays. It was more the lack of a shared goal like they had had during the case and the feeling that they were a team that Emily longed for. She still had a secret hope that one day she, too, might become a public health investigator but, for now, she would have to be content with her work as the director's assistant.

"Is he in, Em?"

Morelli had silently opened the door to the office to speak to her. She had been lost in thought and hadn't noticed the movement.

"Come in, Ed. You startled me," Emily admitted. "He's gone for the day," she added, referring to Director Kent. "He's at a meeting at the mayor's office and won't be back this afternoon."

"Good," said Morelli. "Have you seen the lab report?"

"The lab report? You mean the report on Mr. Wolf's brandy?" Emily asked. "It's on the director's desk. Needless to say, I didn't open it."

"Of course not," Morelli agreed. "Wetherill let me read it. It's quite something."

"What do you mean, Ed?"

"We all assumed that Farkas, that Hungarian farmer Wolf got the brandy from, had been distilling his own alcohol. If you recall, Bill Waters thought he probably had made a mistake in the distillation and contaminated his own product with wood alcohol."

Emily nodded. Waters's explanation of the process had been very clear and had been a revelation to Emily, who had never given any thought to how liquor might be produced.

"Wasn't that what happened?" she asked.

"Yes and no," Morelli explained. "It's pretty clear Farkas was distilling his own brandy, but it looks like it wasn't as strong as he hoped so he added some denatured alcohol to push up the proof."

"Denatured alcohol?"

"Yes, regular ethyl alcohol that has something added to it to make it noxious or even poisonous."

Emily was puzzled. Morelli must have seen this and continued.

"Alcohol is used for several industrial processes. Bill told us about that. It's inexpensive and can be bought in bulk. But they don't want people to drink it. Drinking alcohol, wine, spirits, what have you, is heavily taxed. Or it was, before Prohibition."

"Of course," Emily agreed. She had discussed this with her father, who, like many of his friends, had deeply resented paying this tax before alcohol sales were banned entirely.

"It seems some of this industrial alcohol was added to the brandy," Morelli went on. "The original distillation might have been perfectly safe, but apparently Farkas must have felt it wasn't strong enough, so he added some alcohol of a kind that was never meant to be drunk. There are probably a lot of people who don't realize that alcohol intended for cleaning and as a solvent can't be consumed."

"So, if Farkas had just bottled his original distillation, none of this might have happened," Emily said sadly.

"It's highly likely. The brandy might have been perfectly fine," Morelli said. "It was the extra alcohol that was poison."

Emily did not know what to make of this new twist in the case.

"What will happen to Farkas now?" she asked.

"Most probably nothing at all," Morelli said with a slight smile. "All of this occurred last fall, as Wolf told us. Prohibition was not yet in effect, and it was not illegal to produce or sell alcohol. If the brandy had come from a commercial manufacturer, the law would have been broken and the matter could be pursued, but that would relate to the requirement to produce a safe product.

Farkas distilled that brandy for his own use, or that would be his claim. We know he made a mistake by adding industrial alcohol to the brandy, but there would be no way to prove that under the law, much less that there was intent or negligence involved. He would claim he made the brandy to drink himself, and Wolf admitted no money changed hands. It was a trade for some of his merchandise."

What a strange situation, Emily thought. The whole case had unraveled into a string of unintended consequences that arose from a series of actions taken by people who didn't know each other. If only Farkas hadn't tried to strengthen the brandy he made, if only Dan Wolf had taken something else in trade for his wares, if only the parents of the dead children had tried to treat their cough in some other way, if only the hospital had realized what was wrong with the children when they were brought in. These, and a thousand other possibilities that could have been, occurred to Emily in the space of a moment.

"It's five," Morelli was saying. "What if we go get something to eat, and after that I'll see you home?"

"I'd like that very much, Ed," Emily said, feeling that nothing had ever been more the truth of her feelings. "I'll get my things."

36

"Miss Lowe! Mr. Morelli!" someone called as Emily and Morelli left the health department building. Turning to look, Emily saw Dan Wolf waving frantically at them.

"Mr. Wolf," Morelli greeted the peddler. "What are you doing here?"

"I wanted to see you two before I go away," Wolf explained. "To thank you."

"To thank us?" Emily repeated. "Whatever for?"

"For treating me honestly," the peddler replied. "I did consider that you, all of you I mean, those directors too, were trying to trap me. To get me to say something I could go to jail for."

"Why would we do that, Mr. Wolf?" Morelli asked. "We are not the police. Our only concern, and this includes the directors, is the public's health."

"Well, when something happens, someone's got to pay the price. I thought maybe it was going to be me," Wolf said.

"Not with us," Morelli replied. "Sometimes things just have to be explained. And prevented from happening again."

"I see that now," Wolf said, grinning broadly. "But it's a new one to me."

"You said you're going away," Emily said, hoping the peddler would explain his earlier remark.

"I am. My benefactor and I have come to an agreement. I'm leaving tomorrow," Wolf said. Emily detected a note of true happiness in his voice.

"So soon, Mr. Wolf?" Morelli asked with a smile.

"No time like now. They're itching for city goods up north."

"Where will you go?" Emily wanted to know. She truly hoped this would be a happy change for the peddler.

"Up to Ithaca. I'll settle in some small village near there. My benefactor thinks there's potential," Wolf told them.

"There is a famous university in Ithaca," Morelli told him. "Maybe that's what your benefactor has in mind."

Morelli's words brought back the memory of a trip Emily had taken two summers before in 1918. She and her mother took the train from the city to Buffalo to visit her recently widowed Aunt Helen, her mother's older sister. As the train rolled through the countryside, Emily had watched the moving panorama of black and white dairy cattle grazing in green fields, villages untouched by time and events, and the occasional larger town, seemingly prosperous and well ordered. The scene beyond her window was a stark contrast to the city, which had suffered through the war years, epidemics of disease, and was at the time, sweltering and filthy in the August heat. When the train pulled into the station in Ithaca, Emily would have liked nothing more than to disembark and visit Cornell University's famous campus, but they had to travel on to Buffalo, and she only caught a few tantalizing glimpses of the town.

"How will you get there, Mr. Wolf?" she asked, returning to the present. "Not on foot this time, I hope."

Wolf laughed.

"No such luck," he joked, then added proudly, "My benefactor got us tickets on the Black Diamond Express."

"You're going in style," Morelli commented.

The peddler blushed at this, perhaps thinking Morelli was teasing him. The contrast between the long walk to Binghamton that had caused so much trouble and the ride upstate on "The Handsomest Train in the World," which was owned by the Lehigh Valley Railroad and was a tribute to the black anthracite upon which the company's fortune had been built, was too great.

"What about your family?" Morelli asked, changing the subject. Emily had wondered about this as well, recalling that the peddler had already spent many long years alone in America.

"If not this year, then maybe next," said Wolf with a shrug. The peddler seemed untroubled by what to Emily seemed like must have been an obvious hardship. He really was nothing if not determined, Emily thought.

He stuck out his hand in Morelli's direction as if it were a dare.

"Good luck, Mr. Wolf," said Morelli, shaking the peddler's hand in earnest.

"Have a good trip," Emily added. She still felt a warmth toward the peddler that was difficult to explain.

Wolf raised his hand in a departing gesture, turned, and disappeared into the crowd.

"We'll have to look him up some day," Morelli said to Emily as they watched the peddler vanish among the throng of workers leaving stores and offices for home. "He's an enterprising man. I'm sure he'll make his mark."

Emily had to agree, and she did wonder whether they would hear of Dan Wolf, now former peddler, at some time in the future.

37

"Em, listen to this," Morelli exclaimed. "You won't believe it."

Emily put down one of the cups of coffee she was carrying on the corner of the desk. With her now free hand, she moved a pile of paper slightly and placed a second cup next to the first.

"What are you reading?" she asked.

"*Time* magazine," Morelli replied, holding up the publication so she could see the cover. The Secretary of Labor James J. Davis sat on the front. Emily could see the date was January 10, 1927, the edition for the current week.

"There's an article about Prohibition under National Affairs," Morelli told her.

"That's not unusual, is it?"

In the seven years since they had closed the case of Dan Wolf and the tainted brandy, Prohibition had been a constant topic in the news, as the passage of the Volstead Act had so far failed to stem the trade in alcohol in the United States, even though much of this trade was illegal and had been for almost a decade. In fact, the year before in his annual address to congress, Emily recalled, President Coolidge had called for more vigorous enforcement of the Act, even as public opinion was very much against this position, and antipathy toward the government agents who enforced the law was enormous.

"Not at all. But you've got to hear this. I'll read it to you," Morelli said. "You just will not believe it."

Emily drew a second chair closer to the desk and sat down. She was very curious to know what Morelli had found so interesting.

"I'm reading from page ten," he began. "*Coincidence created a controversy. As everyone knows, a certain amount of spirited celebration goes on between Christmas and New Year's Day. In New York City alone, forty-six deaths due to alcoholism were reported during the holidays this year. A proportionate number occurred throughout the land; the alcohol wards of the hospitals were full. Then on Jan 1, the new Government formula for denaturing industrial ethyl alcohol went into effect. This doubles the amount of poison manufacturers are required to use. The old argument of whether or not the Government has the right to use poison to enforce the Prohibition law raged.*

"*Wayne B. Wheeler, paid advocate of the Anti-Saloon League, at once found himself the villain of the story. His statements through the week fluctuated between the rabid and the sensible arguments of the Drys. Said he, 'The Government is under no obligation to furnish the people with alcohol that is drinkable when the Constitution prohibits it. The person who drinks this industrial alcohol is a deliberate suicide . . .*'"

Morelli turned to the next page.

"There's more," he said. "This from the other side. '*Wet Congressmen, not the least of whom is Senator Edwards of New Jersey, demanded that "legalized murder" by the Government be stopped. Secretary of the Treasury Mellon announced last week that he was opposed to the use of poison to enforce the law but that "Formula No. 5" would have to stay until a non-removable, non-poisonous denaturant could be found by Government chemists.*'"

"Did I understand the correctly?" Emily exclaimed. "The government is deliberately poisoning alcohol to deter people from drinking it?"

"That's what they're saying," Morelli agreed. "But now listen to this. This is in a footnote. '*The new "Formula No. 5" adds four parts methanol (wood alcohol), 2.25 parts pyridine bases, 0.5 parts benzine to 100 parts ethyl alcohol.*

Three ordinary drinks of this may cause blindness.'"

"But that's more or less what happened in our case. Although it wasn't intentional," Emily protested.

"Exactly," Morelli said. "What was a tragedy and a public health problem for us has now become a government tactic to enforce an unenforceable law. The Drys claim Prohibition has saved a million lives, but no one wants to say how many it's killed."

Emily nodded sadly.

"It's unthinkable," she said softly, raising her cup to sip the coffee that had now cooled. Morelli just smiled and picked up his own cup to drink as well. As public healthicans, they were part of the apparatus that enforced the law, and there was no room for either outrage or sympathy in what they did.

Afterword

The 21st Amendment to the US Constitution was ratified on December 5, 1933, bringing to an end the social experiment known commonly as Prohibition. Prohibition was the subject of the 18th Amendment, which passed on January 16, 1919, and took effect one year later. The 18th Amendment was the result of more than a century of social reform movements in the US intended to reduce drunkenness and the disruptive and violent behavior that often accompanied it. Prohibition, however, was widely acknowledged to have been a serious failure that led to the rise of organized crime and a shadowy underworld of illegal alcohol production, importation, and consumption. It did not reduce the availability of alcohol but created a huge black market that generated enormous profits for the criminal elements that ran it.

The 21st Amendment was unprecedented in that it repealed a previous Constitutional Amendment and is the only Amendment ratified by state ratifying committees, rather than by their legislatures. While the temperance movement remained strong, by 1933 social conditions had convinced most Americans that Prohibition had been a mistake. Nonetheless, the laws and regulations on the production, sale, and consumption of alcohol still vary across the United States as the 21st Amendment came to be interpreted as allowing the states to make their own rulings on appropriate prohibitions.

About the Author

Rebecca Fanany is a native New Yorker who has lived in Australia for more than thirty years. She is the author of several academic books, textbooks, numerous articles, and many translations from and into Indonesian and Malay. She has degrees from the University of Minnesota and a PhD from the University of Tasmania. She is currently an Associate Professor of Public Health at a major Australian university and heads the postgraduate public health program. Her first novel, *Emily Lowe, Public Healthican*, reflects her longstanding interest in the history of public health and how the field has evolved.